THE VANISHING POINT

ANDREA HOTERE

Published in 2023 by Ultimo Press,
an imprint of Hardie Grant Publishing

Ultimo Press
Gadigal Country
7, 45 Jones Street
Ultimo, NSW 2007
ultimopress.com.au

Ultimo Press (London)
5th & 6th Floors
52–54 Southwark Street
London SE1 1UN

  ultimopress

 A catalogue record for this
book is available from the
National Library of Australia

The Vanishing Point
ISBN 978 1 76115 275 7 (paperback)

Cover design Sandy Cull
Text design Simon Paterson, Bookhouse
Typesetting Bookhouse, Sydney | 12/18.75 pt Linotype Fairfield
Copyeditor Ali Lavau
Proofreader Rebecca Hamilton

10 9 8 7 6 5 4 3 2 1

Printed in Australia by Griffin Press, an Accredited ISO AS/NZS 14001
Environmental Management System printer.

 The paper this book is printed on is certified against the
Forest Stewardship Council® Standards. Griffin Press holds
chain of custody certification SCS-COC-001185. FSC®
promotes environmentally responsible, socially beneficial
and economically viable management of the world's forests.

Ultimo Press acknowledges the Traditional Owners of the Country on which we work,
the Gadigal People of the Eora Nation and the Wurundjeri People of the Kulin Nation,
and recognises their continuing connection to the land, waters and culture. We pay our
respects to their Elders past and present.

For Richard, J, A and H

MARGARITA'S WORLD

Infanta Margarita – daughter of King Philip IV and Queen Mariana.

Diego Rodríguez de Silva y Velázquez (Diego Velázquez) – Royal artist and King's chamberlain.

José (De) Nieto – in the doorway of *Las Meninas*, the Queen's chamberlain.

King Philip IV.

Queen Mariana – the King's second wife.

Infanta Maria-Theresa – Margarita's older half-sister who will marry Louis XIV of France.

Infantes Felipe and Carlos – younger brothers of Margarita.

Luisa – imagined character, a maid of Margarita.

Agustina – in *Las Meninas*, an attendant.

Pepito – imagined character based on the other dwarves of the court.

Maribárbola – in *Las Meninas*, an attendant.

Nicolas – in *Las Meninas*, with his foot on the dog.

Terrón – the dog in *Las Meninas*.

Duran – imagined character based on churchmen of the Inquisition.

Bernarda – imagined character, gypsy fortune teller.

PROLOGUE

The Royal Alcázar, Madrid, 1656

Diego Velázquez stood alone in the studio. He glanced up at the painting above the mirror. A fair copy – of one of Rubens' finest, even down to the background detail – of the tapestry version of Titian's *The Rape of Europa*. Velázquez knew Rubens' work well, almost as well as he knew Titian's original. Ignoring the goddess and the cowering mortal, Arachne, his eyes rested on the image of the bull, Zeus, bearing away the fair maiden, Europa, on his back, while her friends lament on the shore in the distance. The king of the gods. The resisting maiden. Titian's bold title.

The face of his own king swam before him, pale and sallow. It was a miracle that he was still here, painting King Philip and his new family. He sighed and closed his eyes as his mind travelled back to the night, years past, still haunting him.

A pounding at the front door. The dog barked. Beside him, Juana stirred.

'Go back to sleep,' Velázquez said, patting her linen-clad shoulder. 'I'll go.' He slipped a robe over his nightgown and climbed out of bed, padding over the Turkish rugs on the wooden floor and down the stairs to the entranceway, where the housekeeper was already opening the door. Olivares, his patron – a great beast of a man – entered without ceremony and proceeded into the living room. Trailing him was a younger fellow, dressed as if for a journey.

Velázquez was in his early twenties when the chamberlain had brought him to Madrid and helped to establish him in the royal court. This was back in the 1620s, when the King, an uncertain young man of sixteen, had not long ascended the throne. His Highness still deferred too much to those around him, which, Velázquez knew, was just how Olivares liked it.

At a look from Olivares, Velázquez dismissed the housekeeper.

'He leaves in the morning for Italy,' Olivares told him, gesturing at his companion. 'I need a likeness. Can you do it?'

Velázquez knew better than to question his patron, but he wondered at the strangeness of this urgent request. Why not a daytime commission, with more time, if a portrait was required?

Before he could respond, Olivares inclined his head to the right, as was his habit when he appeared to be making a suggestion but was, in fact, subtly directing their sovereign in his game of puppetry. 'From this we will be able to complete a portrait, to celebrate him on his return,' said Olivares, straight-faced.

Velázquez nodded, steepled his fingers in front of him and pressed them to his lips, studying the younger man who seemed oblivious to his fate. What that fate might be, Velázquez was not sure, but the circumstances of his arrival – covert, late at night, with the patron himself – did not bode well.

Olivares added, 'He goes on an important mission for the King – to the Pope.'

Ah, so that was it. This was the messenger tasked with transporting the evidence to the Pope: a heavy load he would carry in a very small trunk. He would not know its contents. The churchmen of the Inquisition had worked hard to provoke this concession. Evidence had been gathered; perhaps justice would be done. Yet it was to be entrusted to one man? How secure would he be? The enterprise seemed ill-judged . . . or was that intentional?

'Please, sit.' Velázquez could not believe this was all going ahead – and now Olivares had brought him here; was implicating Velázquez in his plan. He cursed internally, felt his innards clenching, recoiling, but fought to keep his outward expression tranquil. 'May I offer some wine, perhaps?'

Olivares sank into a chair with a grunt and, at his nod, the other man, the messenger, took a smaller seat by the window. He sat with his back straight, hands on his knees, the soles of his boots pressing into the floor.

Velázquez unstoppered a carafe and poured some *vino tinto* for his guests.

Olivares flung off his gloves and let them fall, then took the proffered goblet.

The messenger declined the wine.

Velázquez studied his subject. The man wore a short cape and a white shirt open at the neck. There was something of the soldier in his attentive posture.

Olivares was almost smiling, as he twirled the tip of his moustache with one hand and swirled the wine in his cup with the other. 'Make it an exact likeness. His mother loves him, and the King will too.' He laughed, showing his stained teeth.

Velázquez took up some paper on a board and selected a pencil from a pouch inside the sideboard. With his back to his guests, he took a few moments to steady himself. These were the tools he kept at the house, with which he'd drawn his beloved wife, Juana, and even Ignatia. At the thought of her, his little departed angel, he took up another pencil, a new one; those that had sketched her form were sacred. There was nothing sacred about Olivares, and nothing was sacred to him. All was tradeable, even honour. And yet, he, as royal artist, had given his own loyalty to this man, and to the King.

Sighing, he returned, sat on a wooden stool, and considered his subject. He let his hand translate the man's stubby nose and alert eyes onto the paper. Could he see in the dark with eyes like those? He seemed to open them unnaturally wide, as if trying to let more light inside. And he had the eyelashes of a woman, bristly and black. Unluckily for him, his face was a distinctive one; there was even a mole on the side of his nose.

Velázquez made a point in the corner of the lower eyelid, for where the tears would come out. For he suspected, as he drew, that there would be tears; that his drawing might even become a death warrant.

When it was done, Olivares took the drawing and held it in front of him, between him and the messenger. He smiled slyly, pursed his lips and nodded. Then he frowned. 'You've forgotten the . . .' He touched the side of his nose.

'Ah, of course.' Velázquez had left it off on purpose, wanted to give the man a chance.

He brought his pencil to the likeness once more and sketched the raised mole on the side of the fellow's nose into position.

'That will do very well,' said Olivares. 'Instantly recognisable.'

It was true. Poor bugger.

Velázquez released the paper into his patron's eager hands.

Velázquez shivered slightly. A cool breeze drifted across his shoulders. He had been staring at his own reflection in the mirror, lost in the memory of where this had all begun. He took a step back and considered the distance to the door on his right. He then looked up to the two empty hooks in the ceiling, awaiting new lights. Like the Inquisitor's tools, or the meat hooks in the market, he thought. One of them was tantalisingly close to the pictured bull. It was not too great a mental leap.

He checked himself.

Could he do it? Did he dare?

I
IMPASTO

1

CURSES

1991

'*A picture painted with curses . . .*'
PABLO PICASSO

Ping! A button flew off her white shirt as Alex dashed up the front stairs and into the foyer of the auction house. Great. Getting her breasts out on the steps of Christie's. That would thrill the great master. Still, maybe it would distract him from the sweat stains under her arms. There was no time for sartorial repair.

The great wooden doors opened inwards, like the wings of a theatre set in some West End musical. The crispness of the black-and-white tiled floor led to a marble staircase fit for Cinderella and designed to evoke in punters a wallet-opening sense of awe, but, unlike Cinderella, Alex was about to run up, not down. The woman at the reception desk raised an eyebrow. Alex swept a hand over her forehead and brushed her fringe aside. Her skin was damp with sweat. She was late.

'Has it started?'

The woman glared at her. 'Has *what* started?'

'It. Him.' Alex noticed the direction of the woman's gaze and straightened her shirt.

'Sorry – I'm here for the talk by Regi Montano. About Velázquez.' She softened the V, Spanish style, as if she knew what she was talking about. She did know that much. And she knew that Montano was *the* recognised world expert on Velázquez. That he was Italian American, visiting from Rome. But Velázquez, of course, was the *real* great master, not the other guy, the visiting expert. Sometimes people – by which she meant academics and art moths, those who fluttered around the light – seemed to forget that.

The woman sighed.

'Please,' said Alex, pulling out her brand-new ID. 'I'm an intern at the Courtauld.' She'd only been in the job a few weeks. Still couldn't believe it. It was a big jump from Pete's Poster Shop in Wandsworth. 'Which room, please?'

The woman's eyes widened. 'Past the main auction hall, second on the left. I believe they started twenty minutes ago. You may have missed it.'

But Alex was hoofing it up the stairs, two at a time. At the top, she swerved past a man pulling a trolley loaded with Chinese vases towards the main auction room.

'Miss! Watch out!'

'Sorry, sorry!' She knew better than to run around priceless works of art; anything could happen. She couldn't afford to be stuck with the bill. If Greta, her supervisor, could see her now, she'd be mortified, would put her on notice. Alex slowed to a fast walk.

Clutching her manilla folder to her chest to cover the missing button, she took a breath and opened the door.

If she'd been trying to achieve a discreet entrance, she had failed. A ripple went through the room as rows of heads turned towards the source of the interruption. The speaker paused mid-sentence. His eyes alighted upon Alex. She felt like an insect, perhaps a bumbling bee, which couldn't help making a loud buzz and flying in a circuitous route. Could she just turn around and fly right out of there? The room was full of pinstriped suits and studious-looking types in glasses and cashmere. The speaker had a beard like Gandalf, but his face was nothing like Tolkien's genial wizard. This man was as flinty as a granite statue on this podium. Everything about him, from his smart brown brogues to the golden tie with the subtle pattern of blue dots, the impeccably tailored suit, the matching saffron and indigo handkerchief protruding from his breast pocket, but particularly the way he held the sides of the lectern, as if he were preaching from a pulpit, was designed to assert his authority.

Alex shrugged her shoulders, telegraphing apologies to the man on the stage. She'd run halfway across London's West End to hear him speak. She wanted him to continue. Scrambling into a seat at the end of a row, she shrank down so that she could just be a pair of ears, intent on his every word.

The picture, *Las Meninas*, the seventeenth-century Spanish masterpiece, was projected onto a screen behind him, at less than true scale. Diego Velázquez had painted himself into the scene. He stood, brush in hand, behind his easel and close to the Infanta Margarita and her attendants, including the composed and well-dressed dwarf Maribárbola, a boy and a dog. Behind them, in the doorway, silhouetted, was José De Nieto, the Queen's chamberlain. On the back wall, beneath two paintings, was a mirror that showed the blurry reflection of Margarita's parents, the King and Queen of Spain, as if they were in the position of the viewer, while having their likenesses recorded by the artist.

Alex's heartbeat and her breathing were slowing. As usual, coming face to face with this work made her knees weak and she was glad to be sitting down. Was it the eyes that produced this hypnotic effect? Or was it a hallucinogenic effect: the interplay between the pictured past and the imperfectly perspiring present that made you feel you could walk the tightrope between them, as she had? But, no, that was a long time ago. She had probably just imagined it. Weren't there seven stages to grief? What stage was she at now? Would she always miss her mother this much? If they scanned her heart, would it have a hole in it? That was how it felt sometimes. She could even touch the point where it hurt. How could grief be so physically specific? She turned her attention back to the speaker. What did Montano know? Did he understand why *Las Meninas* worked the way it did? How Velázquez had achieved his magic? All her hopes were pinned on this moment, but what the expert said next brought those hopes crashing down.

'What I have concluded is that there is *no* hidden secret in *Las Meninas*,' said Montano. 'No hidden meaning. Rather' – he glanced down and took a moment to adjust his cuffs – 'we can confidently contend that Velázquez was asserting his dominance, his mastery over Titian and Rubens. The work is an exercise in visual mastery designed to demonstrate his superiority. We see how he gestures towards their works on the back wall.' He turned and raised his own arm to indicate the two dark rectangles above the mirror. 'And as I say, this *reference* is not merely an homage – oh no. It is an expression of rivalry.' This last word was enunciated emphatically.

'Competition,' said Montano, placing a closed fist upon the lectern. 'Competition. You all understand it.' He paused, let the word hang in the air. 'It's at the heart of our society. And it's at the heart of this artwork, and I hope that very soon' – here he nodded towards an elegant woman in a Chanel suit, her ankles tucked to the side under her chair – 'the Spanish government will consent to this great work being shown here in London. Where you can guarantee everyone will be *competing* for a glimpse of it.'

Applause and more than a ripple went around the room. As the reaction continued Alex sat up in her seat. This was huge news. *Las Meninas* had *never* left Spain. It was a national treasure, held in the Prado, one of the world's greatest galleries, in Madrid. Perhaps she would see it again, here in London.

But something was very wrong. Montano's words perturbed her deeply. She caught Velázquez's eye, where he stood, working, inside the painting. *There's another truth.* The words were spoken into her mind, but they were so clear she turned to see if someone had spoken in her ear. She swallowed. Remembered her mother's last postcard: *Picasso said* Las Meninas *is a picture painted with curses.* Her mother had been very clear. And Alex knew she had died while trying to discover the nature of those curses.

Alex rose to her feet, feeling her rib cage thrum with her own escalating heartbeat. She tried to remain still as she heard herself repeating those same fateful words aloud, addressing the speaker across the room. 'But Picasso said *Las Meninas* was a painting full of curses – or, to be exact, "a picture painted with curses". I believe he was correct. There *is* a hidden secret inside this painting. It's *not* just about competition. Velázquez wasn't just showing off.'

The room erupted. Heads turned towards Alex.

Montano waved his hand to quieten the audience. 'And what evidence do you have for this assertion?'

Her diaries and the books she had read swam through her brain. She'd been reading about this painting for years, even more so since her dad gave her the postcard six months previously. Where should she begin? It was a feeling. A whole new interpretation hung just on the outer reaches of her mind. Was it possible? She had questions and not enough answers. It was as elusive as a dream. A dream that ended in a smoky haze and with an uncomfortable sense that the painting itself was in danger.

'I . . . I . . . I have a postcard,' she said. Her voice came out as a strangled squeak. People in the row in front laughed outright. Montano smirked. This was not going well – was worse than stage fright or freezing up in a tutorial.

Her boss, Greta, was standing at the side of the room with one of the auction house staff. Greta was meant to be at a long lunch, or so Alex had thought, but of course Greta was here, resplendent with her dark grey hair, bright orange lipstick and green velvet opera coat. Her hands were clasped together under her chin, revealing the golden lining inside her sleeves. Alex paused. Greta had employed her; these other people were potentially her future employers, future colleagues. Alex looked from Montano to the screen, where the young Infanta Margarita sparkled in the middle of the painting in her silver dress and Diego Velázquez waited patiently with his palette.

'I see,' said Montano once the titters had subsided. He cleared his throat. 'A postcard.' He made a doubting face but nodded, as you would to a child. 'Well. That's, ah, very convincing, isn't it?' More giggles from the audience. 'Perhaps you should post it to me.' He turned his attention away and glanced around the room. 'Any further speculations? Theories?' He began to gather his papers.

The MC came forwards to rhapsodically end the session.

⌒

'That was quite an impression you made in there.' A young man stopped Alex as she left the room. He wiggled his hands in the air and grinned. 'Curses, eh? *Wooo.*'

'Don't,' said Alex. She'd had enough humiliation for the day. She tried to move past him.

'Wait, I didn't mean to offend you. Sorry.' The young man shifted from one foot to the other on the thick blue carpet.

'Oh God,' said Alex. 'I've just made such a dick of myself. I shouldn't have done that – I think I'm about to lose my job.' She peered over the balcony and down to the lower level. Greta was there already, networking. She glanced up and caught Alex's eye. Her look meant they would be having words about this.

'Ah, that's not so good,' said the young man. He looked away, running a hand through his wavy brown hair and rubbing the back of his neck, as if he were a cat. Did he fancy himself, or was he just shy? He had freckles on his nose. 'I thought you were more interesting than the big guy, actually. I was hoping he'd talk about the Infanta, but he didn't say anything about her at all.'

In the foyer, Greta was gesturing discreetly for her to come down. Alex pretended she hadn't noticed.

'The Infanta?'

'Yes,' he said. 'I'm researching the background of a musical piece about an infanta, a dead one. Not her – at least, it might be her, but it wasn't written for her. That is . . . I thought maybe we could . . .'

Greta had a hand on her hip.

'Sorry, I've really got to go,' said Alex. She drew a deep breath, then made her way down the stairs.

'Not here,' hissed Greta, when Alex joined her. Greta was still smiling and acknowledging acquaintances as she led Alex to the door.

Outside, Greta hailed a black cab. When they climbed in, Greta was no longer smiling.

'Well, that was hugely embarrassing. *Hugely.*' She took a compact out of her handbag and proceeded to powder her nose.

Alex winced. 'I'm sorry,' she said. 'It just came out. He was so arrogant.'

'Arrogant!' Greta sighed. 'You've got some nerve, young lady. Regi Montano has spent years – his whole career, in fact – studying the paintings of Velázquez. He has dominated the field. He has *expertise*, he is respected, and for good reason.' She replaced her compact in her purse. Alex noticed that the shine had gone from

Greta's nose. It was Greta who had told her that calcite was still being used in cosmetics to make colour appear more translucent, as it had been in paint by Velázquez. Greta had expertise too, she thought.

They turned past the BBC at Bush House and trundled down the Strand. Greta was still fuming.

'I'm your supervisor, which means your ill-judged outburst reflects badly on me. Thankfully, you're so new in the job that not many people will have connected you to the Courtauld. But honestly, Alex, this is not how we work. Art historians are discreet. We are sensitive. We . . .'

Alex wished she could blur her outline and disappear into the taxi seat. Greta had been so good to her, had invited her in for an interview after receiving her letter and was helping her put together a proposal for research work on Picasso. Alex hadn't made it into Oxford or Cambridge; she'd gone to what was considered a second-rate university. She hadn't even majored in art history – instead, she'd chosen history. *Art* history was her mum's thing, and she'd resisted it, but these paintings kept presenting themselves, and when they did it was all that she could see. As if Velázquez himself was adjusting her focal distance, allowing her retinas to reconstitute forms – to optically blend contrasting spots of colour, knowing that she would perceive these differently from colours which had been blended upon his palette. She couldn't help but think he wanted to show her something, somewhere between what was visible and what was not. To communicate. And what about Picasso? He moved around his subjects as he worked, painting them from different angles, offering multiple perspectives simultaneously. Alex's mind was racing. Picasso asked questions of his subject and his viewer. He'd asked questions of Velázquez. Had he found the answers she was seeking?

The taxi pulled up outside the triple-arched entrance of Somerset House, the grand building that housed the Courtauld Institute of Art.

'Alex?' said Greta. 'Are you listening?'

Alex nodded.

'What I'm *most* annoyed about is that you didn't have any evidence. You should never make a claim like that unless you can back it up.'

'I have this,' said Alex. Maybe when Greta read the words her mother had written, she would understand. She opened her manilla folder.

But the folder was empty. The postcard was gone.

⌐

The Spanish woman in the Chanel suit who'd sat on the stage behind Montano had made her way to a side corridor of the auction house, close to the cashier's office. She flipped open her phone and tapped a button.

'*Hola*. It's me – Patrizia. We might have a problem . . . No, no, Montano was fine – as expected. It was a girl, a young woman in the audience. She asked him about the curses. *In public*. She said the painting held hidden secrets . . . Well, a lot of people heard it. It worries me . . . No, they didn't take it seriously; they laughed . . .

Maybe, but what if she takes it further, starts digging? . . . Okay. Yes, I need you to be prepared . . . Let's hope it doesn't come to that.'

She returned the phone to her Dior handbag, closing the metal clasp with a snap.

2

LOOSE ENDS

José pressed the button to end the call. Curses and secrets. Another bitch on the scent. He yanked out a metal chair at one of the outdoor cafe tables that pockmarked the fringes of the Plaza Mayor and placed the speaking device on the table in front of him as he sat and surveyed the scene. The scraping of the chair legs on the cobbles reminded him of times he'd helped position the metal instruments in this very location, or in the tunnels and caves below. Such foul and wonderful things had happened within this quadrangle. He leaned back in his seat and kicked away a pigeon that dared approach his boot. The tiered buildings were much the same as they had always been – the balconies, the tall rectangular windows, the red bricks, the slate roofs. The regimentation was reassuring; you knew where you stood with architecture like this. Everything had its place within the hierarchy: one on top of the other, even the weathercocks were still up there, watching. The statue of Philip III, the one they called 'the pious' – how ironic – was in pride of place on his trotting steed in the centre of the square. It wasn't as good as the one of his son, Philip IV, on a rearing horse – the statue Velázquez had worried would topple, until they'd brought in the Italian stargazer, Galileo, to do the equations. Ha.

An aproned waiter approached. *'Café solo?'*

José nodded. His mind was wandering. Vain Philip had hated the face on his statue so much that they'd decapitated it and ordered a replacement more to his liking. The King had ridden headless for six months till the new visage was installed. Might as well have had a king with no head forever. José smirked and pulled at his sharply trimmed beard.

Up there was the balcony where the royal family had sat to watch the *autos-da-fé*, the spectacles for public expiation of sin; now it was a fashionable apartment with gauzy white curtains. Tourists, aimless pedants, were circling the plaza like goldfish in the ponds of the Buen Retiro, gawping at the hawkers' wares – effigies of flamenco dancers, horse brasses and model toros – remnants from other times.

The waiter returned and placed a cup and saucer in front of him.

Patrizia had left the country without telling him. Her voice was the same, sugar on steel. *How had she travelled?* he wondered. Did the master know? If it weren't for her intercession on his behalf, he wouldn't be here. José played with the gold signet ring on the third finger of his right hand. He swivelled it – had to, so the skin didn't grow over it. All these years he'd worn it. The surface was scratched but the imprint was still clear. He raised Sargatanas's symbol, the moth, to his lips. The lame devil with the power to open any lock – that's how Duran had introduced his master on the day they inducted him. In Sargatanas's service, he'd enjoyed the power of the keys that clinked at his belt. They had omitted to mention what he had since learned at great cost: that locks could be closed, too.

He brought the cup to his mouth, took a sip – good. The Devil's brew, they'd called it – and people were still drinking the stuff. Ha. He grimaced, put down his cup and twisted the ring again.

Duran was dead. José *had* to succeed. Patrizia had sought him out, had asked the master to release *him*. She needed him – perhaps even *wanted* him.

He took another sip of coffee. Oh, the joys of the flesh!

He hissed when his new cell phone rang. A voice, not Patrizia's, uttered the words: 'Her name is Alex Johns.'

José frowned. The name meant nothing to him.

He made a few calls, stabbing at the numbers with his sharp fingernails. No one had heard of an Alex Johns.

But then this: 'Daughter of Rosara Johns.' It was from a contact at the museum. 'You know, the one who died?'

When he heard the name – Rosara Johns – José remembered. 'Died' was such a generic term. So useful. *Eliminated* . . . He made the correction inside his own head. He'd tidied up a lot of loose ends over the years, and he prided himself on never forgetting a target. The job came back to him now. Textbook.

He'd driven his motorbike straight at her car on the winding road near Toledo and flashed his headlight at her, high beam. She had swerved to avoid him, just as he'd planned; launched off the road and down the hill. He had pulled over, parked the bike and walked slowly down the steep slope, leaning back and digging the heels of his boots into the loose dirt to stop himself skidding, wondering if her car, now resting on its back, wheels spinning, would ignite. There was no urgency in his movements. Reaching the vehicle, he crouched down, kicked away some glass and removed her papers from the back seat, hearing her last breaths. She had thought he was there to rescue her, he recalled – she had murmured her thanks. By the time he'd removed a glove, taken a lighter to the papers and burned them, her gurgling had stopped. He passed his palm over her head, sensed the nothingness that was now in her body. He held his hand there just a moment, moved his long fingers delicately – to anyone watching it might have appeared as if he were capturing something as fragile as a spider's web. Only he knew what this moment portended. Rosara Johns was dead. He pulled at the light from the air around her and placed it in his pocket.

But this one, her daughter, was just a girl in her early twenties. Perhaps Patrizia was getting paranoid. He was hers to command. She did not need to restate the instruction: 'perpetual silence'.

Striding down the colonnade, he noticed the absence of shit in his path before he noticed the absence of his own reflection in the shop windows. These things discomfited him. One he missed, the other he did not. A woman with bare arms and shoulders – and a skirt so short he could see her knees – walked past. No shame. He approached the Arco de Cuchilleros on the west side of the square, anticipating the tang of blood in his nostrils. Here was where the knifemakers had gathered, sharpening and selling their knives to butchers. He had bought his own here once, testing it on a slab of meat.

He kicked at a bottle with a red-and-white label that lay in his path. Instead of smashing, it bounced off a pillar. He paused. Things were different. He trotted down the stairs, past the caves where you could still buy a tumbler of cheap *vino tinto* towards what was once the Luján Lagoon and was now the entry to a market. He swung a leg over his Moto Guzzi and set off for Madrid airport. The flight to London left at 10 pm and he would be on it.

3

PIGMENTS

1656

The Infanta Margarita, still in her nightgown, jumped towards Luisa. Luisa caught her and swung her around, then returned her to the bed.

'You'll get me into trouble, Your Highness,' said Luisa. 'We can't be playing like this. De Nieto, and more besides, don't like it. You're a special vessel, he says. Our Infanta, our *princesa*.'

'I am not a ship, I am not a jug,' said Margarita, tipping herself to the side like a ewer. 'I am six.'

'You are too clever,' said Luisa.

José De Nieto was chamberlain to Margarita's mother, Queen Mariana, who said that he should have been a general in the army, because he liked to be organised. Luisa called him the 'nosy one' because he had a pointy nose and liked to know everything. He made it hard for Margarita to see her mother.

'You are strong, Luisa,' Margarita said. 'Give me a horsey ride.'

'From good stock, I am, blended with a dash of knight errant,' said Luisa. She presented her back. Margarita wrapped her arms around her neck and her legs around the maid's waist. Her mouth was close to Luisa's ear.

'What does that mean?'

'It means my mother, bless her, was swept off her feet and under a haystack by a determined gentleman seeking solace before his return to the palace.' Luisa began to puff with the effort of trotting about the room.

'What's solace?'

'Something grown-ups need.' Luisa released Margarita's legs and let her slide onto the bed.

'Your papa?'

'Oh, you are a one for questions. You're too quick. A fine family we were – a fine family.' Luisa shook her head and adjusted her breasts within her bodice. She'd been Margarita's wet nurse and had remained in the Infanta's entourage as a private attendant.

'Enough. Time to get dressed.'

Margarita glanced at her guardainfante, the lashed and hooped willow structure which supported her heavy skirts and now lurked at the side of the room. She poked her tongue at it. Sometimes she climbed inside and pushed it about, pretending to be a caged animal brought by the conquistadors from the Americas, and Luisa would make a show of being scared. But the game usually ended with the thing strapped to Margarita's waist, and from then on movement became more difficult. At night, the frame cast strange shadows. Sometimes in her dreams it chased her around the alcázar and she ran from it, on soundless feet.

'They say the ladies of France are no longer wearing them; maybe you won't have to for much longer either,' said Luisa. 'My ma says they're like something used by the Inquisitor, Duran.' She spat the name, as if it tasted bad.

'Why does he need a skirt?'

Luisa laughed, but a knock at the door made her jump. 'Mercy me, we are all looking over our shoulders these days,' she whispered.

Luisa presented the breakfast tray. As Margarita sipped her chocolate *caliente*, Luisa remarked, 'The cook was in a mood this morning, and there was not much for us in the kitchens. Even the flour bins are nearly empty. When your parents first married, oh, you should have seen the tables then, and the cupboards – they were laden; bending in the middle, they were, with the weight of it all . . . We're all a bit slimmer now, even me.' She patted her hips. 'The cooks had to send out twice this week for supplies.' Margarita held out her half-empty cup, signalling that she was done, and Luisa returned it to the tray. 'You are expected in the studio later.'

Margarita clapped – the studio was one of her favourite places – then pouted as she surveyed her plate with distaste. 'Eggs, eggs, eggs. I am going to turn into a chicken!'

Luisa chuckled. 'You *are* a chicken, little chicken.'

'And you are a hen.'

Luisa trotted about, flapping her bent arms like wings, nearly bumping into the mirror.

Margarita laughed.

'Oh, the enchantment crystal,' said Luisa, stepping back from the looking glass with a worried expression.

'Why do they call them that?'

'The royal playwright called them that; now all the ladies want one,' said Luisa. 'Now, please eat your custard, Your Highness.'

Margarita scooped some golden custard into her mouth with a silver spoon. 'What's that on top?' she asked.

'A little grated nutmeg,' replied Luisa, returning to Margarita's side.

Margarita ran the edge of her finger around the top of the bowl but left half the contents untouched.

'The children in the villages would love to taste one drop of your breakfast,' said Luisa.

'Tell me . . .'

'Well, you needn't bother with them. They live a different life.'

'But are there lots of them, all living together? What games do they play?'

'They run and they hide, like you do.'

'And the others look for them.'

'Yes.'

'How many? How many children?'

'Keep eating. Oh, I don't know, ten or twenty.'

Margarita bounced in her seat. 'So many. Where do they hide?'

'In the forests, or just in the village – not too far away. They don't want to get lost. They like to climb the haystacks and sit up there, or burrow down and fall asleep in the sun.'

'Even the girls?'

Luisa shook her head. 'Mainly it's the boys. They hunt rabbits, too, like your brother used to.'

'I couldn't climb haystacks in my skirts.' She wrinkled her nose at the guardainfante. 'Did Balthazar like to climb?'

At the mention of the King's dead son, Luisa made the sign of the cross at her chest.

Margarita sighed. It was strange how she missed the older half-brother she had never met. At least she had her half-sister, Maria-Theresa, who was kind and brought her sweetmeats, but then she often went away with the Countess.

Margarita knew Balthazar only from Luisa and Maria-Theresa's stories and from Velázquez's portraits. But these were so real his face was imprinted in her memory. He had become a kind of mythological creature in the palace. Velázquez had painted him first as a young boy, on the rearing bay stallion with its round belly, and then as a tall young man with eyes the colour of chestnuts. Sometimes when she passed his portrait Margarita would touch his booted foot.

'Why did he have to die?' Balthazar had died before she was born, before her mother left Vienna and became the second queen.

'It was a tertian fever . . . Only sixteen, bless him.' Luisa touched the crucifix she wore around her neck. 'Holy mother, protect her from the curse . . .' She spoke in an undertone, but Margarita heard her nevertheless.

'What curse?' she demanded. 'Why do you say there's a curse?'

Luisa froze momentarily. 'It's nothing, child. Just a prayer. The death of your brother – it broke the King's heart.'

Margarita considered her father, the King. Most of the time, he was very still and slow, speaking little and staring out of the windows with sad eyes. But sometimes – in his chambers and with Velázquez and with her – he was different, lively. She took pleasure in amusing him.

'Your papa says *you* are the life of the palace,' said Luisa, 'and it is true. Come now, let's get you dressed.'

Luisa poured water from the ewer and wrung out a facecloth. Margarita closed her eyes. The muslin was warm and damp, Luisa's touch gentle.

More meninas arrived carrying the new silver dress and armfuls of petticoats. They strapped the frame of the guardainfante to Margarita's tiny waist. As they lowered the silver skirt over her head, Margarita had to raise her arms and the light disappeared. They slid the bodice around her middle. The sleeves, which were attached next, were a pleasing gauze. She could see her skin through them, even the blonde hairs on her arms. The tiny line of covered buttons up the front of the bodice were like small silver balls that bounced back pleasingly as she ran her fingers up and down.

'Don't fiddle,' said Agustina. 'You'll make them dirty.' She tugged at the laces at Margarita's back, and she had to catch her breath.

Margarita waited until they went to the closet for her shoes and then, while the ladies' backs were turned, slipped out the bedroom door. The corridor was empty. Balancing the swinging skirt with her hands she hurried off, weaving through the narrow passages that led to the heart of the palace. The wooden floors were dusty, and the walls were covered with out-of-favour tapestries and paintings. Margarita knew them all, but today she had no time for them.

Luisa's plaintive voice sounded behind her: '*Niña, niña*, don't play these games. They are not ready for you yet . . .' But after a turn or two, Margarita easily outpaced her. She hurried to Velázquez's studio, which was next to the King's quarters.

She paused on the step, watching. Diego Velázquez was standing before an enormous stretched canvas. She saw how he leaned in, inspecting the base coat: a deep, muddy grey, the colour of the Manzanares River. He tapped the surface with his fingertips, rubbed his fingers together and nodded.

On a trestle table beside the artist were assorted brushes, arranged like flowers in earthenware jugs. On the floor lay tins of various sizes and rags, crumpled with colour and smelling of linseed oil. The mess was glorious, like treasure.

She entered the room.

The studio was a special place, where many of the normal rules of the alcázar did not apply – at least, not to her or the other most frequent visitor, her father. She surveyed the room more closely: there in the corner, Philip IV's leather armchair; leaning against the wall, a large roll of raw canvas. She loved this place of concentration and serenity. Assistants hovered in an adjoining room; sometimes they mixed concoctions for him, but today Velázquez waved them away. Margarita knew Velázquez often liked to blend his own tones. He had told her so. He said she was his best helper.

To her surprise, the boy Nicolas was present again today. He'd come to the palace several times recently. Nicolas seemed to have scant interest in the paintings; he preferred to play with the dogs. The meninas had introduced Nicolas to the Queen as one of the dwarves. They said he came from Italy, which puzzled Margarita, because he seemed like a normal boy to her and he spoke Spanish. Velázquez just called him Nicolas and didn't talk about him any more than that. That was how it was in the alcázar, she was learning: some people told you something was one thing; others told you it was another.

Velázquez took in her new dress with an approving nod and bowed. His thick hair fell forwards over his shoulders, and when he straightened, he flicked it back from his brow with a smile. His brown eyes were soft, with crinkles at the corners. He nodded to someone over her head. Margarita turned to see Luisa, red-faced and panting in the doorway. Luisa frowned at Margarita. She was carrying Margarita's white smock, which she quickly slipped over Margarita's clothing before retiring to a stool in the corner. She took up some knitting. Nicolas went to Luisa, sliding across the floor on his red velvet pants to sit at her feet.

'A stray seed,' muttered Velázquez.

'Weed, more like,' said Luisa.

'He's here at the King's behest.'

Luisa nodded. She handed the boy a ball of wool, which he held for her as she began to knit.

Terrón, a mastiff, had been curled up asleep under Velázquez's table. He sat up, nudged his nose into the artist's leg, and earned a casual caress of his ears. Margarita held out her hand and the dog licked her.

'I'm honoured,' said the artist to Margarita, gesturing for her to join him. 'We had better be careful of your beautiful dress, though . . . Mm, the gleam on that silver thread.' He rummaged among pots, packets, rags and brushes until, with a flourish, he produced a piece of board, which he placed on the table before her.

Velázquez examined her face intently and gestured towards her cheek with his hand. 'How is your colour today? Let me see . . .

Lead *blanco*, iron oxide . . . Help me find the match for your cheeks . . . So pale.' His fingers fluttered among the powdered pigments. He raised a packet to his nose, sniffed it, nodded and scooped some of the contents onto a small wooden platter. Soon he had two tiny mounds: one white, like the ice from the snow pits, and the other a rusty brown. She inched closer as he added a few drops of golden oil and swirled them together with a beech stick.

'But that is not it, you see? There is more. Vermillion – but only a speck.'

The bright red powder shouted for attention. Margarita passed him the jar. He sprinkled a few grains like paprika across the pale beige.

Luisa started up from her chair. 'Mind your sleeve, Your Highness.'

Margarita caught Velázquez's eye.

He selected a small black tin and, with a wink, showed her a collection of deep blue crystals in a twilight powder. He leaned closer. 'The secret ingredient, a touch of the evening sky,' he whispered, adding a pinch to his palette. 'To re-create your royal flesh – azurite: the blue of truth.'

Margarita gasped, for the patch of colour he was mixing now did look very much like her own skin. She held out her hand for comparison.

He nodded. 'Now you try.' He handed her a small square piece of board. He asked, 'Sable, squirrel or humble hog?'

She selected a smooth brown brush, testing its soft bristles against her cheek, as he was wont to do.

'Sable. Very good.'

He chose a brush, twirled the hairs at the tip, dipped it in the white paint and, demonstrating, made a line of little rectangles on the board before her. Then to each patch he added carmine and brown.

'*Blanco, russo, umber* . . . now we blend them like this, *poco a poco*, little by little,' he said.

Margarita dabbed between the colours and the board, creating little painted rectangles, overlapping different hues, each blending towards its neighbour. She painted with him at the table. Each blob of paint – a slick of pigment and oil – had its own character which could be altered slightly, but the precision with which Velázquez achieved this miracle eluded her. Margarita dropped a blob of white onto the board, moved it around a little and blew on it, watching its skin thicken, like the skin on the top of her warm milk. On her piece of board one square was a rose pink and the other a bloodier red. One rectangle followed another, but the colours became tacky and less obliging. She sighed.

'I've been practising all my life, *niña*,' he said, without pausing in his work. 'You must be patient.'

Margarita placed the brush in its jar and touched the paint with her finger. Luisa protested. Margarita ignored her and dabbed her fingertip across the tabletop, leaving a trail of prints. The little swirls and lines of her skin were impressed onto the wood. Velázquez offered her a rag and she tried to wipe the paint away, but it was stubborn. He dabbed the cloth in a solution that smelled like fish and returned it to her. This time the paint came off.

Now he turned away from her, towards the large canvas leaning on his easel. So far it was dull and boring.

'Do not pout – it's the base ground only,' he said. 'Now, if you please, stand here.' He indicated a spot on the floor. 'And turn your head slightly towards the windows.'

Margarita obeyed.

'Yes, but keep your eyes on me – that's right.'

Velázquez began blending burnt umber, grey and bone black. His eyes flicked between her and the canvas. He held his mahlstick up and then positioned it close to the surface and nodded. His brush slid up, down and across; she saw how he repeated this several times. He used his whole body as he worked, bending and stretching. Margarita waited until he paused and then left her position to come to his side of the canvas. Velázquez had sketched the outline of a layered triangle, topped with an upside down V. At first she was puzzled, then she recognised the shape of her dress.

'It will be a family portrait, with you at the centre,' he said. 'That's a start, an outline. You are like the first note. We will call it *La Familia* – no one else knows that yet.'

Margarita smiled and moved her hands through the air, delineating the outline of her skirt. When she looked up, he nodded at her. *La Familia*, she repeated the title in her mind. She liked confidences. Luisa had a way of letting secrets slip out by accident, like peas rolling off a plate.

At a creak in the floorboards, Terrón growled and Margarita turned.

De Nieto had entered the studio. Avoiding her eyes, he stuck his thumbs in his belt and rocked back on his heels, peering at the tapestry on the wall to their left. Margarita sensed he had been listening.

Velázquez raised an eyebrow at De Nieto, murmured to the dog and continued to work.

De Nieto bowed stiffly to Margarita. Then he saw Nicolas, still sitting on the floor by Luisa, his legs spread wide, rolling a ball of wool back and forth between his hands, trying to tempt Terrón.

'What is *he* doing here?'

Luisa shrugged.

'Her Majesty awaits the Infanta,' De Nieto announced.

'A moment,' said Velázquez. He gestured for Margarita to resume her position. She obliged, adjusting her stance as required, and the artist dipped his brush once more into the paint and applied it to the canvas.

Out of the corner of her eye, Margarita watched Terrón. The stump of his tail was standing out behind him and his hackles had risen. He growled at De Nieto. The chamberlain's cheeks reddened and he took a step away from the dog. Velázquez often made him wait like this. *De Nieto does not like Diego*, thought Margarita, *nor the studio, nor Terrón*. Luisa said Velázquez's studio was the beating heart of the palace. Margarita felt it too. The rooms had been Balthazar's. Luisa had told her that her father had lingered here after her brother's death, and eventually he had given them to Velázquez as a studio. De Nieto wore a strange sneer when he came near Velázquez, as if he had a piece of meat stuck between his back teeth and was trying to work it free with his tongue.

The King's armchair had been moved closer to the artist's easel. De Nieto stared at it and frowned. 'Who has moved the chair? There is a danger that His Majesty will get paint on his garments,' he declared, tight-lipped. 'The chair should be returned to its proper position, in front of the tapestry.' The tapestry in question hung on the other side of the room. It was the only one remaining in here, Margarita realised. De Nieto was the keeper of the tapestries. He took great pride in them.

Velázquez continued applying paint to his canvas. 'The King wished his chair to be repositioned,' he said.

De Nieto stalked over to the tapestry and turned his back on them, shoulders hunched.

Velázquez winked at Margarita.

José De Nieto could feel his back teeth grinding together, an old habit from his days in Seville. He rubbed the tight muscles of his jaw and cast a sideways glance at his cousin, Diego Velázquez, who was flicking his brush so casually, this way and that across the canvas. When Diego worked like this, sometimes he seemed in a kind of a trance, so deep was his concentration. The precise tenebrist was becoming more boldly impressionistic as he aged. De Nieto despised such carefree slop. In his domain, as keeper of the luscious hangings, precision was all. The weaver had to know his intention in advance, down to the tiniest detail. Not like these paintings, which the King seemed to favour above the more controlled expression of the weavings. A brushstroke here, a dab of colour there: a painter's trickery.

De Nieto twitched his shoulders and wished for a window he could open. He needed to feel a cool breeze. Perhaps that would calm this angry heat inside him.

'Still wishing you could hold a paintbrush, eh, José?' Diego's eyes didn't leave the canvas, yet he spoke directly to the other man's soul.

De Nieto startled. Did the painter have eyes in the back of his head? His cousin knew him too well, and yet he did not seem to suspect him. It was important that he did not. De Nieto raised his chin. The child inside him, who had once wanted to say, 'Yes, show me,' to that very question, squirmed. His tongue found the groove between two back molars, where one had fallen out. The gum was puffy, swollen, bleeding. He sucked, savouring the comforting taste of his own gore.

Growing up in Seville, he had admired his older cousin, who had emerged as an artistic prodigy, and envied the ease with which Diego wooed his master Pacheco's beautiful daughter, Juana, who was now his wife. When they'd sat down at their marriage feast in Seville, with all the nobles and well-wishers of society, including many artists, De Nieto had watched from the doorway to the kitchens, unable to make himself take a seat at the table. The room was full of love, of bonhomie, with Diego and Juana smiling at each other, besotted, and their guests. De Nieto tried to feel love, but inside he burned and chilled as if in a fever. His veins, he knew, coursed with a thick soup of jealousy. He no longer confessed it as a sin. He no longer confessed anything. He imagined it stiffening him, giving him unholy strength.

He'd found a mask that day and learned to control his features, and had worn it ever since: when he followed his cousin to Madrid; while he helped him into a position at the alcázar; and all through these years as he attended the Queen and oversaw the production of tapestries for her collections. He was truly proud to be her knight within the palace, a neat and direct counterpoint to Diego's role as chief chamberlain to the King. But his position as the keeper of the royal tapestries still did not have the status he craved. Nothing, it seemed, could eclipse Diego's brilliance with the brush, nor his speed. He could produce a painting within a few days, while tapestries took months. Superior spinners and weavers were becoming increasingly hard to find and the Queen was not a patient woman. It was an irksome situation: as De Nieto's team missed deadlines, Diego Velázquez's star continued to rise. De Nieto could feel his place diminishing while Diego, royal artist par excellence, had fast become the right-hand man, even the confidant, of the King. What did the King whisper to Velázquez? He treated him with outrageous tolerance, as if he were a friend. A friend!

Then there was the little Infanta – she adored Diego Velázquez, and he her. De Nieto knew she reminded Diego of his daughter Ignatia, who had died. He could see the resemblance himself. He looked over to her, posing for the artist.

He and Velázquez shared a secret that could not be spoken. How he wished he could use it, but to do so would mean the downfall of them both. Their common grandparents had been Jewish tradespeople, *conversos*. Their country had been torn apart by the expulsion of the Jews and Moriscos around the turn of the century under the King's father. Survival in this era meant adherence to the doctrine of *limpieza de sangre* – purity of blood. Like Diego, De Nieto aspired to the nobility. Nobility required proof of pure blood. Pure blood was a myth that sickened the country, they both knew it. In Madrid, De Nieto had found archivists who would make your blood clean, give your family tree a prune, for a fee. Diego was merely vague about his heritage and did not speak of it. He let his wife attend to family matters and guard his reputation.

De Nieto picked up the edge of the tapestry and rubbed it between his fingers. The threads were so fine, and the border was better than a wooden frame, so much more detailed. Yet he was having trouble getting works finished. The tradespeople were starving; leaving their looms idle in order to scrabble for rice or potatoes. Or, worse, meeting orders for courtiers who were themselves suckling from the King's purse.

Agustina poked her head into the room. She caught De Nieto in the act of rolling his shoulders, pulling them up to his ears and letting them drop, as he did sometimes in his private chambers. She sniggered. 'Oh, you do look a one with those wings up around your ears like a crow.'

There was a snort from the man at the easel.

De Nieto scowled, spun on his heel and left the room.

Agustina followed him into the corridor, shutting the door gently behind her.

'Best we don't disturb the master at work,' she said.

De Nieto stood very still. The hallway was dim and empty. They were alone. Agustina was within arm's reach. He allowed the steel in his eyes to find her and waited while she absorbed the impact of his stare. The respect she gave to his cousin . . . yet how did she address *him*? Never as master. He imagined his thumb in the hollow at the base of her throat. She blanched, put her hand to her neck as if she could feel his touch and took a step backwards. 'I didn't mean anything by it,' she said. 'Oh, not at all. Good day to you, sir.'

He inched closer. 'Master,' he said, leaning over her. 'Say it!'

'Master,' she whispered, bowing.

Hearing her say it to him made him feel taller. He clenched his buttocks then transferred his weight to his heels.

'Well? Report? Nocturnal activities in the Queen's chambers?'

'The King came to my mistress again last night, but he does not seem to find any joy in the sport of it and neither does she.'

While De Nieto knew the fate of the kingdom was hanging on the production of a male heir, the thought of his majesty mounting his mare did not bring joy, but an opposite and liverish sensation.

4

SPACE

Greta had given Alex an ultimatum. Either drop her challenge to Montano altogether or, if she couldn't, take three weeks to see if she could find some evidence. She didn't know if Greta would hold her internship if she failed. It was a risk.

Alex had chosen the second option but now, back in her tiny studio flat, she wondered if she had been too rash. She wasn't capable of something like this, was she? Books were scattered around her on the floor – some from the local library, others purchased over the years at second-hand bookshops, and a few that had belonged to her mum. They were mainly second-hand accounts, or theoretical suppositions about a painting created in 1656, more than three hundred and thirty years ago. Where were the eyewitnesses? Dead. She closed the book in her hand and sighed, leaning her head against the wall. What she needed was something from the man himself, the artist Diego Velázquez, or from a contemporary account by someone who lived around the same time. She'd promised to find evidence but didn't know where to begin. None of the sources she had here mentioned 'curses' in relation to *Las Meninas*; so why had Picasso said what he did about Velázquez's painting? If only her mother were still alive. She'd help Alex look for answers, surely – in fact, she might have already found them.

Alex had made a start on her work on Picasso, trawling through every interview she could find for comments made by the artist. These were written on cards and kept in a pile on top of her desk. For each quotation she'd written the source and the date. Picasso was a prolific artist, who'd inspired great devotion in friends and biographers. Some had written about him so enthusiastically they were almost evangelical in their fervour. But it was Picasso's words that kept running through her head. 'My canvases, finished or not, are the pages of my diary,' his partner François Gilot had recorded him as saying. And, even more intriguing, 'Each time I begin a painting I have the feeling of throwing myself into space. I never know whether I'll land on my feet . . .' What had he meant by that? But she couldn't think about Picasso now. Velázquez was meant to be the focus; if only she had his words as she did Picasso's.

She needed her mother's papers. All her research on the painting *Las Meninas*. Where was it? What had happened to it? She was going to have to get in touch with her dad, which wouldn't be easy, as they'd stopped being able to talk about Rosara a long time ago. The incident at the Prado had set him off – but the problems had really begun earlier, after the accident that killed her mum when Alex was seven.

Standing, Alex went to the kitchenette and took an orange from the small fridge. The studio was the shape of a shoebox and not much bigger. There was one tall sash window and only enough room for a single bed. The room must have been well-proportioned once, but it had been partitioned, badly. She could hear the couple who lived on the other side talking to each other, sometimes with voices raised. If this room had once been a living room, they must have got the fireplace. Alex had a two-bar heater.

She held the orange to her nose and sat on her one big cushion on the floor by the open window. Outside, the street was lined with parked cars, but most residents used the tube. All the houses matched; they would have been grand residences once. Across the street, a woman arrived home carrying plastic shopping bags. Her shoulders were rounded with strain as she dumped the bags at her feet and groped in her handbag for her keys.

Taking up her notes, Alex considered her crossed-out writing. She had been trying to remember the exact wording from her mum's postcard. She had thought she knew it by heart, but it was proving elusive. The start was easy: *Dearest David.* And she remembered the middle – *Picasso said it was a picture painted with curses* – and the end: *I miss you. Love to you both, as always, Rosara.* In between, there'd been a reference to 'paz', which Alex knew meant peace. And her mother had mentioned a name that started with C, but try as she might Alex couldn't recall more than that.

She tossed the notebook aside and dug her thumbnail into the top of the orange, making a crescent, and from there began to peel. Better to dig her nails into the skin of an orange than into her own skin, as she used to do at school in Cornwall when they teased her for being dumb, for losing her voice. Little jets of orange oil launched from the skin of the fruit. She loved the smell. She made a pile of peel on the floor beside her, then split the orange in half and began eating the segments one by one. They were juicy. Better than usual. Maybe this one hadn't sat in Sainsbury's for six weeks. Maybe it had come from a tree in Spain. *Naranja*, she remembered; that was Spanish for 'orange'.

'Nar-an-ja,' she said.

That night, she rang Helen and was happy to hear that her friend would be coming up from Brighton. Helen's cousin, whom Helen said she wanted Alex to meet, had given her two free tickets to a concert. Alex agreed to go with her even though it was some classical thing at St Martin-in-the-Fields. But really she just wanted to see Helen; they didn't have that many opportunities these days, and Alex missed her. Helen had been her best friend ever since Alex had been delivered to Broadhurst, the boarding school where her dad had dumped her before he took off overseas.

'It's a date then – see you Friday.' Helen was about to ring off.

'Do you still have it?' The question had been on her mind for some time.

'Have what?' Helen sounded guarded.

'You know – your photo. The photo.'

'Alex . . .' Helen's tone carried a warning. She was protective of Alex, always had been.

'Can you just bring it, please, when you come to London?'

'Are you sure? You want to bring all that up again?'

All that. She didn't know if Helen would do as she asked. But she had to. Alex's job depended on it.

'Yes,' she said, and quickly hung up the phone before Helen could ask anything more.

5

ALTARPIECE

1659

My mother has a headache and I really deplore it. Margarita put down her quill and studied her writing. The Countess would be pleased with how carefully she had shaped her letters; they all had the same even incline. *Today, my sister and I were allowed to sit on the balcony. Yesterday, we visited the Convent of San Plácido with Mama . . .*

The Countess told her to write in her letters of what happened to her during the course of a day, or a week. In this, her ninth year, she was reading the tales of Ovid from the palace bookshelves, along with passages from the Bible. Diego Velázquez believed girls should be allowed to read and her father, the King, agreed with him. Her mother disagreed but paid little heed.

Her mother's headaches were becoming more frequent. This was the third time in as many weeks that activities had been cancelled due to the Queen becoming indisposed and retreating to her quarters. When the regular dances and theatrical entertainments were cancelled, life was tedious, but her mother's withdrawal gave Margarita more opportunity for writing and visiting the studio and exploring the alcázar (albeit with her attendants in tow) than she would have had otherwise. Luisa, especially, was obliging, letting her process about the palace with herself or Maribárbola for company. 'A girl must have exercise,' she said. The alcázar was like a town in itself, though one purely for the royal family and their attendants.

Margarita fiddled with her quill. She cast her mind back to what had happened yesterday, at the church adjoining the nunnery.

On entering she had found herself momentarily blinded in the gloom and she had to pause to let her eyes adjust. As they did, she noticed a stand of votive candles. Luisa helped her take a taper and light one for Balthazar, the half-brother she'd never met, who had been known as the pride of Spain. They always had to say a prayer for him. Margarita had noticed how the mention of Balthazar caused the Queen's neck to stiffen and her chin to droop; how her mama's hand hovered before her belly, which was flat once more. She had had Margarita when she was fifteen, less than a year after she'd arrived from Austria, and only one baby since, little Felipe, about whose cradle they'd hung amulets for good luck.

The abbess appeared, lips pursed. A cord was wound twice around the waist of her gown. From this hung a collection of keys. The abbess' feet were wide, her bunions scarcely bound by her sandals. She opened her hands towards the Queen.

The Queen and the abbess disappeared into a confessional against the far wall, a little apart from the pews. Margarita wanted to enter the confessional too, and hear the secrets being told in there, or tell her own, but she wasn't yet old enough. However, she wouldn't want to reveal anything to the abbess, whose eyes were strangely furtive.

She followed her older half-sister, Maria-Theresa, towards the front of the church, noticing the sound their skirts made as they swept across the stone floor. They curtsied and genuflected before the altar, with its two brass candlesticks and a silver chalice. Maria-Theresa edged sideways into the front pew and sat. Margarita, with assistance from Luisa, did the same, but the bands of her guardainfante pressed against the base of her spine and pinched under her thighs. She couldn't get comfortable. Wearing the skirt was like sitting inside a pumpkin, and you couldn't go to the toilet. This caused consternation for Mama. Agustina had taken to bringing a jug with them in the carriage and had been known to disappear under the queen's skirt to hold it for her. Margarita bit her lip and glanced at her sister. She shouldn't be thinking such thoughts here. Maria-Theresa took her hand, kissed it, and smiled with a dreamy expression, then bowed her head in apparent prayer. Margarita arranged her own hands on her lap.

Maria-Theresa was twenty-one, nearly as old as Mama, who was twenty-four. Maria-Theresa had been promised to the King of France, which was where *her* mother, Philip's first wife, had come from. Margarita loved Maria-Theresa and wished she wouldn't leave, even if her marriage was to put an end to years and years of war. France and Spain had been at war all of Margarita's short life, and for decades before that. It was normal; everyone accepted it. Spaniards spilled their blood for the King every day and loved him as a father just the same, or so they said. Her mama assured her that even after Maria-Theresa left they would still be able to see her, but Maria-Theresa had warned her that this was unlikely. The revelation that her mama was not telling the truth had come as a shock to Margarita.

The murmuring in the confessional continued. Was she imagining things, or were the voices becoming louder? What sins could her mother have to confess? Surely Mama was above sin? Maybe Margarita should repent her own sins now, but she couldn't think of any. She'd left food for a mouse in the hallway outside her room last week. Crumbs of bread on the floor. Did that count?

She'd not paid much attention to the painting behind the altar before, but now she gazed up, and her eyes travelled over a pair of bare feet. There was a large nail in the centre of each foot, passing through the skin and the bone and into the wood behind. Rivulets of blood were trickling from each nail hole, following the lines of the bones in the man's feet and between his toes. Some of the blood was brighter red, and seemed wet, and some was darker, dry. The blood had dribbled onto the small board beneath his feet, too, and run in two long drips down the base of the cross. A fly buzzed in the church; she could hear it flying above them, as if attracted by the blood. She had seen a bleeding man before, but from far away in the Plaza Mayor, when they made her wait all day for the *auto-da-fé*, but she'd never seen a naked man like this, not even a painted one. This was a naked, crucified, bleeding man. This was intimate, just Christ, with her, and He was *so close*. His weight rested more on his right leg, the left knee was flexed forwards and the left hip slightly dropped. A cloth was tied around his hips and knotted at the front before his man parts, so you couldn't see anything. His body was so simple. His fingers curled over the nails piercing his palms. His hands must hurt. A tiny bit of blood ran down his wrist. She touched her own palms, traced the lines that crisscrossed them and imagined a nail piercing her skin. Her stomach lurched.

Maria-Theresa, head bowed, recited her rosary in a low voice. Behind them, Luisa sat in contemplation. Mama was still with the abbess. Would she care that Margarita was seeing . . . this?

Margarita returned to her study of the man. Someone had cut him, a little angled slice on his chest. Mean. Blood dripped from here too. How much blood did a person have to lose? His hair was brown, hanging long and straight, covering the right side of his face. He was painted as if he were still alive. There were real crosses like this at the gates of the town, and every week fresh sinners and traitors were hung there to die. She wasn't meant to see them. When they went by carriage to Aranjuez, the summer palace outside Madrid, Luisa tried to distract her, but Luisa couldn't hide the foul smells or mask the sound of the crows.

She wondered which artist had painted him, but then knew immediately that it was her own Velázquez. Velázquez had spent hours with Christ in his mind, rendering His flesh in his magical way. But when had he had time? These days his main job was to paint Margarita and her family.

Christ's skin seemed smooth, almost hairless, like hers, pale like the candles on the stand, the ones you had to press upon a spike to make them stand up.

What did the nuns think as they prayed under this naked man who accepted his fate like this? She sat here within her guardainfante of lashed willow and her padded skirt and her boned corset, bound inside her carapace of a dress. But for Him there were no leggings, no doublet, no cape, just a rag around his hips and a crown of thorns. There were words written on a board above his head. She tried but could not read them. She nudged Maria-Theresa and pointed.

Her sister paused in her devotions and craned her head.

'It's Latin,' said Maria-Theresa. After a few moments, she said: 'Jesus . . . something of the Jews.'

'It says "Jesus of Nazareth, the King of the Jews",' said Luisa from the pew behind them. 'Your papa commissioned the work years ago, as a gift to the nunnery.'

A gift that called Jesus the King of the Jews? That must be a mistake. Her father hated the Jews. No one was allowed to be Jewish in the court; they all had to have pure blood.

They sat in silence for some time longer. Margarita heard the singing murmur of the abbess' voice. She must be doing the blessing. But then her mother said very clearly, 'I *will* find out!' and everybody jolted upright. The curtain was flung back and the Queen appeared, her mouth in a straight line, her chin high. She tilted her head towards the door. It was time to go.

Back in her chamber, Margarita put her quill down. What was the abbess hiding? Why was her mama, the Queen, so perturbed?

6

PAPERCHASE

Alex forced herself to call Bettina, her dad's old girlfriend. They hadn't spoken for some time, but Bettina was likely to know some of the people with whom he was working. David's last letter to Alex had been sent from Greece; he'd been planning to head to Turkey and the Middle East, with a team documenting Byzantine mosaics. Eventually, with Bettina's help, Alex got a number for his latest hotel, and left a message.

Alex was at her aunt Flora's place in Clapham. They had dinner together at least once a week. On the kitchen table, beside a copy of *The Guardian*, was a dental pick, a few pens and pencils, a small trowel and a magnifying glass. Alex picked up the magnifying glass and looked through it at Flora, who had her hands in the sink.

'Looks like you have another dig coming up,' said Alex.

Flora turned her head and grinned. 'Mm, Portugal – next month.' Flora was an archaeologist.

Alex grabbed a tea towel and began to dry the plates. She was still at it when the phone rang.

'There you go,' said Flora. As if to say, *See* . . .

Alex hadn't seen her dad in six months. He'd popped by when she was at the poster shop and seemed a bit lost for words when he saw her circumstances. At least she'd been earning her own money, she'd been proud of that. He had looked at her feet, the floor, the walls, even the cash register – everywhere except into her eyes. Before he left, he'd thrust her mum's postcard at her, as if it was hot. Without that she might never have gone to see Montano talk.

On the phone, he responded to her question. 'Yes, Rosara had a lot of notes. She was writing a paper, something about the Hapsburgs – Spanish branch, royal family . . .'

'That's it,' said Alex. This was going to be a big help. Maybe she would have some of her mother's research soon. There had been many times when her aunt Flora had tried to encourage Alex's dad to talk more about Rosara. The fact that he wouldn't, or couldn't, was a sore point for all of them. Alex had given up trying – until now.

Flora was smiling, nodding.

'There was something wrong with them, Rosara thought – more than the inbreeding.'

'Where are Mum's notes now, Dad? What happened to them?' She could barely get the words out in the right order.

'She must have taken them with her to Spain; I know she didn't leave them at home in Cornwall. I suppose they're still there some- where, in Spain. I have no idea where. If she had them with her, they would have been destroyed in the . . .' His speech slowed, like a 45 rpm record played on 33. As if, like Alex, he could somehow see the car leaving the road, see it rolling over and over, past olive trees and thyme bushes, down the hill.

'Car crash . . .' She said it for him. They had to face it. They never really had. Not together.

'Accident.'

Her father ended the call quickly after that. Their own wheels had left the road, in a different way, after Rosara's death. Life became harder; her dad had softened the edges with alcohol for a while. The more he drank, the quieter Alex had become. Then they'd gone to the Prado and seen the painting, *Las Meninas*, and . . .

She felt Flora's hand on her shoulder.

'It was tough for him when you went missing,' said Flora.

'It wasn't for that long.'

'Well, yes, but to a parent it can seem an eternity. He thought he'd lost you too.'

'But he didn't.'

'Didn't he? He blamed himself.'

Flora came and sat down opposite Alex at the table and took one of her hands.

'I think there might be something in my attic,' she said.

Something? Flora could be forgetful. She frequently lost her car keys and her glasses.

'Some things Rosara posted – and a notebook. I'd forgotten until now. Rosara and David had been thinking of moving house around that time, so she sent them to me, asked me to keep them for her. I must have mentioned them to David, but he never got around to collecting them. He had other . . . er, issues, to deal with and so did I. I'm sorry, I should have thought of this before.'

Alex pushed herself back from the table and leapt to her feet. They had to find whatever it was that Flora was talking about. *Now.*

An hour later they had moved numerous boxes and unpacked several others and still not found anything. Flora had cobwebs in her hair and Alex was sneezing from the dust.

'Why didn't you tell your dad about your internship?' Flora asked as they searched. 'You know he'd be thrilled.'

'I, ah . . .' Alex could not come up with an answer but she knew Flora was right.

Suddenly, Flora launched herself towards a bookshelf on the far wall and seized a brown envelope from the bottom shelf.

'Yes! This is it,' she said, dusting it off and handing it to Alex.

Inside the envelope, which was addressed to Flora, she found a spiral-bound notebook and an old *Vogue* magazine. On the cover was a woman in a voluminous red dress. Alex frowned; her mum hadn't really been into fashion, had she? And then there was the date: 1956. 'This is *old*,' she said.

'Not *that* old,' Flora protested.

Alex opened the magazine at a black-and-white photo of Picasso. He gazed challengingly into the camera lens, his dark eyes swimming in his large round head above the horizontal lines of his striped Breton shirt.

Perhaps this was significant, but there were no obvious notes on the accompanying text. Scanning rapidly, she saw no mention of anything connected to *Las Meninas*, certainly no images of it, although there was quite a bit about the author's visit to Picasso and a long lunch. Alex dropped the magazine on the floor and took up the notebook. She felt Flora's hand on her shoulder as she opened the cover, emblazoned with an 'R', and saw her mum's name written neatly inside: *Rosara Johns.*

'I never read it,' Flora said. 'I think it was private. I'll leave you.'

Alex perched on a single bed, between an old vacuum cleaner and a beer crate full of tools wrapped in cloth. Alex was familiar with the implements Flora used on her digs. She had even helped her occasionally in her holidays. Alex took a deep breath and turned to the first page. She was looking at a rough pencil sketch of combinations of rectangles. Five rectangles, to be exact: two above, which were horizontal, and three more below, of similar proportions, but vertical. Maybe her mum had been doodling? She turned the page. It was the same. She sighed. The same pattern repeated for several more pages. The shapes meant nothing. A subsequent page included a series of numbers: 16381734 . . . but there was no indication of what they meant. Was it a phone number? A reference? Or dates? Then there were a few blank pages, followed by an actual drawing, a good one, of a street scene, with old stone buildings on either side, one of which had a bell tower. Her mother could have been an artist, like her dad. They had met at art school. David had stopped painting after Rosara died. Before they left the Cornwall house, he had wrapped all his brushes in green baize and stashed them on a high shelf at the top of the stairs. His movements had been forceful and jerky, she recalled, as he'd stuffed them out of sight. Those brushes had previously been freely used and shared. They were probably still there. Alex spent some time studying her mother's sketch, noting the vanishing point at the end of the street. Her father had taught her about this effect. They'd been sitting in a cafe and she was eating a caramel flan, swinging her legs, which didn't reach the floor. They must have been in Spain – a place that, for a short time, had seemed like home. There was a house with wide-planked floors, and they had eaten outdoors at a table with a green-checked cloth, under a grapevine. She remembered feeding figs to the goat tethered in the garden, while the grown-ups chatted and drank wine on the terrace. She remembered how her mother used to speak to her in snatches of Spanish.

Quashing a pang of grief, she brought her mind back to her dad and what he'd shown her that day in the cafe; how he'd pulled a pencil stub from his pocket and sketched a few lines on a paper serviette, explaining as he drew, 'It gives a picture perspective, depth of field. If you are drawing three-dimensional space, the parallel lines appear to converge in the distance, and where they converge is called the vanishing point.' His four lines on the serviette represented the floor, ceiling and walls of a room. At the back of the room he added a small rectangle. 'In this case, it's a single-point perspective,' he said, 'and the vanishing point is here, in the doorway.' He marked this with an X. 'See how this point is exactly where, if you continued this line here from this side and this one from the floor, these lines would meet . . .'

Alex adjusted her position on the bed in Flora's attic and gazed at her mum's drawing. Her pencil had recorded the outlines of the stone blocks on the walls, even a little plaque, which might have included a street name, but the detail was an indecipherable squiggle. In the bottom right-hand corner, though, Rosara had written: *Madrid*. Somewhere in Madrid, her mother had sat to do a drawing. *Thanks, Mum*, Alex thought, sighing.

She turned the page and found another drawing, this time of a square-fronted tower with a wooden door and ornate metal hinges. This too was old, historic, but it could be from anywhere. Nothing in the notebook seemed to relate specifically to *Las Meninas*. The first pages, the rectangles, were like the kind of doodles someone did while they were talking on the phone, and the drawings could have been travel sketches. Alex flicked through the remaining pages. Most were blank, but on one her mother had written: *A painting is a search*. What did that mean? And towards the end of the note-book was another drawing. A hook, hanging from the top of the page, like a question mark. Or was it a noose? Following this was a cartoon-like sketch of a couple of stick figures, with cloud-shaped thought bubbles above their heads. But those 'bubbles' were empty. Was this a joke? She frowned and bit her lip.

This wasn't what she needed. These were barely notes and didn't contain the information she required. Maybe her faith in her mum was misguided and her own search was all a terrible mistake. She sat forwards, hands on her knees, her eyes prickling. She sniffed, brushed her hair out of her eyes. What was she going to tell Greta? Her plan was a feeble, hopeless thing. Who was she kidding? She had no plan. She surveyed the jumbled furniture and tools. Although the attic seemed chaotic, Flora was not chaotic – she had purpose. As an archaeologist, she kept on digging and brushing, methodically, layer-by-layer. Alex had a purpose here too, she reminded herself.

As she reached down to pick up the magazine from the floor, she noticed the protruding corner of a folded piece of paper. Alex picked it up. The paper was flimsy, designed for airmail letters.

She unfolded it. Within quote marks and with scribbles and crossings out, were the following words:

'The light from my candle throws the chisel marks of the masons who built this chamber into sharp relief. The bumps and undulations of the dun-coloured stone put me in mind of the plains I knew so well, and every trail upon those plains leads to Madrid . . .'

Alex frowned. The plains I knew so well? Madrid? Who had written this? Her mother? The handwriting was hers, but the quote marks suggested that it was an extract, a quotation. Beside it were a few words in both Spanish and English, as if her mother had been translating – *light/ligera, candle/vela*. Who had been writing by candlelight in a stone chamber?

Alex read the words again, folded the paper slowly and slipped it back into the magazine. Carefully she turned the few remaining pages of the notebook. On the second-to-last page were three lines:

I'm heading to Toledo tomorrow . . . Someone has been following me, I think. I've told David. He thinks I'm being paranoid. Let's hope he's right.

Then:

Toledo . . . I was right. He is following me!
He mustn't learn about Paz, or F . . .

This last note was an urgent scrawl and Alex's pulse began to race as she read it. Someone had followed Rosara to Toledo – it had to be because of what she was working on. *He mustn't learn about Paz.* Paz – like in the postcard. She'd thought it meant 'peace', but her mother had used a capital letter; could it be that Paz was a person? Someone in Toledo, perhaps? And who or what was F?

Rosara had been followed to Toledo, and then she had died. Alex's hand flew to her mouth as the certainty hit her: her mother's death had not been an accident.

For a moment she couldn't breathe.

With trembling hands she picked up the notebook again, tracing the outline of her mother's 'R' with her finger. Turning the notebook over in her hands, she flicked it open from the back, and her eye was caught by a name scrawled on the inside cover: *Prof Leadbeater, Oxford.* Her mother had studied at Oxford. Had she known this professor? Was the professor somehow connected to the research Rosara had been doing in Spain?

Alex jumped up, returned the items to the envelope and headed for the door. She would have to go to Oxford and find out.

7

A SKETCH

The Courtauld Institute of Art, arranged around a stately courtyard, was a veritable palace of art and art analysis. Inside,
all was orderly and air-conditioned, to a precise temperature of
between eighteen to twenty-four degrees celsius. Greta's office was
in the rear of the building, which was no reflection of her status. She
had retreated here after the furore at Christie's. Her green opera
coat was now on a coathanger on the back of the door and Greta,
in her black poloneck and skirt, picked up a fresh pair of white
cotton gloves and slid them onto her manicured hands. Work always
soothed her. A client had sent a nineteenth-century watercolour for
assessment earlier that week. The minor work now lay face down
on her workbench. Beside it was an old drawing, which she had
just discovered hidden inside the frame.

The drawing was in pencil or charcoal, unsigned, but she
recognised instantly that it could be special. The paper was soft,
and it had seen better days, but it was the confidence of the hand
that excited her.

It was a sketch, the head and shoulders of a man, with gleaming eyes. The gleam was no trick of the light. This was skill, a rarely seen skill. The drawing was gestural and free; the face that now stared at her was well rounded – but there was something perturbing in his gaze.

Though unsigned, she mentally compared it to drawings by the Flemish master, Peter Paul Rubens – there was a similarity in style – but the odds of it being a work by one such master were slim. Reproductions and copies were increasingly common. Copyists in Asia and Europe had learned techniques for ageing paper. They were also attempting to slip them into established collections in order to gain more credence. She shouldn't get ahead of herself; it wouldn't do to go making brash assertions. The girl, Alex, came to mind. Greta shook her head, and chuckled. Alex reminded her of herself at that age. But Greta had learned caution. Evidence was the thing. Provenance, a trail that would prove ownership, validated by bills of sale, testaments and the eventual connection to an artist. Letters, signatures – this work had none of these things. She checked again. The right-hand corner of the work was unsigned. There were no evident initials. All the same, Montano *was* in town and although she disliked the idea, for the vendor's sake, she should see if he had any thoughts. He might be intrigued, as she was. She imagined herself bringing him into the room, practised in her mind the pitch of her voice. The intern, Alex, had caused quite a stir, and Montano had been irked. She must be going soft, giving the girl time to go on what was probably a wild-goose chase. She winced. Challenging dogma? There was a time when that was *her* modus operandi. 'No sudden movements' was the rule in the conservation studio. It was the unwritten rule in the literature of the field, too. Sometimes she worried that in the course of her career she'd ended up saying more and more about less and less, rather than saying what she really thought.

8

ORANGES

1659

Margarita and Luisa were sitting under the east wall of the alcázar, in the orchard of the prioress, when Pepito came leaping across the grass towards them. 'Pick-a-nicking under an orange tree with only bread and cheese, Your Royal Highness – what a to-do!'

Margarita stood up. Luisa would not let her climb the tree.

Pepito, who was dressed in a green doublet with a lace collar and wide culottes, was one of the most energetic dwarves – the Queen called them 'buffoons' or 'foundlings' – who enlivened the court. At the whim of her father, the King, Pepito and his compatriots wove nimbly through heavy, etiquette-laden seas, poking fun at the stiffest of the courtiers and least-popular royal rules. While her father walked around as rigid as a statue and all the attendants were so careful in their every move and word, Pepito and his friends could fire barbed arrows from their mouths, and everyone would simply laugh. Pepito was the one to watch during gatherings; he said things no one else dared. Sometimes Luisa explained his ripostes to Margarita; other times she declined to do so. 'Not for your ears, child,' she would say, which only made Margarita listen harder.

Luisa had explained it once: 'When you are trussed up like a chicken, my darling, every now and then you have to sneeze. Pepito helps us all to sneeze.'

'But you don't sneeze, you laugh.'

'Well, yes, we have to laugh like we have to sneeze. Everyone needs to laugh sometimes,' she said. 'It releases the pressure.'

Pepito went down on one knee before Margarita, his close-cropped fringe crowning his bowed head. 'Though I am not of great stature, Your Highness, I can climb like a goat, and I have the heart of a lion,' he declared, slapping his chest, then feigning pain. 'I see the object of your heart's desire; this shining orange jewel above us. Command me, and I shall fetch it for you.'

'Do goats climb trees?' Margarita asked.

'They do now!' He swung himself up the trunk and into the higher branches, where he stopped and emitted a strange bleat. Plucking a leaf from the tree, he placed it in his mouth and chewed, his jaw moving sideways like that of a goat.

Margarita giggled.

With his hand shading his eyes, he peered into the distance. 'Your Majesty, I see the table-lands and I see the sierras . . . Yonder are the villagers who marvel at royal Madrid, the Spanish Babylon. Luckily, they do not see that the fabulous alcázar itself is patched here and there with brick and even mud; that the splendid court struggles to pay its bills; that the displays of wealth and power are mere reflections of a grandeur which once was . . . Your loyal subjects are toiling in the heat of the sun. They ply their fields – the fields of the nobles of the court, that is – to bring a little wheat to make your bread. But in these lean years, the *vacas flacas* – the poor, thin cows – are struggling to produce even a little milk for your cup.'

Luisa was shaking her head.

Pepito continued. 'You know they are talking in the *mentideros*, Luisa, in the gossip parlours; they ask what price the King would pay for another son. Perhaps you know the answer? They are betting on my lady's belly.'

Luisa frowned.

'*Naranja!*' Impatient, Margarita pointed at the golden fruit.

Pepito plucked the baubles, launched into a backwards somer-sault from the branch on which he was balanced, and landed, smiling, at Margarita's feet, holding a scented orange in each hand.

'Arise, Sir Orange-fetcher,' she said, anointing his shoulders with an imaginary glove.

Pepito drew the knife worn in a scabbard at his belt and offered its black-and-silver handle to Margarita. She took the knife and tapped him lightly on each shoulder.

'Yours to command,' he said.

Margarita returned his knife and he cut the orange, which he'd described as a shining jewel. Margarita took several bites, until the juice ran down her chin.

'My special . . .' Margarita loved that Pepito had called the oranges 'jewels'. She wanted to mention her own jewel, the blue diamond her parents had given her, which she thought of as her star, but Luisa stopped her with a look.

'What's the matter, Luisa, you can trust me,' said Pepito. 'Don't worry; I don't report to De Nieto, much as he would like me to . . .'

'No one in their right mind would trust you!' Luisa retorted. 'You're hardly famous for your discretion.'

Pepito pouted. 'I'm not renowned yet, Luisa. But I will be. The master, Velázquez, has said he will paint my portrait. He sees something special in me, and I too will be immortalised . . . People will see this fabulous countenance' – here he squeezed his cheeks together – 'in a hundred years.'

Pepito bent down and picked up some earth from beneath the tree and studied it, then he held it out to Margarita, trickling it into her outstretched hands.

She rubbed the dirt across her soft white palm. It was a deep *marrón* mix, dry and grainy; it filled the tiny grooves and lines in her palm, which Luisa had said contained the story of her future.

'The master paints us from the ground up,' said Pepito. 'He starts with dirt like this, but especially with the red soil of Seville, mixed to a paste to prime his canvas, and on that ground he creates us in light and shade and then he moulds our flesh from lead *blanco*, from carmine our blood, and under his hand our forms become plump and round and begin to breathe and verily to sprout hair, all within his vision of who we really are.' He paused. 'There is one other who creates us from the clay, and that is the Heavenly Father himself.'

'You are full of talk, Pepito,' said Luisa, making the sign of the cross, then raising a pinch of grit from the ground and tossing it over her shoulder, as if to ward off the spirits. 'Do you want the churchmen of the Inquisition to visit with us in the Plaza Mayor? Do not assume young ears cannot hear you.'

Margarita took a bite of orange.

Pepito continued, 'The monks, Luisa, they whisper that there will be a cost to this invigorated art of his, that the forces emanating from his divining rod can corrupt or distort those whose spirits are weak, those who gather around him to fawn and feed on the drips from his easel.'

Luisa was listening intently now and nodding, head tilted. Margarita stood quietly, for she did not want Pepito to stop. He was speaking of Velázquez, her favourite within the court, and of the power of his art. This much she knew.

'Velázquez paints the truth,' said Margarita. 'He tells me so.'

Luisa placed a hand over her mouth.

'Our artist must watch out,' Pepito went on, 'for there are those who are afraid of the truth. Those who resent his influence – his *friendship* – with the King; to them he will never escape his humble origins, never be a true noble. They love that his duties give him less and less time to create masterpieces; that he is owed more than a year's worth of wages but can say nothing. De Nieto . . .'

Luisa nodded. 'Aye, De Nieto is jealous. It's eating him up . . .'

Pepito clutched at the front of his jerkin, scrunching the fabric between his fingers. 'It *devours* him.'

Luisa rolled her eyes and sighed. 'I am wary of him,' she whispered. 'His eyes are blank. There is nothing there.'

Margarita wondered what Luisa meant. She abhorred De Nieto, and she had sensed he did not like Velázquez.

'Ah yes: as we know, the keeper of the royal tapestries likes to weave in more ways than one. Duran is encouraging his . . . spinning. It's the jealousy which has made him a husk of himself,' said Pepito. He began skipping in circles around them and the tree, then he paused, saying, 'Her Highness the Queen is expecting a visitor sent by her brother in Vienna. The man has reached Italy, they say. A nuptial reconnaissance mission. You know he wants our treasure.' At this he waved his arms towards Margarita, bowed, and then skipped off.

After Pepito had gone, Margarita and Luisa peeled the remaining orange. Luisa fed her segment after segment, and they sat for a long time in juicy silence. There would be no such hasty eating allowed in the royal dining hall, where each mouthful was tasted before it passed royal lips, and where those lips were dabbed after each unappetising portion.

Luisa picked sprigs of orange blossom and wove them through her hair. The scent of the oranges was all around them. Margarita's chin was still sticky with juice when Luisa led her back to the arched side door through which they had emerged earlier. Margarita trailed her fingers over the patched mud and stones of the castle wall, then halted.

'Let's not go in,' she said. 'Let's run away, over there, to the fields. You could take me to your village. I will meet your family.'

Luisa chuckled. 'You wouldn't like it there, my dear.'

'I would like to see for myself,' said Margarita.

They surveyed the lands below, bathed now in a golden light. Smoke was drifting from distant chimneys, low to the ground. The sun was sinking, a hot disc in the sky.

Luisa was staring into the distance, holding her knuckles to her lips.

'The fields are red, Luisa,' said Margarita.

Luisa did not reply.

Margarita pulled at her sleeve and pointed. 'See? They need a wash from the rain.'

'The rain will come, sweet one,' said Luisa.

9

PAVANE

Alex came to an abrupt halt in front of a boy sitting on the bottom step of the entrance to the National Gallery. His head was bowed, and dark hair obscured his face. A battered fedora lay upturned on the footpath in front of him and he held a piece of cardboard on his lap.

She rummaged in her pocket, found fifty pence and dropped it into his hat. At this, he thrust his cardboard sign at her. It read: SHE NEEDS YOU.

She? thought Alex.

When he tilted his head to peer up at her, she realised he wasn't a boy, but a very short man. He was dressed in a dusty smock, with what might once have been a white collar around his neck.

Alex was still puzzling over the words SHE NEEDS YOU as she crossed the road to meet Helen, who was waving to her from the steps of St Martin-in-the-Fields.

They hugged and then Alex asked, 'Did you see him – the little man? His sign?'

'Hi! No, who?' said Helen, linking her arm through Alex's. 'Come on, it's about to start. I want to introduce you to . . .'

They passed through the columned portico. Inside, the church was smaller than Alex expected. Electric candle chandeliers hung on long wires from the arched ceiling. It was a peaceful oasis after the busyness of the streets. A collection of musicians sat up the front, tuning strings and tightening bows. Sidling past those who had already found their seats, Alex followed Helen to the middle of a pew.

'This is going to be a bit different from what I've been listening to,' whispered Helen, smoothing her long brown hair. Then she leaned forwards, grinning, and waved at one of the musicians, the young man sitting in front of a piano. He nodded at Helen. He had freckles and wavy brown hair.

'Oh!' said Alex. It was the guy from the auction house. The one who'd stopped her to talk about the Infanta.

'That's him! Oscar, my cousin, the one I was telling you about.'

'I've seen him before,' said Alex.

'Really? Where?'

Before Alex could explain, a woman in a black dress stepped onto the stage, bowed to the audience and tapped her baton on a music stand. The musicians came to attention.

There were a few coughs from someone in the row behind them, and shuffles and creaks from the seats, then the audience fell silent.

The first notes were from the French horn, followed by what sounded like plucked violin strings but was actually the piano, and then a lone clarinet, slow and sinuous. Alex could see the young man – Oscar – from side on, his hands soft and fluid above the piano keys. The music curled like a cat around her legs and then swept across her chest, around her neck and through her mind. Soon she was falling in slow motion, unable to regain her footing.

The air chilled. Time slowed and unfurled itself in Alex's ear. The sound was the sound of a girl in a wide skirt dancing alone in a large room in an empty palace. Alex could see her as if through a blue prism, a kaleidoscope, quietly turning as she processed, stepping, first one foot, then a pause, then the next. There was a mirror or a doorway at the end of the room and the girl was dancing towards it but could not seem to reach it.

Then Helen was shaking her shoulder and speaking in her ear. 'Alex . . . Alex . . . It's over.'

The music had stopped. The woman next to her was clapping. Gradually the applause faded. Alex rubbed her arms. Her fingers were numb; she could barely move her hands. Around her people were shuffling out of the pews, heading for the exit.

'Margarita – she needs me,' said Alex, feeling her lips move, hearing herself speak, but it seemed the words were not her own.

Helen was looking at her, concerned. 'What are you saying?'

'Did I fall asleep?' asked Alex.

'No, not exactly – you were in, like, a trance or something. It was weird. Your eyes were open but there was no one home. Are you okay? You look pale. Let's get some air.'

'It was her! Helen, it was her – Margarita! – the Infanta Margarita . . .'

Alex's palms were damp. She pressed her hand against her forehead. Her skin was clammy.

'Let's get out of here,' Helen repeated.

They made their way outside. Alex stopped at the top of the wide steps, craning her head, trying to see over the shoulders of the crowd. She was looking for the small man, but he was gone.

Someone bumped into her and muttered an apology.

'Come on, we need to move,' said Helen, tugging at her arm.

And then Oscar appeared at the bottom of the steps and called to Helen, signalling that they should follow him.

They found him waiting around the corner, leaning against a tall wrought-iron fence. Helen gave him a hug. 'You were great.'

'Thanks.' Oscar's face lit up as he recognised Alex. 'Hello again!'

'Again?' said Helen. 'Sorry, but we need a place where we can sit down. Do you know somewhere close? Alex is feeling a bit faint.'

He snapped to attention. 'Of course,' he said. 'We can go in here: the Café in the Crypt.'

A deep-set doorway cut into the side of the church opened onto steep stone steps leading to a vaulted basement. Framed rubbings of tombstones hung on either side. Down below, it was dim. A serving counter with a coffee machine and small bar stood in the centre, lit by a few electric lights. The farthest recesses of the space leached into blackness. Tables were lit with candles. Some of the flagstones were engraved with names. Alex didn't know where to put her feet. Didn't want to stand on anyone's grave.

Oscar ushered them to a table. 'So *you're* Helen's friend, Alex — it's good to see you again. Thanks for coming. Are you okay?'

Alex nodded and slipped into a seat.

'What's this, *again?*' said Helen, taking off her jacket.

'Mm, at a lecture . . .' Alex replied.

'Glass of water? Juice? Wine?' Oscar was still looking at Alex. 'Was it too hot in there?' he asked.

She shook her head and tried to smile. 'Water, please.'

'I'll have a sangria,' said Helen, reading the blackboard menu.

When Oscar returned with the drinks, Helen said, 'Alex has a thing for Spain.'

Oscar immediately turned to Alex. 'Do you speak Spanish?' he asked. 'I don't, but I'll be doing a student exchange there soon.'

Alex shook her head. 'I can understand a little, but I don't really speak it.'

'Yes, she can, when she wants to,' said Helen.

'That could be helpful . . .' He was reading philosophy and music at the University of London, he explained. 'Our conductor told us about this piece – the one we played earlier – and I'm working on it for my assessment. My supervisor wants me to learn as much about it as I can.'

'What *is* the piece?' asked Alex.

Oscar leaned back in his chair and brushed a curl of brown hair out of his eyes. 'It was written for a Spanish princess, an infanta,' he explained. 'It's called *Pavane pour une Infante Défunte – Pavane for a Dead Princess* – by Maurice Ravel.'

Alex sat forwards in her seat. He had mentioned this when they first met. 'An infanta? Which infanta?'

'We don't know. Ravel didn't say. He was French but his mother was Spanish, and he described it as an evocation of a pavane a little Spanish princess *might* have danced. I'm trying to find out if he was referring to a specific princess,' said Oscar.

A familiar feeling, as if someone or something was coming up behind her, made Alex glance over her shoulder and pull her chair even closer to the table.

'You were great, by the way,' Helen said to Oscar. 'But I didn't know you were playing Spanish music.' She leaned in. 'Tell him about Margarita,' she said to Alex, then, to Oscar, 'That's her ghost.'

Oscar raised his eyebrows.

'She's not my ghost, she's . . .' Alex hesitated.

Oscar leaned down and pulled a small square book from his backpack. 'This is her, isn't it?'

Although Alex had become an avid collector of books about Velázquez, she'd not seen this one before. On the dustjacket, which was slightly torn, was an image of a painted girl, perhaps ten or eleven, with shoulder-length blonde hair, swept to the side. She was wearing an ornate blue dress with a gauzy collar. Her eyes were round, almost owl-like, and on her chest was a blue-and-gold brooch, surrounded by a ribbon.

Hello again, thought Alex. 'Yes, that's her. That's Margarita,' she said.

'Her ghost,' Helen cut in.

'Does this have any connection to the curses you mentioned at Christie's?' Oscar asked.

Alex groaned. He was going to think she was nuts; maybe Helen would too.

'You dropped a postcard when you hurried away. A Picasso version of *Las Meninas*. I'm sorry, but I read it, because I was trying to find you. It said that, according to Picasso, *Las Meninas* was a picture painted with curses – which is what you said at the lecture.'

Alex stared at him. 'Do you still have it?' she asked urgently.

'Yes, but I don't have it with me. I wanted to return it, but I didn't know how to find you . . .'

'Christies? And what's this about curses?' Helen was looking from one to the other.

'Yes, we met a few days ago, at a talk at Christie's,' said Oscar.

Alex pressed her hands together and glanced towards the counter and blackboards. She looked across the other tables, then at the floor and the flagstones, which were tombstones. There was a small bowl with sachets of sugar on their table. She picked one up and turned it over, feeling the grains of sugar moving inside, then put the sachet back in the bowl.

'Once, Helen took a photo of me, a portrait, in front of an old mirror. It was while we were at boarding school . . .'

Helen couldn't help herself. 'When we developed it, there was something strange in the picture – it looked like there was another face behind her, watching. It freaked us out!'

Oscar was leaning in. Alex met his eyes. They were brown, gold-flecked. He was not laughing but was concentrating hard – on her. She took a deep breath. 'Her name was the Infanta Margarita. There's something else. I'm not sure how, but I know what a pavane is; it's a dance, an old-fashioned one, sixteenth or seventeenth century . . .'

Oscar nodded and, conducting with his hand in the air, he began to hum a tune. It was the same music that had so entranced her in the concert upstairs. As it echoed around the crypt, a vibration began in Alex's head. Helen was staring at her, her forehead crinkling. Alex began to hum with Oscar, then she stood, staring over their heads, and turned. Taking one purposeful step, and then another, she brought her feet together for a beat, bending her knees slightly, and then repeated the movement, one foot and then the next, moving in a straight line away from the table. As she danced, the trace of the music in her head seemed to become louder. Her movements were automatic, instinctive, as if she were dancing inside someone else's shoes, weighed down by a cumbersome skirt. The cafe around her disappeared; all she could see were large flagstones, an arched stone ceiling, and rows of columns stretching into the darkness.

Helen's hand on her shoulder halted her progression across the floor.

'Alex – stop! You look like Princess Diana walking down the aisle.'

Alex blinked and turned. She was twenty feet away from the table.

Oscar was coming towards her. 'That's it,' he said. 'You've got it absolutely right; the pavane . . .'

They guided her back to the table and sat down.

'The pavane is a procession dance – it doesn't really look like what we would call a dance,' said Oscar. 'It's the basis of the wedding march. Where did you learn it?'

'That's the thing,' said Alex. 'I didn't learn it – I just know.'

❧

In the shadows at the back of the crypt, a man with a neatly trimmed beard and a widow's peak sat watching the three young people at the table by the stairs. When one of them processed across the floor, the hairs stood up on the back of his neck. He recognised that dance – and the infanta whom the girl was invoking. And, though it had been some years, he'd seen the girl before, too; a younger version of her had slipped through his fingers. Alex Johns. Her mother's daughter. He took a sip from a glass of red liquid. Then he adjusted the sleeves of his black shirt. Churches still made him sweat.

10

BLUE

1659

Margarita gazed across the sea of faces in the royal greeting chamber. She sat straight-backed, swinging her legs slightly under her large skirt. Luisa smiled encouragement from Margarita's left, but was positioned too far away for comfort.

Velázquez, in his role as chamberlain, was helping to oversee the comings and goings of those who would petition the King. Many courtiers were trying to gain his attention. Velázquez, positioned near the entrance, spent most of his time listening, head inclined, and spoke little. Occasionally he crossed the room to stand at the right hand of the King, who was dressed in a dark suit. De Nieto, his beard clipped and sharp, hovered behind the Queen and Margarita, occasionally whispering in the Queen's ear. The room was warm. The Queen used a fan, and every now and then a waft of stale air lifted the stray strands of hair around Margarita's face. Margarita wished she would also waft away De Nieto's onion-scented breath.

The herald stepped forwards.

'Your Majesties, may I present Count Franz Eusebius von Pötting, Imperial Ambassador to Spain, emissary of the Holy Roman Emperor Leopold I, Archduke of Austria, King of Germany and Bohemia, King of Hungary and Croatia.'

Pepito had mentioned a visitor from Vienna while she ate oranges in the orchard, Margarita remembered. Her stomach gurgled and she shifted in her seat. She wished she were in the orchard now.

Von Pötting wore a pigeon-grey doublet, buttoned high, with frilled breeches and beribboned shoes. As he bowed, the white lace of his collar flopped around his neck. Lowering one knee to accommodate the girth of his waist, he nearly swept his hat upon the floor.

Pepito was behind the ambassador. He bowed in unison, as if he were the man's shadow, then placed a hand over his bottom, feigning a rip in his breeches. Von Pötting's breeches were satin, and rather tight.

The courtiers who had a good view of both men's posteriors began to smirk. Margarita bit her lip. Pepito was so naughty. He winked, then gazed innocently out of the window.

Von Pötting returned to standing, dabbed his brow, and proceeded to address the King and Queen. After the usual salutations, he began. 'My master, His Royal Highness, Emperor Leopold I –'

The Queen, her hands clasped in her lap, interrupted to ask after the health of her brother, the Emperor.

'He is in excellent health, and is anxious for news of yourself, Your Highness, and the Infanta Margarita.'

His gaze shifted to Margarita, who tapped her slippers together and tried to catch Velázquez's eye, but he was watching the ambassador. The man, von Pötting, might be measuring her for a dress, so intent was he upon her figure.

'The Emperor relishes the earlier portrait sent of his niece and cousin, the Infanta Margarita. It is one of his most prized possessions and takes pride of place within his privy chambers.'

A picture of her? A prized possession? Margarita clasped and reclasped her hands in her lap, squeezing her fingers.

A murmur rippled around the room, which was filling with more courtiers. Those at the back were tiptoeing and craning for a glimpse of the visitor. The ambassador continued to speak. He mentioned letters. He spoke of empires, of contracts and agreements. Margarita stifled a yawn. Von Pötting paused and gripped his hat. He dabbed the sweat from his brow with a kerchief and took a deep breath.

'It is the Emperor's heartfelt wish,' he continued, stumbling a little in his Spanish, 'that another, more recent portrait be created and sent, and that the engagement treaty – about which there has been considerable correspondence – be signed.'

Another murmur went around the salon, louder this time. Everyone was looking at Margarita. She felt eyes scanning from the top of her head to the tip of her satin slippers. She had thought they were talking about Maria-Theresa, her sister who was to marry the French king, but no – it was *her* they were discussing. Her cheeks burned. She shot a glance at Luisa, who made a calming gesture with her hand. Margarita rubbed a small piece of the brocade of her skirt with a fingertip, out of sight, where no one could see. She wished for one moment that was hers alone.

The Queen's profile was turned in the direction of the ambassador. Margarita watched as her mother inclined her long white neck, like a swan, gracious in assent. Her mother loved Austria. She was ignoring Margarita. Didn't she care what her daughter wanted?

The man continued, emboldened, complimenting Margarita, saying she grew more beautiful every day. His master, her uncle, would be delighted that his niece was in such good health, and he humbly passed on to her his master's ardent best wishes. Margarita noticed Luisa's downcast gaze and saw that Velázquez, who had a hand on his cheek, was looking out of a window.

Von Pötting presented gifts, as well as letters and fabrics for the Queen. An attendant appeared behind him holding what appeared to be an animal with brown fur on a cushion. Margarita hoped it might be a rabbit. But, no, it was a muff – the pelt of some eastern bear. She stroked the soft fur and slid an arm inside the satin lining. The Queen commended the gift. There were plenty of deerskins around the palace, but not many furs like this, she said. Margarita held the muff on her knees and then allowed it to slide from her lap. A footman picked it up and presented it again.

Once von Pötting had completed his ceremonial exertions, Margarita was excused. She exited the chamber, with Luisa in her wake, carrying the muff ceremoniously. Velázquez met them in a room adjoining the main salon. His expression was serious, but he winked at Margarita. 'A new pet, eh?' He grinned. 'Does it bite?' He extended a hand towards it and then pretended to rear back. Margarita laughed.

The artist handed a folded sheet of paper to Luisa. 'Could you give this to our friend Fuendacia? Some further items I require for the new commission – he knows where to get the pigments for me.'

Luisa nodded and tucked the note into her sleeve.

Fuendacia was the keeper of the royal records and worked in the archive of the alcázar. Margarita had seen him once or twice while she was with Luisa. Velázquez often met with him.

Pepito cantered into the room and gambolled about behind them, pretending to try to pat the fur, but Luisa hissed and whispered that it was not the time for his antics.

'They are talking of the Viennese visitor in the *mentideros*, Luisa,' Pepito said in a singsong voice. 'It is everywhere; gossip is fleet of foot. You cannot ignore it. The King will sign . . .'

'Trust you to know the news before the rest of us,' said Luisa wryly. To Velázquez she added quietly, 'This news does not bring me joy.'

The artist sighed and shook his head.

Luisa sniffed. 'She grows towards womanhood, and I wish for her sake that she would not. Why must they send her away?'

'Send me away?' said Margarita. 'Papa wouldn't want that.'

'No, he loves you, of course,' said Velázquez. 'I'm sure there will be many suitors for your hand . . . The King will choose wisely.'

'But what about the Queen and her plans?' Luisa dabbed at her eyes with her overskirt. Velázquez touched Luisa's shoulder. Pepito made as if to hug the maid, but he only reached her waist.

Terrón was asleep under a table. Margarita wanted to give the dog a pat but, constrained by the guardainfante, she couldn't bend far enough. She would not marry. She intended to stay in the alcázar forever.

'Von Ponty-pony from Vienna at your service, senorita.' Pepito bowed to Margarita, mimicking von Pötting's clipped accent and pulling his chin down to his chest.

Margarita batted his arm and Luisa frowned. 'Shh.'

Pepito touched Velázquez's sleeve. 'Best you make her ugly this time, master.'

'Hm, difficult.'

Pepito continued, 'She must wear the *blue* dress; it is the Queen's wish. All the ladies are wanting blue now, it's coming from Nîmes, *very* expensive. Only for *very* precious goods.' Pepito began walking in a circle around them, hands clasped behind his back, his words marking time with his steps.

'Stop,' said Velázquez, waving him away. He seemed distracted, almost angry. Perhaps he had too much work to do. Margarita sighed. She felt Luisa's hand cup her elbow, guiding her away from Pepito and back to her quarters.

⌐

Later that week, word came that Velázquez was ready. At the request of the Queen, Margarita wore a lustrous blue satin and taffeta dress. The gown was trimmed with velvet ribbon and had a gauzy lace collar and cuffs. Her hair had been washed and brushed and swept from a side part to her ear, where it was held with an elaborate ribbon. A golden sash extended diagonally from her left shoulder to her waist.

Her special blue diamond, a present from her parents which had come all the way from the mines of India, was pinned to her chest. Today the diamond had been surrounded with a swirl of gold filigree and a blue ribbon, as a brooch.

De Nieto ushered her into the studio. Margarita had to turn sideways to get her skirts through the door. De Nieto stared at the diamond. She was glad when Luisa shut the door behind her, leaving the Queen's chamberlain outside.

Velázquez greeted her with a bow. Her fingers reached for the diamond. She'd kept her hand over it as they dressed her before the glass.

'May I examine it more closely?' said Velázquez. She nodded. He dropped to one knee before her. 'It is the same colour as your eyes,' he said.

'Yes, but sometimes it glows red inside,' she said. And she remembered when she first held the stone, how it had lifted her out of her body and up to the ceiling, so she could see herself from above. It had been a blue eye in the palm of her hand.

He raised an eyebrow and inclined his head. 'Interesting.'

'Do you see the star?'

He nodded. 'I see it. Eight points – the number of perfection or of eternity.' He studied in silence. 'Not unlike a compass,' he said, returning to standing.

'To find my way?'

'To find your way indeed. To find your way home, perchance,' he said.

The afternoon sun fell across his table of paints and pigments. Velázquez's worktable was like none other in the palace. In the

King's and Queen's chambers the tabletops were inlaid with onyx, lapis and jasper, but this was simple timber and its surface was covered in drops of dried paint.

He added powdered indigo to a pale oil and used a thin beech stick to mix the paint. Then he dipped his thumb into the blue mixture and pressed it onto the table, leaving a dense print. He sprinkled more powder into the mix, added a drop more oil, adjusting the proportions again and again till he was satisfied with the way the paint stood in crests and did not fall. She held a portion of her skirt towards him and he considered it, then nodded. Margarita was no longer allowed to paint. Her mother had forbidden it.

A special background had been prepared for the portrait. The setting included a red-hued painting and an oval mirror above a tall console. Below the mirror was a golden statuette of a lion. The easel was nearby.

'Will he be in my picture?' she asked, nodding at the lion.

'Yes, I think so. At your shoulder. Would you like that? It is a fitting royal symbol.'

The artist picked up his palette. 'Like that. Stay there – perfect,' he said.

Behind him, Luisa cleared her throat and he put the palette down again. 'I almost forgot. Her Highness requested that you hold this present from Vienna in your portrait.' Luisa gave the muff to Velázquez, who handed it to Margarita.

Margarita dangled the muff from one hand, wishing she could fling it across the room. 'Can't I have a dog in my picture instead? Terrón? He's furry.'

The dog was sleeping nearby. He raised his tawny head at the sound of his name, then flopped down. Velázquez rubbed the dog's shank with the toe of his leather shoe and smiled. Soon Terrón's legs were twitching in time with his dreams.

'Sorry.' The artist shook his head. Then, 'Oof, dog hairs get everywhere,' as he brushed them off his sleeve.

'Well, he *will* be in my painting then.'

'Ha, yes, in spirit. And you have the golden lion, no less,' he reminded her, as he returned to the canvas and began to sketch her form in shadow upon the grey basecoat, 'and that represents your home.' Velázquez's voice was soothing. He added small details to his story as he worked the paint onto the canvas, his intent gaze moving between Margarita and the portrait.

His voice helped her to remain still. While she posed, Margarita's eyes travelled to a medium-sized painting that hung above one of the doors behind him. She amused herself by studying it while he painted her. Two women seemed to be having an argument. One, wearing a helmet, was standing over the other, who was cowering on the floor. Behind them was a loom, and in the corner was a hanging tapestry, which formed another tiny picture inside the painting. In this she could see the figure of a woman, half-draped in a sheet, being carried away on the back of an animal – a bull.

Velázquez paused, following the direction of her gaze. 'Ah, a tale from our friend Ovid. Have you studied him?'

She nodded. 'A little.'

'Mortals and gods, eh? The mortals with skills who challenge the gods – it's not an equal contest.'

'Who are they?'

'It's a copy of Rubens' *Pallas and Arachne*,' he said. 'Pallas, the goddess – the one with the helmet – was displeased by Arachne's subject matter and by her weaving; Arachne was so skilled she challenged the skill of the goddess. As a punishment, Pallas doomed her to spin forever, but as a spider.'

'But she's not a spider in the painting.'

'No, that happens later . . . The little picture in the background is meant to be a tapestry, it's a copy of Titian's *R*—' He broke off, as if distracted by something on the canvas, then continued. 'It's based on a work of Titian about . . . about Europa. And Zeus. Zeus is represented by the bull and he, ah, carries her off.'

'Carries her off?'

'Mm.' Velázquez coughed a little, glanced up at the painting and then back to his canvas, pushed his hair back from his forehead and painted in silence for some time.

Margarita had the sense he had left something out of the story. She frowned. Something about the very dim image of the woman and the bull was familiar.

'I know!' she shouted. 'I've seen it before!' She had, in another of Velázquez's works: *Las Hilanderas – The Spinners*. 'She is in the background of *Las Hilanderas* too. Europa, isn't she?'

Velázquez's eyebrows shot up.

Luisa's head appeared from the adjacent alcove where she had settled with her needlework. When Luisa had retreated to her divan, he murmured to Margarita, 'You have a good eye. Too good! Don't tell all my secrets.' He feigned shock, and they both laughed, though Margarita wasn't sure what was funny.

He returned his attention to the easel and held his palette to the side. Margarita fidgeted with the fur muff then, noticing him frown, held still once more. His eyes traversed to and fro, between her and the canvas. There was a slight scuffing sound as the brushes scumbled across the surface, then moments when he blended colours on his palette. He was absorbed, intent.

'What are you painting now?' she asked.

'Hm? Ah, the light that comes from inside *you*. Leonardo called it the Universal Light.'

'What does that mean?'

He placed the end of his mahlstick against his cheek and considered. 'I'm trying to catch the shimmer of your soul,' he said.

He only talked like this when they were alone. He always made her feel special.

'Have you?' she asked.

'I don't know yet. Perhaps in that one . . .' And here he pointed to *La Familia*, the large work leaning against the wall, the one in which he had included her and himself. All of them. 'You are the light in that one.'

Margarita nodded and studied her younger self. Her cheeks were rounder then.

She noticed something else. The shadowy rectangles high on the wall inside *La Familia* matched those on the wall that they had been discussing.

'Those paintings on the wall in our painting *La Familia* are the same ones here in the studio now, up there behind you!'

Velázquez inclined his head and touched his fingertip to his lips.

He cleared his throat. 'Hmm, yes,' he said. 'They hang over our heads every day. But we all need a light in the darkness. You are ours.'

A rapping at the door made them both start. Luisa stood.

An attendant entered, bowed, and announced the arrival of the King.

Philip IV was tall and long-limbed. He paused, filling the carved doorway, half-man, half-shadow. Margarita curtsied.

'Ah, there you are again, my dear,' the King said to Margarita. 'You like it here as much as I do. And today Velázquez paints *your* portrait. Excellent.'

Velázquez bowed, but the King waved him up. As the chief chamberlain, the artist's first duty was to the King, but the King bade him work on.

To her surprise, rather than considering her blue portrait, the King walked away from them and stood, hands clasped behind his back, in front of the enormous work standing at the side of the studio.

'Ah, *La Familia* indeed. It is supreme. A phenomenon,' he said. 'I will never tire of it. I am there and yet I am not there – you play tricks with our eyes and our hearts. You have been kind to me and obeyed my wish for no more portraits.'

'You are omnipresent, Majesty,' said Velázquez.

'And look, Margarita – you! As if you were breathing . . . You *have* captured her,' he said to Velázquez.

'Captured?' Margarita asked.

The artist raised his hands, palms upwards. 'She is as quick as Ignatia was.' He turned to look out of the window. The King put his hand on the artist's shoulder and they stood together in silence. Margarita wanted to ask about Ignatia, but the King said, 'And Balthazar.'

Margarita crossed the room to stand before her own image in the picture they were discussing. She was younger in that picture, in her silver dress.

Her attention turned to the boy with his foot on the dog, Terrón. She frowned. Why was *he*, Nicolas, in their family portrait? Why did she have to share Terrón, and Velázquez, and the rest of them, with him?

The King turned back to *La Familia*. 'There am I, reflected in the mirror . . . It is miraculous. You have fulfilled my wish, my friend.' He swept a hand across his face, as if wiping a window on a foggy day. 'Thank you. Your eyes, they see. And you show our thoughts, and reflect them back at us . . . You are too clever, my confessor . . .' Here he bit his knuckle and lowered his head.

Velázquez bowed again, deeply. 'It is an honour, Your Highness.'

The King *has* a confessor. *So why does he call Velázquez his confessor?* Margarita wondered.

Philip lowered himself into his armchair. 'Nicolas is a little like Balthazar, is he not?'

Velázquez inclined his head. 'And Infante Felipe will be too,' he said.

Felipe was, to Margarita, a disappointment. There seemed little chance that he would ever play with her. The creases of skin around his neck smelled of sour milk.

As if reading her unspoken thought, the King raised his hand towards her in a kind of benediction and, emboldened, Margarita approached him. 'This one is our tonic.' He kissed Margarita's hand. Noticing the diamond on her chest, he said, 'You are my diamond.'

The artist smiled his agreement, then, taking up his mahlstick, continued to work.

Margarita returned to her position and resumed her pose.

'Papa,' she said, 'may we keep this blue portrait, please? For me?' She liked what she had seen of this new version of herself, but point was there in having a beautiful portrait made and then giving it away?

At her question, Velázquez's hand froze, suspended in mid-air.

Luisa, who had been scrabbling inside her sewing bag, stopped and was still.

Terrón sat up.

The King leaned one elbow on the side of his chair and placed his head in his hand. No reply came. No one spoke. Not long after that, her papa, the King, left the salon.

The sitting was over.

II
CHIAROSCURO

11

ANTIQUES

'I never do a painting as a work of art. All of them are researches. I search incessantly . . .'

PABLO PICASSO

Alex groped inside her red backpack for the address Oscar had given her. She rolled and unrolled the soft paper as she walked through the amniotic air and white-tiled tunnels of the underground. A man played electric guitar with his hat on the ground, and proclaimed he'd spent his last pound and would be happy with pence, in the name of world peace. Alex rode the moving steel stairs with Sloaney girls in preppy leather shoes who pulled at their collars and tossed their pretty manes.

Alex had spent the morning in the library at the Courtauld, searching books and catalogues for every Velázquez quote she could find. She wanted to learn everything she could about what Diego Velázquez the artist had said himself, but mostly she found explanations from other people. She left the library having garnered just *one* direct quote from the man himself: 'I would rather be an ordinary painter working from life than be the greatest copyist on earth.'

He didn't want to copy. What would he have made of Montano's assertion that he had replicated the works of Rubens – and Titian – in order to prove he was better than them, as a kind of one-upmanship? If that was the case, why were Velázquez's versions of those other artists' works so blurry? They were barely copies. Again, she was sure that this was not his intention. She pictured him laughing, bemused and – what? Frustrated, maybe?

Her destination, Pimlico Road, was lined with antique shops – posh ones. It seemed a strange place for a flat. Did she have the right address? It must be; Oscar had written it down himself. She needed her postcard back – for those precious words of her mum – and she wanted to talk to Oscar about the music. She wished for a moment that Helen had come with her. Then she was glad it would just be her and Oscar. As her reflection paced along beside her in the large shop windows, she had to admit there was a tingling in her chest, and it seemed easier to smile at strangers, who responded with expressions of bafflement or polite neutrality. A man wheeling a trolley laden with boxes between a shop door and a truck lurched into her path. She swerved around him and walked on, combing her hair with her fingers while scanning for street numbers.

The gingerbread-terraced building was three storeys high, plus the garrets. A discreet brass plate on the bricks bore the name EVERSON'S ANTIQUES. This was repeated above in gold-painted lettering. Alex turned the art nouveau doorhandle and entered a carpeted hush. Tapestries, etchings and paintings hung on the walls.

There were no price tags. Alex recognised Canaletto's pale-yellow sky over Venice, some somnolent Turner cows sleeping in an English meadow, and another work that emulated a muscular and frothy Delacroix. A woman in a camel cashmere twin-set and tweed skirt was seated at a desk. She acknowledged Alex with a chilly nod. On the walls behind her and draped over a large screen were two large drops of thick plum wallpaper, embossed with flowers and heraldic figures. Alex moved closer.

'It's leather; very old . . .'

Alex clutched her bag as she felt the woman's eyes taking in her scuffed lace-up shoes, black tights and flared black skirt. The woman's superior manner made her want to play the customer.

'Ah, how much for the wallpaper?' she asked.

'Approximately a hundred thousand pounds a roll,' said the woman, her voice sibilant. She held Alex's gaze across the green leather surface of her desk, as Alex imagined a bank manager might. Not that Alex had ever approached a bank manager. She'd never got further than the tellers.

'I'm sorry,' she said, laughing. 'I'm not really a customer. I'm looking for Oscar . . .'

'Indeed,' said the woman, unamused.

When she said nothing further, Alex stammered, 'Is he . . . Could you . . . ?'

'He's downstairs.' The woman gestured towards the rear of the showroom, raising one eyebrow as well as her voice. 'Oscar,' she called, 'one of your' – her gaze took in Alex's appearance once more – 'one of your student friends is here.'

'He's expecting me,' Alex said awkwardly.

'I see,' said the woman. 'Oscar?' she called again.

A moment later his head and shoulders emerged through a trap-door behind her.

'Alex! Hi!' He was beaming.

'I'm about to lock up,' said the older woman, standing and gathering her handbag and gloves. 'Will you set the lights and check the alarms for the evening, please, Oscar?'

'Yes, of course, Mrs Crawford. Let me get the door for you.' Oscar winked at Alex and strode across the shop to reach the door ahead of her.

Mrs Crawford hesitated before stepping out. 'I noticed a man outside earlier today, watching the shop. He could have been a customer, I suppose, but . . . I saw him go past again this afternoon. For some reason he caught my eye.'

'No one out there now,' said Oscar, peering up and down the street. 'Maybe *you* caught *his* eye . . .'

Mrs Crawford sniffed. 'Don't be ridiculous, Oscar. But please be sure to lock up. You can't be too careful.'

'Sorry if I've come at a bad time,' said Alex, as Oscar closed the door behind Mrs Crawford.

'No, no, it's great that you've come. I didn't know if you would. Did she give you the frosty treatment? She's okay, really – she's worked here for years. Come below decks.'

Alex bent her head to follow him down the stairs to a cosy low-ceilinged basement space filled with antiques – armoires, wardrobes, desks and side tables. Two old leather chairs and a coffee table – much used – were positioned in front of a white marble fireplace in which, to Alex's surprise, a fire was burning.

'Who buys wallpaper for a hundred thousand pounds a roll?' she asked.

'Texans,' said Oscar. 'And footballers.' He used the poker to adjust the coals, and a flare of sparks whisked up the chimney.

'Is that a real elephant's foot?' She was staring at a stuffed stool.

Oscar nodded and she made a face.

'I know,' he said. 'It's ancient. Poor elephant.'

'I didn't think you'd be allowed a fire down here,' she said.

'We're not, but it's okay if you have the back vents open. Otherwise, we'd asphyxiate like some Spanish king did with his brazier in his bedroom. Roger Everson, who owns the place, likes to tell that story.'

'Spain again!' said Alex.

'Yes,' said Oscar. 'Synchronicity.'

Oscar took her coat and hung it on a hook under the stairs while Alex continued her perusal.

Lamps with heavy brass bases and fluted columns threw pools of light over jumbled armchairs, a chaise longue, even a partial suit of armour. A tall black screen took up a lot of space.

As she drew closer, Alex realised it was a large box, like a small house, with carved screens for walls.

'It's a seventeenth-century box bed,' said Oscar. 'Quite amazing, isn't it? A room within a room. You can go to bed and shut the doors on the world.'

The bed had a roof as well as walls, all carved in filigree and painted black, but the paint was worn, and here and there the red of an earlier incarnation peeped through, and under that was the odd glimpse of a natural wood. Screen doors closed off the front.

Alex ran her fingers over the fine timbers and slid open the door. Inside, a small backpack stood at the end of the neatly made bed and a paperback and watch lay on a little shelf.

'Oh, I'm sorry!' she said, her face flushing. 'You're sleeping in here?' She had barged straight into his bedroom.

Oscar was leaning against the mantelpiece. Alex closed the sliders and moved back across the room towards him, weaving through the furniture, keeping polished mahogany, marble, teak between them. She touched the curtain of tiny threaded beads hanging in a fringe around the bottom of a pretty silk lampshade. She stroked them gently, and they swung like wild pendulums. Oscar shovelled coal onto the fire. Alex edged closer and stood behind a chair, rubbing the striped velvet, the bristles moving minutely under her fingers. The fire crackled.

'Have a seat,' said Oscar. 'Would you like a tea or something?'

She nodded – please – and he disappeared through a door in the corner, beneath the stairs. Alex stretched her hands out towards the flames. She heard water running, a fridge opening, and the clank of cups. She sat and unwound her scarf. Her skirt seemed too short; she arranged her scarf to cover her legs. It looked silly. She placed it on the back of the chair.

'It's like a treasure cave down here,' she said when he returned with two mugs.

While they sipped their tea, Oscar explained that Everson was a friend of his parents, and was letting him use the place in exchange for help restoring assorted musical instruments and antiques, skills Oscar had learned from an uncle. 'It's much closer to the uni than my old flat, which has been handy while I've been working on pieces for the ensemble.'

'You're lucky,' said Alex. 'I'm living in a shoebox. Well, not literally . . . but sometimes it feels like it.'

'I keep thinking of you when we play the Ravel piece; the pavane,' he said.

'For a dead princess,' Alex noted. 'Hmm.'

'Yes. But you're very much alive.'

She smiled. 'It was quite amazing hearing that at St Martin's.'

'It was amazing *playing* it at St Martin's. The painting, *Las Meninas*, means a lot to you, doesn't it? When did you first see it?'

The coals glowing in the grate reminded her of the coal range in their old home in Cornwall. She hadn't been there for ages. It had been rented out after they left.

'I saw it in Madrid at the Prado when I was twelve,' said Alex. 'With my dad.'

Oscar's face was expectant, attentive. 'Tell me . . .'

That day unspooled in her mind. Twelve-year-old Alex tapped the book she was carrying against her leg as she trailed her dad and his girlfriend, Bettina, up a sweeping staircase. Visiting art galleries was what David did on sabbatical. The galleries were like a sweet shop, he said. If you had too much at once you felt sick, so he focused on just a few works at a time.

On this particular day, David's determined footsteps echoed off the pink marble and polished wooden floors as he passed quickly through the first few galleries then through an arched doorway, where he finally came to a halt.

The room they had entered held only one huge picture in a wide frame; a big dark painting of a large, high-ceilinged room hung with paintings, and a cluster of people – a painting of people in a gallery, within a gallery. Alex sensed her dad watching her. She shrugged. David sighed. Alex plumped herself down on a bench and opened her book. She was sick of paintings. They were like ancient wall-paper. She began to read, but a few minutes later, her dad sat down beside her.

'Do have a good look at this one. It's one of the most famous paintings ever made.'

'Dad,' she said, gesturing to her book, but he continued.

'Velázquez had a rare ability; he had empathy and he had insight. See, that's him there with the cross on his chest – he's included himself in the picture, working. Picasso's father brought him to see this painting when he was not much older than you – fourteen, I think. *This* was the painting that made Picasso want to become an artist. I wanted you to see it. Rosara loved it. She was researching it when she died. She even pinned a poster of it by your bed when you were little. The girl reminded us of you.'

Alex had been seven when her mum died, and her memories of Rosara were blurred, but she did sometimes remember her voice, rolling over waves of words as she read to Alex in bed at night. She hadn't heard her father say her mother's name for ages.

He leaned forwards. 'Picasso returned to it in later life,' he said. 'He painted fifty-eight versions of it in his studio in Cannes. He said it was a painting full of –'

He stopped.

David stared into the painting, his head cocked to the side, nostrils flaring. He reminded her of their old dog, who would sit listening by the front door of the cottage. She followed the direction of his gaze, taking in the static canvas, which gleamed dully.

'Full of what, Dad?'

'*Curses*,' he said. 'A painting full of curses.'

He touched the corner of his eye and sighed, adding quietly, 'Rosara was fascinated by that.'

Alex took a deep breath. Her chest felt hot. She swallowed. Maybe it was finally time to ask David what she most wanted to know.

He was a good dad, but whenever the subject of Alex's mother came up, he would get really sad, and Alex had learned it was better to avoid talking about her. Sometimes she'd felt that since her mum's death *they* had been cursed, because everything had changed, especially him. His mood had lifted a bit once he had started working at the university again, though. This trip was like a fresh start. But then Bettina was saying her dad's name, beckoning him over. She had a knack for interrupting the two of them at the worst, or most important, moments. David stood, adjusting his jacket and feeling for his cigarettes.

'But, Dad,' she said, 'what about . . .' The word 'Mum' was too much for her mouth.

Bettina wanted to move on; Alex asked if she could stay and read.

'That's fine, but don't leave this room.'

Alex nodded. They'd done this before. She could read for hours, but mostly she didn't want to be near Bettina right now.

'She was an infanta, a princess . . .' Bettina was repeating David's words and nodding authoritatively towards the painting as she left. Bettina often used David's words as if they were her own, pretending she knew more than she did. Alex couldn't stand it.

Alex was alone in the quiet gallery. She moved her tongue around her mouth and sniffed. Was it possible that the air tasted different, almost milky and slightly thicker? The massive, dark painting *was* familiar. You had to tilt your head back to take it all in and even then you still couldn't. She tried to locate the source of the light pooling in the foreground of the painting, falling upon the young girl poised in the centre. Alex's skin tingled as if the available light around her and this other girl was beginning to bounce back and forth between them and all the tiniest points of it were touching her, nudging at her senses, while at the same time the girl and the other people gathered near her inside the painting were shuffling minutely forwards into an increasing luminosity.

The bench creaked and Alex froze, catching her breath and forcing herself to glance left and right. A cool breath caressed her cheek, and a colder sigh tickled the hairs on the back of her neck. She rose to face the painting.

Everything seemed to revolve around the girl, the Infanta. She was bright, full of life, and paint swirled about her flowering heart, which was as red as her lips, her pale arms plump inside gauzy lace sleeves. She was younger than Alex, though similarly blonde and blue-eyed, with a petulance about her mouth. The light in her eyes flickered. Her dad had been right. Alex could see something of her younger self in this other child, a girl with quick hands and feet who held still with some difficulty.

Someone else was also watching Alex intently. When their eyes met she could not look away. He held a long thin paintbrush in one hand and a curved wooden palette in the other, and he was gazing up and out, standing back from the stretched frame of canvas on which he was working. But he was inside the painting. He dabbed his brush on the palette then reached towards his work in progress. As he drew the brush down the canvas, she felt a corresponding tingle down her spine. Her arm moved of its own accord with a snap of static electricity.

The rays of the late afternoon sun caught the end of the artist's nose and his silver belt buckle. It caught too the silver of the Infanta's hair – almost as pale as her forehead – and the silver threads on her dress. She glowed like a candle. Beside the Infanta were young women, or maids, in pretty dresses – one of whom was bending low to offer the girl something in a red jug. Then there was a short, stocky woman with a boxy face in a blue dress, and a boy with red pantaloons and long brown hair. In front of them lay a brindled dog, with a proud chest and a stumpy tail. The boy was stroking the dog's back with the sole of his brown slipper, and the creature's eyes closed in rumpled bliss. The two ladies, one in fawn, the other in grey, were bending towards the young Infanta, whose pearly skirt curved bell-like from her tiny waist. Behind the first row of figures was a woman with a white headscarf. In the doorway behind her was a man with a pointed beard and a cape.

Alex forced herself to turn and see if there was someone else with her in the gallery. A woman in a silky yellow shirt with headphones on was fiddling with her tape recorder by the arched doorway, but it was as if she were miles away. She was not looking at Alex or the painting. Alex turned back, paused, then, holding her skirt, she curtsied to the girl and the artist. She found herself moving forwards, and as she did so, the painting began to glisten, yet held its form, as if there were a smooth slick of water pouring over it. The Infanta and the man with the brush were standing out from the canvas in a misty haze. A small glass rectangle at the back of the room was shining; Alex noticed her own face in the reflection at the same time she realised it was a mirror hanging on the wall between two doorways, one open, the other closed. The artist reminded her of the conductor of an orchestra; he beat the time with his paintbrush as she approached. He was on the threshold. The Infanta's hand and her arm in her gossamer sleeve were reaching out towards her. The hand, when she grasped it, was firm enough to pull her up . . .

Alex left her reverie and came back to the present. The fire had burned low. A coal fell inside the grate. Oscar leaned back in his chair, hands clasped behind his head. She slipped off her shoes and tucked her legs up underneath her. Having him listening helped, somehow.

'Then what?'

'They found me later in a different part of the museum. There was a fuss. Dad and the staff were running around looking for me. Later, he freaked out. He felt bad. We left Spain, came back to London, to my aunt's, and not long after that he sent me off to boarding school; he decided he wasn't capable of caring for me on his own. He had a sort of breakdown.'

'That's where you met Helen – at boarding school?'

'Yes. Broadhurst. My mum went there too.'

'Do you remember anything else? Between standing in front of the painting and when you were found?'

The memories were like oil on water, floating, drifting and impossible to catch. 'Glimpses,' was all she said. How could she tell him? Yet she wanted to; she wanted to say that she remembered Margarita holding a blue diamond, drips of water on rose satin from a wet, grey hand, and a mirror drizzled with mercury. And being told by Margarita that her mother was with the Dead.

They sat in silence before the fire for some time and then Oscar stood suddenly. 'Hey, here's your postcard.' He retrieved it from the mantelpiece and handed it to her.

Alex examined the image, turned it over and re-read the words. She held it to her chest. She couldn't speak.

'You miss her,' he said. 'Your mum . . .'

Alex nodded. 'Yes.' Just one word. Something lifted, like a breeze under the edge of a curtain.

'What happened to her?'

Alex hated this question. But with him, it was different. She didn't fidget, or get up and walk away; instead she sat very still, and so did he. 'She died in a car accident. She was researching what Picasso called the curses in *Las Meninas*. Supposedly her car just left the road and rolled down a hillside near Toledo.'

He raised both eyebrows. 'What do you mean *supposedly*?'

'I've just found out that she was being followed; I think it was because of her work. She was afraid.'

He was watching her intently. 'You mean maybe her death wasn't an accident?'

Alex nodded.

'Did they investigate it? The police?'

'I don't know. My dad never talked about it.'

'Where were you at the time?'

'I was at home in Cornwall, with Dad.'

'So it's possible someone was chasing her and drove her off the road on purpose. Or they tampered with her brakes or something . . .'

She had been thinking along these lines herself. Hearing him say it aloud made her chest ache. 'It sounds like a movie, but . . . maybe?'

'But why? Why would anyone want to kill your mum?'

'That's what I want to find out: how the curses in the painting and her death are connected – if they are. I believe there's a secret hidden in the painting, and I want to know what it is. I think Velázquez wanted us to know . . . I feel like whatever it is, it was a big deal.'

'What does your dad think?'

Alex had considered sharing her suspicions with her dad, but something had stopped her – more than the fact of his absence. She swallowed, rubbed her arm. Oscar was right to ask. Why hadn't she? She swallowed again, touched her throat. Remembered the sound of David pouring gin from a big rectangular bottle and then gulping it down. The spirits bottle, he used to call it. Drowning his sorrows. She didn't want to make him sad again.

She turned the postcard over in her hands.

'I'm sorry I read it.'

'That's okay.'

Oscar pulled his chair closer. She held the postcard out, so they could both see.

'I've never seen this Picasso painting before,' said Oscar. 'It's pretty intense, isn't it?'

And Alex was able to see it through his eyes, as well as her own.

Picasso's version of *Las Meninas* was a collection of angular lines, in black and white. It contained a sense of menace, but it wasn't a straight copy. The image was horizontal, rather than vertical, and as the ceiling had lowered, so Velázquez had become taller, towering towards the roof. The cross on his chest and his brush and mahlstick seemed electrified, as if exuding a kind of creative lightning. The Infanta Margarita became a triangle, square and a circle-headed girl in the middle, and in the light-filled doorway was a black silhouetted figure. Alex traced his outline with her fingernail. Here was another difference.

'He's turned him to the right, and his cape has become a wing,' she said.

'The same but different,' said Oscar. 'Who is he?'

'That's José De Nieto, the Queen's chamberlain,' said Alex.

'He's like a dark angel,' said Oscar.

'Exactly,' said Alex, and she shivered.

'What about this guy?' Oscar pointed to the figure in the front right corner, whom Picasso had enlarged in size and turned into an outline, like a cardboard cut-out.

'He's supposed to be a dwarf; that's how he's been identified in catalogues. But I think he was a boy.'

'How do you know that?'

Alex remembered the boy beside her in his red velvet suit, his delicate neck and slender chest. And on the other side, Maribárbola, short, squat, yet somehow grand, with her elaborate dress and large head.

'I just know,' she said, 'Picasso's version is like a lens on the original. He did more than one . . .'

She flipped the card over and scanned the caption in tiny print: *Picasso's* Las Meninas, *Cannes, 1957.*

'Read it to me?' said Oscar, sitting forwards in his seat.

The handwriting was small and sloping. Alex cleared her throat and read aloud:

'Dearest David . . . It's been six months and I am still engrossed. I'm intrigued by everything that's in there! C has been a great help. I'm learning so much. Picasso said a painting is always a search and that it's a picture painted with curses. He was right! I give thanks for Paz. Still a lot of work to do. I miss you. So looking forward to joining you and Alex soon. Love to you both, as always, Rosara.'

It was hard to say her name. Alex heard her mother's voice in her own as she read, like an echo. Her mum had written this card. She ran her fingers over the words.

'A painting is always a search,' Alex repeated. What had Picasso searched for? Alex's mum had been on a search for the curses. Her mum had loved her. Loved them. Had wanted to see them again. Who was C?

'Is that what you are doing?' asked Oscar. 'Searching?'

She nodded and explained about Greta's insistence that she find evidence to substantiate her claim.

'What's next?'

'Oxford. I've got a name – a professor there who I think Mum might have known. I want to find him or her.'

'Can I come?' said Oscar. 'Maybe he'll know about the Ravel piece.'

'Oh . . . Um . . .'

Her mind was already moving to the next day, she needed to make progress and find something to report back to Greta. Oscar might slow her down, but he seemed so keen and, she had to admit, she liked his enthusiasm.

'I'm leaving tomorrow morning, from Paddington station,' she said.

'I'll be there, like the Bear and you'll have to take me with you,' he said, grinning.

12

STAGE PLAY AND CARTOMANCY

1659

'Finally, a boy!'

Now nearly two years old, Infante Felipe Prosper had a face like a walnut and smelled of tepid milk. Margarita thought he looked more like a monkey than a boy. They were still celebrating his birth. The next event was to be a performance by a troupe of actors in the courtyard of the alcázar. Margarita, accompanied by Pepito and Maribárbola, made her way to the golden tower to observe the preparations.

She peered out of a narrow window on the second floor. Below, the public courtyard of the palace was brimming with hawkers and traders selling everything from fish to lace. Pepito was standing on the step below, looking out another window, and Maribárbola was behind him.

The golden tower designed by the architect from Toledo shone, they said, and was a beacon for the city. Each of the four towers of the palace was different, because they'd been built during the reigns of various monarchs. Margarita's mother said the towers were *al azar*, haphazard, and that God preferred symmetry.

Gentlemen began spilling forth from the doorways below.

'Those fine sirs have come from the councils of Castile and the Indies,' said Pepito. 'The decisions they make in there affect the whole world. Their administration is as slow as a tortoise, the wheels are made of paper . . .'

Maribárbola tittered and, encouraged, he continued. 'See those ones with the mouths tight like their purse strings? If you see them smiling when they leave, you can be sure they've levered more coins from the King's coffers. They are pursued by their pages. And there – those men with flapping capes – are the *lestrados*, the magistrates . . .'

The commoners swerved away from them.

With a blast of trumpets, the courtyard gates swung open and a trio of wagons drawn by oxen with painted horns and flowers about their necks careened into the yard. The wagons were exploding with dancers, giants and stuffed creatures, including a dragon's tail that hung over the side. Margarita jiggled up and down in excitement. Men began extracting planks, ladders and trestles from the wagons. A stage began to take shape.

De Nieto strode across the courtyard, his cape billowing behind him. The actors bowed to him. He was joined by a tall man in a red gown – a man of the church. The man in red flexed his fingers at his side, as if gathering some invisible reins.

Maribárbola said, 'Ugh, there's Duran, the Inquisitor.'

'The Devil and his henchman,' added Pepito.

'He's talking about the actors,' said Maribárbola to Margarita, giving Pepito a warning look; Margarita had the impression this wasn't what he had meant at all.

◦—

De Nieto joined Duran in an antechamber near the empty meeting room of the council of Castile.

The friar closed the door behind him. 'I have secured another source of labour for you. Now that we have, er, purified them, they are very – how should I put it? – malleable.'

De Nieto sniggered at Duran's creative language. *Purified*. The punishments were most impure. He shivered as he recalled a recent visit to the Inquisitor's chambers with his fearsome associate. Men's scalps had been partially prised from their heads; hot wax or tallow poured on bare skin; knees were hammered with mallets. Three severed fingers had lain on the floor. The blood was fresh and not yet attracting flies. Several rats had feasted on a creamy lump in the corner that was not cheese.

Just this week Duran had had the soles of a woman's feet burned off and then she was deposited in the countryside. She had been reported to the Inquisition by her husband for cooking a chicken too close to midnight. Such 'reporting' was becoming commonplace as a way to get rid of tiresome wives.

Duran continued: 'Labour, yes. I've decided I don't like waste. Their families will not take them back. They are weak, but with feeding they will recover somewhat and can still be used to make more looms for your workshops. They will position the warp . . .'

Duran had come closer and was drawing lines of warp down De Nieto's own chest with his beringed forefinger as he spoke.

'They will weave the weft, and they will tie the Spanish knot.'

At this, the friar undid his sash from his waist and threaded it under and around De Nieto's arm, completing a Spanish knot. De Nieto felt the other man's usually assured grip become light and suggestive. Fetid breath moistened his cheek. He resisted the urge to move away and instead allowed the whispered words to evoke a vision: rows and rows of workers producing acres of luscious tapestries with woollen and silken threads, and colours which would rival those of the paints. His chest lifted. He *would* please his Queen and outdo his cousin. The plaudits would be his. It would be worth it, he thought.

Blood pulsed in his wrist, for Duran was still applying pressure on the cord.

'Tonight, you will do it to me,' said Duran.

De Nieto half-closed his eyes and studied Duran's fleshy lips and the crease of skin beneath his jowls. He touched the perspiration there, then placed his fingertip inside the fat friar's mouth and watched him suck like a baby.

᠉

That evening, Margarita took her place on the dais, adjacent to the stage.

The crowds were milling about.

'The musketeers are getting restless,' said Agustina, who was behind Margarita and Luisa. 'They go to all the plays and are the best critics. If they don't like it, they'll abuse the actors. They scald them with their wit.'

Margarita was to the left of her parents. Usually, they watched plays from the confines of the royal box, and thus she could slip unseen from her seat when the speeches became too tedious, but tonight there was no possibility of this and no need. The arrangement was novel – a special concession from the King.

Nobles and lesser grandees dressed in their finery were posing on the balconies, or on the lower stands behind the royal family. Women in the *cazuela* – the women's screened area, known as the 'stew pan' – were 'simmering', relishing their freedom to chide all within range.

Agustina nudged Luisa. 'Ah, and there is La Calderana, the famous actress, the playwright's muse and one of the King's . . .' She didn't finish her sentence.

Margarita followed Luisa's glance towards a nearby balcony, where an elegant woman dressed all in black, with an elaborate lace mantilla, sat waving a fan. Margarita had seen her at the palace and in the royal park, Buen Retiro. Her father loved the theatre and the actors and actresses. He was a great patron of the arts.

Luisa harrumphed. 'They shouldn't have put her there; she's practically above the Queen.'

Nicolas, the one who had been in Velázquez's studio, and whom they insisted on calling a dwarf, was with La Calderana on the balcony. The woman raised her hand to his head and idly stroked his long hair as he leaned against her. *She is his mother, and he's a boy, not a dwarf*, thought Margarita.

Luisa had seen him too. 'Good Lord preserve us,' she said. She caught Margarita's eye and raised her finger to her lips, then glanced at the Queen.

Margarita turned and saw that her mother was oblivious to the woman and Nicolas, and was waiting eagerly for the play to begin.

***

The actors and the crowd were engaged in a push-pull game; the voyeurs leaned in and applauded, and the actors raised their voices and made their characters larger and more fabulous in reply. The commoners cheered and booed. Some were drinking, others shaded their eyes from the setting sun. An actor playing Gitano, a bedraggled and wizened gypsy, roved about the stage, which changed into a village, a high mountain pass and, eventually, after much laughter, a palace.

The actors were so close to the royal dais, Margarita could see where the make-up finished around the edges of their faces.

A character called Bernarda approached Gitano, who was sweating with his exertions.

'What fortune will the King have with the Queen?' Bernarda asked.

Gitano replied: 'He will not desire any other fortune than to have her.'

The crowd murmured their approval. The Queen smiled.

Bernarda: 'What will you say about the beautiful Margarita?'

Margarita sat forwards in her seat. She sensed eyes upon her.

There was a pause, then: 'That love made the maiden in order to kill.'

Margarita gasped. To kill? What did he mean by that?

'It is a compliment to you,' the Queen whispered in her ear. 'He is saying that your beauty will slay men.'

'Why is that good?'

'It means you will have power,' her mother explained.

'But –'

'Quiet,' said her mother.

The gypsy walked to the edge of the stage and began to smoke a cheroot and count the coins extracted from a leather pouch.

Bernarda asked: 'What fortune do you promise to the ladies?'

High-pitched laughter came from the *cazuela*.

'That all be aware of the dangers in naming them.'

The woman with the black mantilla rearranged the lace veil to cover her face. Margarita could hear murmurs from those standing before the stage. A man called out, 'No name, no shame!' and some people laughed and the women of the *cazuela* cried out, 'For you! For you!'

As the curtain fell, one of the actors came forwards to offer his good wishes to young Felipe, who was at that moment asleep in his bed with his nurse.

'I soon hope to be saying to the little one, *el chiquillo*, "Walk, walk, I say, you beautiful child."'

Margarita wished they would let her brother be. Her mother barely breathed around the boy, so intently did she watch him.

On the way back to her quarters, Margarita found Luisa's sleeve and tugged, 'Why did they say, "Love made the maiden in order to kill." Is it the curse?' More than once Margarita had heard Luisa beseeching the holy Mary to protect the young infante from a curse.

Pepito appeared. 'Plague, famine, never-ending warfare – why would anyone think we were cursed?' he quipped.

Agustina, who was behind her, said, 'Life and death walk hand in hand. You will see. One day, when you are in Vienna –'

Margarita placed her hands over her ears to block out the rest of the woman's words. She would never leave Madrid! Never!

After the performance, De Nieto followed Duran on his horse to the workshop on the outskirts of town. The convenience of the location soon became apparent. It was close to the gate at the wall of the city, beyond which sinners were set up upon crucifixes. The simple fact was that the agents of the inquisition were discovering more sinners than there were crosses on which to impale them.

Once they had dismounted and left their horses in the care of the stable boys, Duran unlocked the door of the building, and then handed De Nieto the key.

'A better way to go, is it not? Out there they piss themselves with fear, and then they find themselves cleaned and handling precious linen and silk. They are so grateful, they will do anything. Suddenly they remember how to work. They will do it for naught. And a little inducement, why it just makes them pass the shuttle faster.'

They passed through a flagstoned foyer and into the workshop proper, which was dim, save for the light from tallow lanterns along each wall. Rows and rows of workers extended right to the back of the warehouse. It was the largest loom studio De Nieto had ever seen.

The women were not as buxom and plump as they once might have been, and their feet were bare. They wore shirts, which perhaps once were white, and long skirts. Some were old; the older ones wore headscarves. The women held the skeins of silken thread and passed them to each other. Their spinning wheels were blurs of motion, as bony feet pumped the pedals up and down. But the faces of those at the looms were set and their eyes sunken. As shuttles flew, here and there a tear fell.

'No salt on the fabrics, or they will bleach,' De Nieto barked.

Duran came closer. 'Pleased, my sweet?'

De Nieto curled his lip. 'Very,' he said. 'You will be rewarded.'

The factory master paced up and down the rows, with a lash attached to his belt.

De Nieto did some quick calculations in his head. With this many fingers and this many threads, production time would halve or better. He would be able to produce more tapestries, more quickly. There was hope for his fortunes at court! He kicked the dung from his boot.

'There's more,' said Duran.

He led De Nieto to a room at the back. The foreman drew the bolt. A pile of bodies lay against one wall, limbs jutting out at all angles, here an outstretched hand, there a swathe of long matted hair over a twisted ankle. De Nieto covered his nose and gagged. The place stank of rotten flesh.

Duran ignored the bodies and strode to the corner, where a woman was strapped to a chair.

'Observe this,' he said.

The woman's head had sunk forwards upon her chest, her mouth open.

'A fresh one,' said Duran. 'Died just an hour ago. The soul has not left yet – see how it lingers above her, how those strands still attach it?'

De Nieto approached the corpse and peered into the dim light, but saw no strands. He shook his head.

There was a low fireplace in the room. On a shelf above it were two candles. Duran reached into his robes and extracted a clay figurine of a hunched man, with a gnarled face and a crutch. This he placed upon the shelf between the candles. As Duran kneeled and paid obeisance before the figure, whom he referred to as Your Highness Sargatanas, De Nieto moved closer, noticing strange markings on the plank beneath where the figure now stood. Then Duran gestured for him to also kneel before 'the master'.

De Nieto went along with the charade, he kneeled, he bowed his head. Sargatanas was, De Nieto thought, the stuff of folktales, he had heard tell of the lame demon who had the power to open any lock, they all had. He wondered how long this ritual was going to take, but he sensed he needed to appease Duran who was uttering a series of incantations. Yet, as these continued, De Nieto felt a stiffening within the fibres of his being. He could not stop the sensation. An involuntary cry escaped his lips as he found himself expressing allegiance to his new master.

When it was over, they stood. De Nieto began dusting the dirt from his knees, but Duran stopped him and ushered him back to the corpse.

'Let me touch your eyes.'

De Nieto took a step back. He had witnessed Duran blind someone, knew him to be capable of great cruelty. But Duran's touch was like a woman's, soft and gentle, on his eyelids. His strong fingertips caressed De Nieto's temples as he spoke of service to Sargatanas. Duran was giving himself away. If they were caught . . . But, as if Duran's words had granted his eyes a special gift, when De Nieto looked again he could indeed see strands of silver silk, like cobwebs, glinting, attached to a silvery pool which floated above the woman's head. He gasped.

'And this,' said Duran, reaching out with a flick of his wrist, quickly winding the thread like fishing line around his finger and thumb, 'is how you catch them.' Then he whisked the silver wraith into a black cloth bag. The contents wriggled and trembled as he passed it to De Nieto.

'The first of your ethereal servants, my dear,' he said. 'Don't open it until you have a loom to tether it to. But with the master's help, tether them you will.'

⌒

The cartomancer who came to tell the Queen's fortune wore a grey silk scarf around her shoulders. Margarita perched in the window seat with Maribárbola and Luisa; the Queen had denied entry to

Agustina, whom she said was a gossip. The Queen did not want her chamberlain to hear of the woman's visit, said Luisa. Her mother said the card reading was like a game, but Luisa said the cards would tell the future.

The rays of the late afternoon sun gleamed on the cartomancer's black hair as she spread her grey silk scarf on the table between herself and the Queen. Then she lit a candle, although it was not yet dark. She shuffled a pack of large cards with dexterous hands, but it seemed to Margarita that she struggled to hold them, as if they had a will of their own.

The Queen cut the deck, from left to right. The dark-haired woman dealt the cards face up. Margarita wanted to be closer to them, to see the destiny they foretold. Pulling free of Luisa's grip on her wrist, she tiptoed across the room to stand at the Queen's shoulder. Maribárbola followed her.

A series of picture cards were arranged in a pattern. They reminded Margarita of paintings filling a wall. The cards were well worn, with mysterious images. Margarita longed to touch them.

'The Queen of Cups, the Ten of Swords and the Tower,' the cartomancer said, nodding. The first card showed a dark-haired woman on a golden throne, holding a goblet.

'Queen of Cups. This card represents one's hopes and fears,' said the woman. She spoke of the Greeks and of Zeus's wife, Hera, whom she said was jealous of the child sired by her husband out of wedlock. 'This card may represent a rival — a woman who is strangely disturbing, a catalyst.' The woman's eyes reminded Margarita of those of a cat.

Margarita's mother sat perfectly still. A slight crease appeared in her forehead and she wrinkled her nose, as if offended by a scent. 'La Calderana . . .' she whispered.

The woman raised her eyebrows, glanced at Margarita over the Queen's shoulder and paused. 'Best Her Highness the Infanta does not see the cards,' she said.

Margarita felt Maribárbola's hand on her back, ushering her back to her seat by the window. She could no longer see the cards, but she could still hear what was being said.

'Hmm. This refers to the River Styx.'

Luisa gasped and crossed herself, pleading with her eyes for Margarita to join her.

'The river of death?' said the Queen.

'These are forbidding waters – the river over which the souls of the dead are carried. This card represents a state of mourning and sadness, and it is as necessary to life as joy and celebration. Life is a procession of births and deaths. You must let go of something, or someone . . .' The Queen crossed herself and clasped her hands together over her belly.

The cartomancer tapped another card with a long fingernail. 'Here we see the Tower,' she said. She spoke of a structure of false values, like those put on by actors in a play, to impress but to hide the truth. The *alcázar*, thought Margarita, with its feet of clay, but she loved its forgotten corners, secret passages and cool courtyards.

'Ah. The goddess and the ancient curse . . .'

Margarita could stand it no more; at the word 'curse', she rushed back to the table.

On the card in question, she saw a woman in a robe with an upright sword. To her right crouched three crones, surrounded by sticks. A boy lay unconscious on the ground, beneath a blackened sky.

'It is a dark time, when we see something as it truly is, and it is like death. A family curse is passed down from one generation to the next. The children must suffer until insight is gained.' The woman began to rock on her chair, and the flame of the candle flickered.

'Enough,' said the Queen, pushing her chair back from the table. 'I have heard enough!'

Passed down from one generation to the next. The children must suffer . . . Margarita ran the words through her mind and watched her mother's quivering lips. At any minute they might insist she leave.

'Do not be alarmed, Majesty; the cards speak in metaphors, to teach us to follow what is inside.'

But the Queen stood and began pacing the room, wringing her hands.

Margarita hurried to her mother's side. 'What is the curse, Mama? Tell me!'

The Queen brushed her daughter aside, her face strained. 'It is because of *him*,' she said.

Who does she mean? Margarita wondered.

'I prefer the word of our Lord, and the devotion of our Lady,' said Luisa. 'These cards make me afraid.'

Luisa – afraid? Margarita no longer wanted to touch the cards. She hoped the woman would leave and take these strange cards with her. Soon.

13

MIRRORS

Despite Alex's protestations, she and Helen were on the bus to Camden Market. They were both slightly hungover, having shared more than a bottle of wine in Alex's flat the night before.

Helen had told her about an older man who kept inviting her out for dinner. She'd gone once but he had tried to grope her in the taxi and she'd turned down subsequent invites. For her part, Alex had recounted the events at Montano's lecture and admitted that she'd been to see Oscar at the antique shop. At this, Helen's shrieks evoked several thumps on the wall from the flat next door.

'I just wanted to get my postcard back,' said Alex.

'Uh-huh.' Helen, sitting on Alex's bed, widened her eyes. 'And?' she prompted.

'I did get it back.'

'Come on, that can't be all! You look very happy about it.'

Alex wriggled deeper into her beanbag and took a sip of wine.

'I am,' she said. 'I needed that postcard.'

Helen opened a packet of crisps, ate one and passed the bag to Alex. 'I knew you guys would like each other.'

'Nothing happened, he just wants to help. He's interested in the Ravel piece, and in Margarita.'

'In *Margarita*.' Helen gave an exaggerated nod.

Now they were on a packed bus and Alex was feeling slightly queasy. Every time the driver braked all the passengers lurched, and so did Alex's stomach. She had insisted that she had too much work to do to go to the market – she was going to Oxford the next day – but Helen had begged, so Alex relented. As a compromise she'd brought along her red backpack, with her journal and notes, so that she could go straight to the library after the market.

As the bus stopped and started in the traffic, Helen shared her other news. 'I've decided to go for it with the photography.' She had applied to art school in London and was considering pulling out of the accountancy course she'd enrolled in to please her parents. Some friends who produced a small magazine had invited her to come and have a chat. It was a start.

'That's cool!' said Alex. 'You have a great eye. I love your shots.' The accounting course had made Helen miserable.

Helen suggested that when she came up to London the two of them could find a flat together.

'*If* my internship turns into a job, I'd love to,' said Alex. 'But that's a big *if* unless I find evidence to support my, ah, theory about *Las Meninas*.'

'Then find it,' said Helen. 'I know you can do it.'

They alighted from the bus and joined the stream of pedestrians passing under the metal railway bridge that marked the entrance to Camden Lock.

They strolled past racks of T-shirts, pausing to browse at a stall selling handmade leather bags and belts.

'So . . . Oscar wants to come with me to Oxford tomorrow,' Alex said.

'You see! I knew he liked you.'

Alex ducked her head to hide her blush. 'He wants to help me with the search for the curses in *Las Meninas*.'

'You and that painting and Margarita – it's freaky, isn't it? I didn't believe in ghosts before I took that photo.'

The photo. Alex had seen it again the night before.

Helen had taken Alex's picture as part of a school assignment, and she had brought it with her to London, as Alex had asked her to do.

❧

Alex had been the new girl at Broadhurst, alone and lonely, till Helen had sat beside her at breakfast and showed her how to break her toast, and other important and ridiculous techniques for avoiding the ire of the matron. In return, Helen had asked Alex if she could photograph her for an art assignment she was working on. She'd led Alex towards the kitchen gardens, explaining that she had the perfect backdrop in mind.

'There,' she had said, pointing to an ivy-swathed wall beyond the glasshouses.

Something gleamed among the green. As Alex moved closer, she realised an old mirror, streaked with silver and spotted with lichen, had been hung amid the foliage. The sight of it gave her a start. She'd seen a mirror like this before; a far older mirror, in fact. Margarita's mirror, in Margarita's room. Alex turned to share the discovery with Helen but realised from the other girl's nod that she had known the mirror was there.

'Don't break it or you'll have seven years' bad luck!' said Helen.

'I don't need bad luck,' said Alex. 'I'm already cursed.'

Helen stared at her. 'What do you mean?'

'Nothing,' Alex muttered, wishing she could take the words back.

Helen gestured towards the mirror with her camera. 'Can you stand there? . . . Move a bit to the right . . . and maybe open your eyes a bit wider?'

Alex followed Helen's instructions. Why had she said that about a curse? Clouds were scudding about. The sun broke through and made her squint. She missed her dad and her mum. She shifted from one foot to the other restlessly.

Helen swayed behind the cyclops eye of her camera, her hand adjusting the lens. 'Stand still – you keep moving as if you have to pee.'

Alex tried to focus. Helen had been kind; she wanted to oblige her, hoped they might become friends.

'I'll take lots,' said Helen. 'I'm trying to get the mirror behind you as well.'

Alex turned and glanced into the mirror. The glass was flecked with tiny specks of black and melting grey among the silver.

'Go on, get a bit closer, it won't bite,' said Helen.

Alex inched backwards. The hairs on her arms were standing up; she rubbed them and shivered. 'I'm cold.'

'Don't be silly, it's warm as anything . . . Now, face me.' Helen clicked away. 'Relax! You look terrified. It's only a camera . . . That's better. A bit mysterious. So, tell me about this curse.'

Alex stiffened. She recalled the other mirror, Margarita's mirror. In her mind's eye, she saw the blue diamond lying in Margarita's palm, not twinkling, but emitting a soft red flare, a pulse of chiffon – that was the moment before she heard the footsteps and saw herself in the glass. The point at which she lost sight of Margarita, lost the fusty smell of her, the seashell sounds of her – the vanishing point.

Helen's camera lens was an eye, coming closer and closer, blinking and clicking and blinking and clicking.

Later, in the school darkroom, Helen had filled three white plastic trays with different liquids. 'You're my prisoner now,' Helen said, grinning. 'You can't leave now that I've exposed the film.' Helen tilted the tray, gently swishing the water backwards and forwards over the submerged photographic paper. In the pale red light, a face appeared. Two eyes and a mouth, black holes on a white moon became Alex, complete with freckles, eyebrows and nostrils. Helen seemed pleased, but then she frowned.

'Hang on – what's that?' She bent over the tray. 'Behind you . . .'

In the mirror over Alex's shoulder was a face.

Alex's heart started to pound. 'A reflection?'

'No,' said Helen. 'It should be the back of your head, but it's not. This is so weird. I don't understand how it would have happened. And it's not even *your* face!'

The face in the mirror was pale, the chin turned to the right, the eyes large. Silver candy-floss hair; a round cheek. Alex gripped the bench. There was not enough air in the room. A thumping noise filled her ears. Little ripples were pulsing across the tray of developing liquid. She touched her chest. The reverberation was coming from her.

'I know who it is,' she whispered.

Helen turned to stare at her. 'Who?'

'Margarita.'

The crowds heading towards the market were becoming increasingly dense.

'Watch where you're going!' said a check-shirted man with whom Alex had collided. Helen was outside a second-hand clothes stall, trying on a black leather jacket. Some punks with striking mohawks, one of them dyed bright pink, were clustered near the Doc Martens shop on the other side of the street. One of them was talking to a man in black trousers and a poloneck with slicked-back hair. Alex moved closer to Helen.

Helen, who was also watching the men, nudged her in the ribs. 'Drug deal,' she said.

Helen had mentioned a few chemically assisted adventures in nightclubs over the last few months. Maybe she was right.

'Don't stare,' said Helen.

They moved on to a second-hand book stall. Alex flicked her eyes over the few art books, as she always did. Nothing on Velázquez.

For lunch, Alex ordered a plate of paella, wondering if her mother had enjoyed this special Spanish dish or even cooked it herself. She must have, but she had never made it for them in Cornwall. The stallholder sprinkled on some paprika from a red tin. He squeezed lemon over the rice and added an extra wedge to Alex's plate. Helen queued for a falafel kebab.

They sat eating with their backs against the railings and the canal behind them. The paella was delicious.

'This is good,' said Alex.

Helen shrugged. 'It's just a kebab, but it's okay.'

'I meant this. Us. Everything,' said Alex.

'Uh-huh,' said Helen through a mouthful of falafel. Then, 'Oh, look – a tarot reader.'

'Ooo,' said Alex.

'Go on. Do it. You'll be surprised, I bet,' said Helen. 'I want to try and find myself a big woolly scarf – I've seen handknitted ones here before.'

When they'd finished their lunch they parted, and agreed to meet in twenty minutes. Alex approached the small tent tucked in at the end of a row of stalls. A little table outside had a bell and a sign written in a spidery script: TAROT – APPLY WITHIN.

Alex rang the bell. A woman emerged. She had smudged black eye make-up on a tanned face, and wore a loose purple top and black skirt.

'Ah,' she said in a husky voice. 'So glad you could make it. Come in, my dear. My name is Bernarda.'

Bernarda closed the curtain behind her, the movement making the bracelets on her wrists jangle, and took a seat at a table, nodding

134

for Alex to do the same. She lit a candle. The flame flickered, then grew taller and stronger. She held out her hands.

'You smell of saffron. You've had the paella? I like saffron. You like Spain?'

'Ah, yes,' said Alex, thinking, *Here we go: she's trawling for clues to work out what to tell me.*

But Bernarda asked no further questions. She took Alex's hands and rubbed them, then turned them over. Could she see anything about her mum in her hands? It wasn't possible, was it?

Bernarda picked up a pack of large cards and began to shuffle. After some moments she handed them to Alex. They were heavy, the edges soft, blurred by touch. 'Cut them to the left,' came the instruction. Alex obeyed. Bernarda gathered them up and laid them out, picture side up, three above, two in the middle and three more below, then a few to the side.

'We start here,' said Bernarda, tapping a card. 'This is the base of the matter. The Ace of Wands . . . a card of promise. You are on a great journey. You must trust your imagination. You are in pursuit of a vision.' She studied the card thoughtfully. 'Something is hidden which must be revealed.'

Alex thought of the painting: its curses and its hidden secrets.

Bernarda continued, 'The crowning card, the situation hanging over your head.' She raised an eyebrow. 'And you have lost someone.' It wasn't a question.

Alex swallowed.

'I feel her pain,' Bernarda continued, lowering her voice. 'Your mother . . . Ah, I see.' She nodded, as if to someone else. 'She is caught in a nowhere place by a gatherer of souls. She is trying to find the thread so that she may finish; so that she may rest.'

'What do you mean?' Alex whispered.

Bernarda pointed to another card. 'Be careful. There is a frame or . . . a window? Or it could be a mirror. A reflection. The way is dangerous. There is a tunnel. A dark force blocks your path.'

Alex exhaled slowly. A mirror! A tunnel?

Bernarda peered at Alex again, then her eyes flicked to a point behind her. A prickling sensation rippled down Alex's neck and between her shoulder blades. Alex shifted in her seat. She had had that sensation before.

'Here, girl,' commanded Bernarda. She rubbed her hands together, clapped sharply twice, and said, 'Leave us,' to no one in particular. The candle flame trembled, and then began to burn straight and true once more.

Bernarda leaned forwards, resting her palms on the table. 'Grief attracts them. It makes you more accessible, more vulnerable. You need to be strong, face the sadness. Don't be afraid of it.' She raised two fists, shaking one. 'Here's love.' Shaking the other, 'Here's grief.' She clasped her hands together. 'They are linked, you see? Always remember the love. This is for you . . .' She turned a card over and placed it in front of Alex. The card showed a tall woman with long dark hair, dressed in silver. She had a beacon of light above her and a greyhound with three heads by her side.

Bernarda was nodding. 'Hmm. This is Hecate, ruler of the moon, of magic and enchantment. She frequented crossroads, tombs . . . She presides over magic, childbirth, death, the underworld . . . and fate.'

'She's very busy,' said Alex.

Bernarda gave her a hard look. 'Do not belittle the cards or your unconscious mind; the watery depths can be treacherous. In some cultures they call this the Void. This is the place before birth, before light, the place of potential, the place where artists go fishing. It is only for the brave.'

Alex made as if to get up from the table but Bernarda grasped her wrist. 'This is your hand,' she said. 'Someone else is watching you. I see a bird's wing. I don't know why. We choose which threads we will take up. Trust yourself. Make your own decisions.'

Alex nodded. Her mouth was dry. She muttered her thanks and paid Bernarda hurriedly. Outside she took several deep breaths. Everything seemed louder and brighter than before, more garish. Where was Helen?

The woman had mentioned artists – that was strange. And somehow she had known about Alex's mother! How could she? Was her absence written all over Alex's face? Still? She had said Rosara was in a nowhere place. What did that mean? It sounded horrible.

Alex extracted her notebook and pencil from her bag and, leaning against the fence, drew a quick sketch of Bernarda with a trembling hand. Then she wrote: *A frame, a window, a mirror. The Void. Make your own decisions. A wing?* Picasso had given the man in the doorway a wing.

She slipped the pencil back inside the elastic loop on the edge of the notebook and returned them together to the bag at her feet.

At a nearby caravan a woman in a hand-knitted jersey and jeans was selling enamel teapots decorated with brightly painted flowers.

They were cheerful. Made for living and drinking tea with friends and family. She thought of her aunt Flora; what a rock she had been during David's frequent absences. Gratitude welled up inside her. Perhaps she could buy a teapot for Flora. Maybe she could also get one as a Christmas present for her dad. Maybe this year they'd have Christmas together.

She spotted Helen, and waved, then something brushed against her legs. She thought it was a dog at first, but when she glanced down she realised her bag had gone. A skinny guy with spiky hair was hurrying down some stairs towards the edge of the canal, stuffing something red – her backpack! – into a large black plastic bag. Dodging a man eating a pie, she sprinted towards the stairs.

'Hey! Stop!' she yelled.

She hurried down the slippery steps to the old towpath that ran alongside the canal. The thief had a head start, was disappearing around a bend; she took off after him.

As she came around the corner an overbridge loomed. Alex saw the skinny man silhouetted at the mouth of a tunnel; she paused for a moment, her heart thudding, then she followed him into the darkness.

The canal water was black and silver. Her pulse was pounding in her ears. She could no longer see the bag-snatcher. Unless . . . unless he was there in the dark, waiting, watching. She stopped running abruptly. What was she doing? No one knew she was here. Helen would be wondering where she'd gone. The *drip, drip, drip* of water from the underside of the bridge matched her breathing. Every step, every scrape, echoed. Should she continue, or go back?

There was an alcove near her in the brick wall, and there were others she had passed and must now pass again. He could be hiding in any one of those.

She turned, forcing herself to move in the direction of the market, but, as if in a dream, she was too slow, speed eluding her. She laboured on, was about to break into sunlight, when she heard him behind her. Fingers locked onto her hips, Alex struggled out of his grasp but landed heavily on her chest and chin. She felt his knee press into the small of her back.

'Give it up, bitch,' a voice growled in her ear.

She tasted slime on wet concrete and heard his boots pounding as he ran off. He had her bag, her journal. Her notes on the Infanta, thoughts about *Las Meninas*. All those trips to the library, requesting books and encyclopedias; the research she'd done at the Courtauld. Gone. She sat up and saw the man crossing the canal lock as if he were running across the balance beam in a gym. He bounded up another set of stairs, with the plastic bag bouncing on his shoulder, then leapt the fence and disappeared.

She climbed to her feet. Her palms were scratched. There were drops of blood and streaks of moss on her white T-shirt. She touched her chin. It was sticky. Then she remembered the postcard. She'd re-read it with Oscar and later placed it in her journal. Now it was gone again, for good. How stupid she'd been to bring it to the market. She trudged back down the path.

Helen met her at the bottom of the stairs. Alex's ribs hurt when they hugged.

14

MANIFESTATION

'Art is a lie that makes us realise the truth.'
PABLO PICASSO

Alex and Oscar were standing in front of the honours board of Balliol College, Oxford. Professor Leadbeater's name was listed on the board, but a receptionist informed them that he'd retired, and his details were not to be given out. 'Not under any circumstances,' replied the woman when Alex protested, her eyes on Alex's scraped chin.

'Does it hurt?' asked Oscar as they walked away.

She shook her head. 'Does it look bad?'

'No.'

She'd told him all about it as they sat opposite each other on the train. He'd been reassuring about her journal. 'You'll be surprised how much you remember. You've written it down, you know it, it's in your head – it's not like you have to start all over again.'

They wandered down by the river where a few tourists were attempting to propel themselves along on wooden punts. Alex sat and Oscar flopped beside her on the newly cut grass. The clouds were suspended in a blue sky which went all the way up. 'Maybe Professor Leadbeater is dead,' Alex said.

Oscar picked a daisy. 'Or not. He could be making himself a cup of tea right now.' He moved to lie on his side, facing her, leaning his head on his hand, with his elbow on the grass. She noticed the fine hairs on his arm.

'Daisy or buttercup?' he said, as if they were at a picnic.

'Um? Oh, buttercup, of course,' said Alex. He loves me, he loves me not – that could be embarrassing.

If he was disappointed by her choice, he didn't show it. He picked a glossy yellow flower and held it under her chin. His eyes were intent on her neck. She could see the hollow where his collarbones almost met.

'Butter wins,' he said.

She closed her eyes and opened them again. Remembered why she was there. Buttercups wouldn't help her find Leadbeater. Her eyes travelled across the sandstone bridge to a bright red phone box on the other side of the river. 'I'll be right back.'

The cover had been ripped off the dog-eared phone book. She leafed through the pages until she came to the L's, traced her fingernail down the page. Leacroft, Leacutt, Leacy, Leadall . . . and there it was: Leadbeater, Prof. G. She memorised the address and jogged back to Oscar. He was right; she did have a good memory.

'I found him,' she said, extending a hand and pulling Oscar to his feet.

She recited the address, and Oscar unfolded the map they'd picked up at the information centre. They studied it.

'Bingo,' he said, stabbing at the street. 'It's not far. Let's go.'

The professor's stone cottage was surrounded by a frenzy of roses and long grasses. A lavender bush gave off a delicious scent. Carved onto a block beside the door was the image of an open book.

'That's from the Oxford crest,' said Alex. 'It was on the map.'

She tapped the curved doorknocker.

After a wait of several minutes that seemed to Alex to stretch interminably, a man in tweedy trousers, a blue shirt and waistcoat opened the door and peered at them over his reading glasses. 'Can I help you?' he asked.

'Sorry to bother you, but are you Professor Leadbeater?' Alex asked.

'I am. And you are . . . ?'

Alex introduced herself and Oscar, and explained that she thought the professor might have known her mother, who had studied at Oxford. She might have been one of his students, perhaps?

'And is there a reason you are asking me this question and not your mother?'

Alex took a breath. 'She . . . she died when I was seven.'

'Oh, I see. I am sorry. Well, you'd better come in.'

He beckoned for them to follow, and led them into the house.

'I miss their energy – the students, I mean,' the professor said as he lowered himself into a high-backed armchair. They were in the living room, but it seemed the whole house was really a study. The dining room table served as an expansive desk covered in neat piles of books, apart from a small oasis of space in the middle, where rested several sheets of paper. A fountain pen waited, uncapped, for the professor's hand. Alex glanced around for a chair that wasn't piled with newspapers or books. A Burmese cat opened one eye from atop a faded plum velvet cushion and yawned. Alex moved a small cane footstool close to the professor's seat, while Oscar opted for a couch in the bay window.

'I try to keep up the work,' said Professor Leadbeater, 'but my eyes let me down these days. My nephew says he'll get me one of those new recording devices – but for me there's something special about the connection of the thought and the flow of the ink which I am loath to forgo.'

'So, you said your mother may have been a student of mine?' The professor fixed a piercing pair of grey eyes on Alex.

'Yes. Rosara Johns.'

Leadbeater's brow creased in thought. He shook his head. 'I can't say I remember the name, I'm sorry.'

'She was interested in Velázquez – *Las Meninas*, in particular.'

'Oh, *that* one.' He looked out into the garden as the memory came back. 'Yes, I do remember her. Rosara Johns, eh? A very promising student. She did a good piece of work. Got a top mark, I seem to recall. I wanted her to do more. We offered her a postgraduate scholarship to the college, but – and this was a rum thing – she accepted, then we never saw her again. I believe she may have embarked on some further research but she didn't come back to Oxford. And now you tell me she died. Most sad . . .'

'Could you tell me more about what she wrote?' said Alex. 'About the painting, I mean? I have an interest in *Las Meninas*, too.'

'Ah, well, you're not alone there. Some great minds have grappled with that one. Whole careers have been swallowed by it, including those of a few of my colleagues. Let me see . . . As far as I can remember, your mother's work related to royal portraits, specifically those of Velázquez, and beliefs at the time – we're talking about the seventeenth century – that portraits captured people's essences. Leon Battista Alberti wrote about it; let me see if I can remember . . .' He narrowed his eyes, finger tapping his chin. 'Painting possesses a "divine power" – that's how he put it – in that it makes "the absent present, but also represents the dead to the living, many centuries later". He wrote of one of Alexander the Great's commanders – Cassandrus, I think it was – who "trembled all over at the sight of a portrait of the deceased Alexander". He recognised the majesty of the King, you see. That was much earlier, of course, but in Velázquez's time, too, the portraits were considered *living* portraits, "so excellent that the canvas had life itself".'

His words were tumbling in Alex's mind. *So excellent that the canvas had life itself.* The words 'captured people's essences' hung in the air.

The professor continued, 'Foucault, of course, cogitated upon *Las Meninas*. Oscar Wilde had a crack at it, too; he empathised with the dwarf, feeling himself "the other". Even Francis Bacon had a stab – oh no, no, sorry, that was in relation to Velázquez's portrait

of the Pope. But Dalí had a go at *Las Meninas*. He had his own . . .
theories. He gave each of the characters in the painting a number.'

'Numbers are also figures, and figures are people,' said Alex.

'Exactly,' said the professor. 'But beyond that not many people
were able to follow his thinking.'

'What number was the Infanta?'

'Eight,' said the professor.

'The number of infinity.' This was from Oscar.

'Oh, I do miss teaching,' said the professor. 'It's such fun watching
people catch up!' He went on, 'Now there was a connection that
Rosara noticed, something about Picasso . . . I can't quite recall the
detail. But I do remember that she was certain that it resonated
with grief.'

'Does grief have a sound?' asked Oscar.

The professor shifted in his chair. 'Interesting question,' he said.
'What makes you ask that?'

'When I look at the painting, I keep noticing their hands. To me
they're like a flight of musical notes.'

'*Very* interesting,' said the professor. 'Do you happen to have a
reproduction with you?'

Alex pulled Oscar's small book on Velázquez out of the cotton
shoulder bag she'd scrounged from Flora's place. They took turns
studying the picture of *Las Meninas*. The hands of each of the
people in the painting were at different levels. 'I see what you
mean,' Alex said.

'Ah, the open book. Manifestation,' said the professor cryptically.
'Yes. What note would Margarita be?'

'Well, I can't really say, but I think she'd be C, the tonic note, the one that holds it all together,' said Oscar.

The professor was nodding. 'Cross-medium connections – delightful. *Las Meninas* is a most fascinating work: as famous as the *Mona Lisa*, and as mysterious, but I prefer it – so much more complex. One of the more intriguing analyses was by a German philosopher, Gadamer. He wrote about *Las Meninas* in relation to what he termed "the playing field"; the space between the person viewing the work and those in the frame. The viewer enters "the playing field", of course, at their own risk! Ha!'

At the word 'risk', Alex felt a chill run through her. Had she entered that field?

'Picasso said it was a painting full of curses – or, to be exact, "a picture painted with curses",' she said.

The professor nodded. 'Picasso also said: "Art is a lie that makes us realise the truth." What do you make of that?'

'We have art in order not to die from the truth,' said Oscar. 'I think that's Nietzsche.'

'Nietzsche,' said the professor, nodding. 'Very good.'

What secrets, what truths, had Velázquez and, after him, Picasso painted into their canvases? Alex wondered. 'My mum wrote something about a painting being a search,' she noted.

'Yes, a search,' Leadbeater said. 'That's Picasso. You need to do your own search. We each ask different questions. Picasso also reputedly said that each human is a colony of souls. Not to get all superstitious, but I have the impression that he felt the dead walked alongside him. He would not be alone in that, though our rational world doesn't like to consider that.'

The dead walking alongside them. Alex swallowed. She was visited by a flash of Rosara reading to her at night from a large book of Greek legends. Her bedside lamp a round globe beside them, and her mum's hand, turning out the light.

Oscar, who was sitting forwards on the couch, gave her a little nod. Alex met his eye – it was if he could tell what she was thinking – then turned back to the professor, who was warming to his own theme.

'The Spanish court at the time Velázquez painted *Las Meninas* was fascinated by the relationship between illusion and reality. The artist holds up a mirror to society, and what do they show in the mirror? Why does their work intrigue us? Do they show the reality that we can see, that we can touch, or do they show us what lies beneath, that which we can feel but not touch, that which remains unsaid . . . hidden.'

'What is hidden . . .' Alex repeated, almost to herself.

'That was where Picasso wanted to go, and I think Velázquez, in his way, also travelled that path; he had an empathetic eye, one which subtly subverted and perhaps challenged the power structures he saw around him.'

'You mean he cared about the dwarves and the animals as well as the Infanta and the royal family?' asked Alex.

'Precisely,' said the professor.

'Was he saying they were all equal?'

'Perhaps . . .'

'When you stand looking at *Las Meninas*, it's like you are in the position of the King and Queen. You could almost see yourself in the mirror, in the middle, instead of them.'

The professor smiled. Nodded. 'The viewer would be standing where the King and Queen are standing. A radical concept. It's driven the academics mad.'

'What about the curses?' said Alex.

'You tell me,' replied the professor.

'Well,' said Alex, uncertain, 'I suppose the Spanish Empire had been great but was in decline.'

'Good,' said the professor. 'You've read a little of the history then. Go on.'

'The girl, the Infanta, the light is on her; she is literally silvery, golden, but her parents, the King and Queen, are merely reflections in the mirror – pale shadows – at the back of the room.'

The professor steepled his fingers. 'Yes, at the time that painting was made, *she* was the one in line for the throne. Her parents were royals on the way out. There was a vacuum of leadership, a crisis of succession – they were obsessed with male heirs.' The professor gestured to Alex. 'Go on.'

'I wondered what happened to the Infanta Margarita,' said Alex. 'I read that in Spain they called her the life of the palace. But she was sent to marry someone in Austria and it seems in Vienna that spark went out. She had lots of babies, most of whom died.'

'Her husband was Leopold, Emperor of the Hapsburg Empire, and he was also her uncle, the brother of her mother, and her cousin,' said the professor.

'That's sick,' said Oscar. 'You can't marry your cousin – it's illegal.'

'One cannot do it these days,' said the professor. 'But seventeenth-century European royal families all intermarried; it was the done thing. Margarita's mother married her own uncle at fourteen, though she was initially betrothed to his son. Very confusing. Young girls being wedded to their relatives, married to men decades older than themselves, in order to keep thrones in the family. The Hapsburgs were terribly inbred.'

'Like pedigree dogs,' said Alex. 'They become inbred and get funny hips and problems with their teeth.'

'Quite. My sister has one of those – impotent and incontinent. Always making a blasted mess on the carpet.'

They laughed.

'The curse of inbreeding,' said Alex. 'A line breeding itself into extinction – perhaps that's the curse! Or one of the curses, anyway.'

'Well, yes, absolutely! The Hapsburgs were on the way out in Spain, due to the succession crisis, as many of their children died in infancy, especially the boys. As I said, the Infanta you are interested in was heir to the throne at the time *Las Meninas* was painted. But she was a girl . . .'

'Why couldn't she be queen?'

'Well, actually she *could* have been. It wasn't until later that Salic law came into play – that's the law that stopped female royal succession.'

'They married her off?'

'Correct. Her second surviving younger brother was the last surviving child of Philip IV, the Planet King, and Queen Mariana, Margarita's mother. He was the classic case: they called him Carlos the Hexed, the "bewitched"; he could barely walk, he had an oversized tongue, he drooled, he had myriad deformities. No one expected him to survive childhood, but he did, with all sorts of troubles, including mental illness. Later on, he saw fit to have himself exorcised – twice, I believe.'

'You mean exorcised by a priest?' said Oscar, shifting further forwards on the couch.

'Oh yes; he thought he was possessed. He thought – and he was not alone – his line was cursed. His father, the King, was also exorcised, right before he died, for the same reason. Which takes us back to your question about the curses, and your mother's research, doesn't it?' He turned to Alex.

'She – the Infanta – thought they were cursed too,' said Alex.

'Well, we can't know that,' he said.

Yes, we can, thought Alex. Margarita had been afraid of a curse.

'Speaking of hereditary traits,' said the professor, 'isn't it interesting how passions continue down through the generations?' He considered Alex. 'You are clearly your mother's daughter. I remember her now because I can see her in you as you speak. "Each human a colony of souls," eh. You must look at Velázquez's painting – really *examine* it – and look at Picasso's at the same time, then compare and contrast. Make your own interpretations, ask yourself what truth they wanted you to see.'

'You mentioned Foucault,' said Oscar. 'We've read some of his work in my philosophy course. He said to look at art archaeologically, didn't he?'

'Yes, he did.'

'Has anyone actually done that?' said Alex. She thought of Flora's tools and her techniques, making grid lines on the earth, digging down, one layer at a time. She would do that – metaphorically – with *Las Meninas*; the artist's symbols were there to be discovered.

Alex looked at the image in the book on her lap, at the great dark wall of paintings and the ceiling above the heads of the people in the foreground, the Infanta and her attendants and the artist.

'It's almost like a waste of space, isn't it?' said Oscar, getting up and coming to look over her shoulder. 'Why didn't he just zoom in on them? Why waste all that effort on the back wall and the ceiling?'

Why indeed, thought Alex. She must find out about those blurry paintings in the background.

At that moment, there was a loud rap at the door. The professor excused himself and went to answer it.

Alex heard his voice, quiet at first, then indignant. And then another voice. Whoever it was seemed to want to enter the house. The accent, Alex realised, was Spanish.

The professor said, 'No, no, I must insist. Not possible. I'm sorry, I really don't know. That's not my area at all.'

Alex went to the window, which was slightly open, and peered out. A man with dark hair, a short beard and a black knee-length coat was standing on the doorstep, talking to the professor. *Though talking* at *him might be a more accurate description*, Alex thought. The man placed a foot on the threshold, as if about to enter, but Professor Leadbeater, whom Alex could not see from her vantage point, must have been barring the way.

'No, no,' said the professor. 'Try the history department, ask for Humphreys. I'm retired. Can't remember a thing. Suffering from early dementia . . . Goodbye!'

As the door closed, Alex looked at Oscar. The professor had been faking; there was no lack of mental agility on his part.

The man had turned on his heel and was walking back up the path. As he passed through the gateway, he paused, placing a black-gloved hand on the gatepost. His figure was silhouetted against the sun. Who was he? He seemed familiar. His head swivelled towards her and Alex ducked out of sight behind the curtain, aware of the thudding of her heart. She remembered sliding behind a tapestry with Margarita, trying to avoid a man dressed in a black cape. The pounding of her heart. A clutch of keys jangling on the man's belt. How he raised his nose, sniffing the air.

The professor reappeared and collapsed into his chair. He was puffing, as if he'd walked up a hill. 'Harrumph. Get me a glass of water, will you, my dear? What an unpleasant fellow. Good riddance. He's quite knocked the wind out of my sails. Do you know, I get the feeling he'd been out there listening to our conversation. Eavesdropping!'

In the scullery kitchen Alex found a glass and filled it. She had to grip the bench for a moment, her knees were liquid, unreliable. A memory of a wet grey hand reaching towards her and Margarita as they sat within her curtained bed flipped through her mind like a fish then disappeared. They had been bathed in blue light.

'Oh dear, oh dear,' said Leadbeater, as she handed the glass to him. 'Well, isn't the Infanta Margarita popular today? What's brought all this on? I didn't like that fellow one bit, though. You know, he didn't even give me his name. Most perturbing.'

Leadbeater took a sip of water and studied Alex over the rim of the glass.

'One of my predecessors – a scholar from that *other* place – spent much of his life researching the Hapsburgs. Did a tonne of work, but little of it was actually published. He died early this century. His great-nephew wrote to me at one point about finding a repository for the old fellow's papers – at that time they were still at the house, which he'd inherited. What was his name? That's right: Blunt. By name and nature. Ha. I'll put you in touch. He might be able to help you with a thing or two . . .'

'That other place?' said Alex, not understanding and still absorbing the information about this man, 'Blunt'.

The professor rolled his eyes. 'Yes, it's bad, isn't it? I'm going to have to send you to the opposition.'

Alex shook her head. *What did he mean?*

Leadbeater laughed. 'You know – Cambridge.' He turned his attention to Oscar. 'So, Alex's interest is hereditary, but what brings you here?'

'I'm keeping Alex company, mainly, but there's also a Ravel piece . . . it's kind of what brought us together.'

Alex glanced at Oscar. *Together?*

'Let me guess,' said the professor. 'It has to be *Pavane pour une Infante Défunte*, surely?'

Oscar nodded. 'The dead princess. Yes.'

'There's no evidence that it was written specifically for the Infanta Margarita, but she would have known a pavane or been taught it. It's not exactly a happy piece, is it? Written early last century, long after she died but possibly inspired by her. Quite haunting. As I understand it, it wasn't a funeral lament but it feels like one, doesn't it? A speculative and sad little dance for one of Velázquez's princesses.'

Alex remembered St Martin-in-the-Fields, and the cool chill of dancing in Margarita's footsteps; how from the first note she couldn't stop, as if her shoes were not her own. She wrapped her hands around her elbows and shivered.

'Haunting, hmm,' said Oscar.

The professor was beginning to look tired and Alex was aware that they had been there a while. 'We should probably leave you in peace,' she said, standing. 'You've been so generous with your time.'

Leadbeater didn't argue, but as he rose to his feet he said, 'One moment.' He moved to the dining table that served as his desk and rummaged around, muttering, until he found a small address book. Taking up his fountain pen, he quickly dashed off two letters, waved the pages about for the ink to dry, then folded them carefully and placed them each in an envelope. He also copied out an address.

'Here you are: two letters of introduction. One is for Eva Pierre at La Californie, in Cannes, which she is looking after these days; the other is to introduce you to Carla Mertez, who studied here at Oxford with your mother. She became a well-known museum curator in Spain. And this,' he handed the notepaper to Alex, 'is an address for Blunt. He's an academic too. Or he was . . .'

Alex took the crisp white envelopes and slip of paper and thanked him.

Carla Mertez . . . Alex was reminded of her mother's postcard. *C has been a great help*, Rosara had written. Could C be Carla Mertez? Surely it must be her!

'Remember,' the professor counselled, 'don't get distracted by all the academic noise around the works. Many of your answers will be in the paintings themselves. You just have to be able to see them. But perhaps you will find more of your mother's sources. That would prove worthwhile. I would be interested to know if you do. I sense she may have a successor herself.' He chuckled. 'If you want to take it up – academically, I mean – do let me know. Rosara Johns, eh . . . It's such a shame to lose the brightest minds. I'd hoped to hear from her again someday.' He suddenly stood upright, as though struck. 'Goodness, I'd quite forgotten – I *did* hear from her. Your mother sent me a poem at one point. I don't really understand why. I did keep it, but goodness knows where. I'll try to find it. A budding poet, was she?'

Alex shook her head. She didn't think so, but she scribbled down her contact details, both at her flat and at Flora's where she would be the following night. An uncomfortable thought played on her mind as she and Oscar headed back to the train station, talking excitedly about the leads the professor had provided. The thought was this: she didn't want to see the man in black again.

15

LUNCH DATE

Greta leaned back in the grey velvet booth and raised her glass of golden chardonnay towards her lunching companion, Regi Montano. The leadlight windows in this old Tudor building were kind to him. He had suggested the restaurant. It was a popular place for discreet meetings, where whispers and wine soaked into the soft furnishings.

Montano took his linen napkin to his moist lip, returned it to his lap, and raised his own glass in return. 'You look good, Greta. After all this time, still the best-looking woman in the room.'

'It's a very small restaurant, Regi.' Crikey, was he still sexually active? He had that look in his eye she remembered from a long-ago conference in Chicago.

The booth was curved. He moved a little closer and touched her wrist.

'So tell me, are some of your colleagues still insisting that the Kingston Lacy painting is a real Velázquez, or have they come to accept it's a copy?'

This disputed replica of *Las Meninas* had hung in a mansion in Dorset for two hundred years. She'd seen it. It seemed a poor copy to her. Not at all the same.

'There are those who still believe,' said Greta, spiking three capers with her fork. 'Our colleagues at the Prado are definite, though: it's a copy.'

'And you – what do you think?'

'Bad copy.'

'On this we agree,' he said.

'And on the salmon.' She smiled.

They'd both had the smoked salmon, with scattered capers and finely sliced red onions, marinated in lemon.

'Indeed – you have exquisite taste.'

'Regi, I have to apologise for the, ah, interruption at Christie's.'

'You mean the brash young woman?' He grimaced. 'Occupational hazard.'

'The thing is, she's an intern of mine.'

'Is that so? Not a very experienced one, then, I take it.' His shoulders had stiffened. He hadn't liked it. He tore his bread in half.

'No. But she has potential. Anyway, enough about her; that's not why I invited you to lunch. There's something I want you to see – a drawing I found secreted in the backing of another framed work.'

'Secreted!'

'Hmm.' She raised an eyebrow.

'You're getting my juices going!' He swallowed and adjusted his collar. 'I could spend all my time assessing the copies being brought to market; you wouldn't believe it.'

Greta nodded. 'I do believe it, Regi.' *And so could I*, she thought, but he was unlikely to be cognisant of that fact, or to acknowledge it if he was.

They were both aware that there were only around a hundred and twenty recognised Velázquez paintings in the world.

'The Prado has over fifty of his, obviously the masterworks: *Las Meninas, Las Hilanderas, The Christ, The Siege of Breda* and so forth.'

'That's not many when you consider that over forty thousand works are attributed to Picasso. Astounding!'

'Indeed, indeed. Sometimes I feel there are forty thousand people asking *me* to attest that their minor works or copies from their dear old uncle's attic are by the great master!'

'Well, Velázquez was a busy man, too, wasn't he?' said Greta. 'What was it – royal artist for thirty years?'

'Ah, we can do better than that. Let's see . . .' Montano began counting on his fingers. 'Court painter; usher to the King's bedchamber, 1627; gentleman of the wardrobe and then of the bedchamber, then chief chamberlain, in 1643 . . .' He tilted his head towards the ornately plastered ceiling. 'And, of course, he was granted the sought-after Order of Santiago in 1659.' Montano congratulated himself for this feat of memory with another sip of wine.

'Impressive,' said Greta.

He inclined his head in a mock bow. Greta wondered if her massaging of his ego was too obvious, but apparently not. The man was practically purring like a cat.

'I have a favour to ask,' she said, mentally reminding herself to get some more cat food. She glanced at the remains of salmon on Montano's plate. Shame she couldn't take it home for Thompson, her prized tabby.

'Oh yes.' He gazed at her over the rim of his glass. 'Shall we have another?' He turned and signalled to the waiter, who hurried over and cleared their dishes.

'Another bottle? The Californian chardonnay? Certainly, sir.'

Greta played with the silver bracelet on her wrist. 'I wouldn't ask if I didn't think it was worthy of your opinion.'

He leaned back, raised an eyebrow. 'Age?'

'Well, it was hidden in a minor nineteenth-century work, but I'd have to say we are talking old, Regi. Seventeenth or eighteenth century. On paper. Pencil sketch.'

Their mains arrived. French onion soup for Greta and the rump steak for Montano. As the waiter slipped a steak knife beside his plate, Montano nodded approvingly at the blade, then sliced into the meat. Red juices began seeping into his mashed potato.

Greta sipped her wine, while Montano chewed, then swallowed.

'Of course, for you, I'd be willing to take a look. I'm hoping you're going to say it's at your apartment.'

'Oh, Regi,' she said. 'Stop flirting and tell me about your latest project. It sounds fascinating.'

'Now *you* are flirting with *me*,' he said. And he was off.

She placed her hand on her chin. It was amazing how freely some men could talk about themselves, and for so long – even while eating. Eventually, he paused and took a sip of wine.

'And now that it's finished, can you come out of the shadows?' she said. 'Sometimes we speak of standing on the shoulders of giants, of developing what they've done.'

'Being in the shadow is a long way from being on the shoulders, unfortunately,' he said. 'Maybe I should have been an artist myself.'

'Didn't we all want that? Back in the day?'

~

After lunch, they went back to her office. As soon as she had closed the door, he moved towards her, placing his chest hard up against hers and gazing down upon her prominent bosom in delight. He reached around, squeezed her buttock and breathed steak and wine into her neck.

'Regi! The drawing! Stop it.'

She moved away from him, lifted the tissue paper from the drawing and laid it carefully to one side.

He was attempting to nuzzle her neck. 'I've missed you, my darling. It's delicious to see you. It's been too long.'

'No, Regi . . . no!' she said, pushing him away and straightening her shirt.

'Admit it, the drawing's a ruse to get me into your lair.' He pressed his hips against hers. For a moment she thought he was going to flip her over onto her worktable, on her front, as he had done when she was in her twenties. She should have pressed charges.

'Regi,' she said, summoning her best matronly voice. 'Stop. I will shout in a minute. You are going to crumple the paper! *And* I'm in a relationship.'

'So am I,' he murmured. 'No one needs to know.'

'*No!* I don't want this.'

He groaned. 'It's not my fault you are so fuckable,' he said. 'Come on, I want to be your Zeus! I've taken a Viagra. Climb aboard!'

'I do not want to be your Europa, or your Leda, or your whichever other poor woman got carried away and raped!' There, she'd said it. He pulled back.

'Oh, I love it when you get angry,' he said, but he took a breath.

'Get *out*. I mean it.'

'But the drawing, darling?' He cast a quick glance over her shoulder.

'I'm not your darling. Leave! Now!'

The door clicked behind him. She sat down at her desk. Still fighting them off at fifty. God. Fucking men.

16

CLOSING TIME

José reclined in the back seat of the car and fiddled with his high collar. It helped to hide the dark red rash that speckled his neck and chest. Some days the itching was so intense he could almost tear his own skin. It never used to bother him. This new skin was unstable – that was the word. He reached into his pocket for another painkiller and his fingernails snagged on a thread. They needed a trim. They'd become hoary and grey. His nails were growing fast. One of his colleagues had called them talons. That's why he needed the gloves; he didn't want Patrizia to see them. He wondered if she would meet him this time. He swallowed the pill, gulping it down with his own saliva, and tapped his foot. He wished he had his motorbike; imagined the feel of the pedal under his foot and the accelerator under his hand. It was one of the few pieces of modern technology he enjoyed, as it brought him close to flight. He studied the profile of his driver. Waiting again. But José was patient. It was one of his strengths.

The upstairs light went off in the professor's house. About time; the old man was slow to go to bed. Too much damn reading. He'd been recalcitrant today, too busy talking to the girl and her boyfriend.

'Take me around the block a few times,' he told his driver. He slipped his fingers into his gloves and flexed them. Yes, like a second skin. As was his to his master.

When they paid him for this job he would buy a hundred pairs of gloves. All kidskin. But it wasn't over yet. The professor was a loose end.

It was dark. A few drunken students stumbled out of a corner pub – closing time. Privileged snivellers. He toyed with the idea of sending his driver to do the job. But he wouldn't know what to look for and might miss something useful. No, José would have to do it himself. He fastened the button at the wrist of his glove.

He left the car and walked in the park till midnight, remembering the tall trees outside the Prado in Madrid and the warm Spanish night air, lapping at him. Here in England there was a chill in the night. A dampness.

He returned to the professor's cottage and let himself in the front gate, lifting it so it didn't squeak. Luckily there was no dog. The cat he'd seen earlier that day would hardly sound the alarm. Cats only cared about themselves. Pushing his way through some vegetation, he found a side path and then a rear scullery entrance, where he grasped the round metal doorhandle, turned it, and pushed. Unlocked; *fool*, he thought.

José moved through the tiny kitchen. Soon he was leafing through the files in the professor's office, struggling with the man's illogical filing system, then yanking folders and their contents onto the floor, scattering and kicking them about. All the writing was in English, illegible to him. There were envelopes with notes scrawled on one side and addresses on the other, none of which he could read. Who was this so-called professor? Fuendacia had kept order in the archive of the alcázar. There was no such order here. The modern world was a mess of laxity.

He backed away from the folders and stood on something small and round. Something alive, which now screamed like a banshee in Sargatanas' waiting room. José jumped, staggered and ran for the door. He wasn't going back there. Please, let her not send him back!

17

FAREWELLS

1660

M argarita clung to her sister's hand. 'Don't go! Please don't go! You don't have to marry him.'

They were in Margarita's chamber. Maria-Theresa had come to say goodbye. Margarita's cheeks were wet.

Her sister gently prised her fingers away. 'I do. We will meet again. I'm sure . . .' Her voice faltered.

'It is too far! We won't. They won't let us,' wailed Margarita. 'Luisa! Don't let her go!' To her sister: 'You mustn't! I forbid it!'

Luisa sighed and shook her head. 'All the grandees are headed to Bidassoa, including young Louis XIV. Imagine how sad he would be if his bride did not appear . . . Your papa will lead the way; Velázquez will supervise and oversee the decorations. They will look after her. You must let her go. It will be a beautiful sight.'

'I will write,' said Maria-Theresa as she left the room.

Later, Margarita watched from a window as the carriages lined up across the courtyard. Her sister was handed inside one. Attendant dwarves and a menina climbed in with her.

Velázquez sat straight-backed upon his horse. A large hat shaded his face. He turned the horse's curved neck and rode around several wagons full of rolled-up tapestries and bolts of cloth. He leaned over and tested the ropes securing each load.

Margarita would be lonely without them. At least Velázquez and the King would return.

The anticipated wedding had set Spanish hearts murmuring. It was vital that the young Felipe, Margarita's baby brother, grow to strapping manhood.

'We cannot have the son of a Frenchman taking the throne,' said the Queen, within Margarita's hearing.

The Queen's cheeks were plump and her stays had been loosened. She was with child once more.

What is a succession crisis? Margarita wondered, as they rode to church.

She said her prayers in the chapel with Luisa. It didn't help. The curse was upon them.

A few weeks later, Margarita was in the gardens, sitting among hedges of thyme and lavender, when the King and Velázquez returned from Bidassoa. Velázquez had returned in a carriage, his horse tied behind it by the reins. Servants helped him inside.

It was Luisa who gave her the grim news. 'Our artist developed a fever. He has a terrible thirst and has retired to his chambers.' The King had sent his personal physicians to treat him, she assured the Infanta.

Margarita sent a sprig of rosemary and lavender but was not allowed to see him. The King and Queen were terrified that she would catch a fever, like Balthazar, and confined her to her rooms. But still, she walked the passages between Velázquez's salon and the studio, moving quietly so as not to disturb the patient.

On the sixth day the bells were rung.

Candles were lit. Velázquez was gone.

Marooned in the corridors, Margarita hovered, examining his paintings for succour.

Luisa placed an arm around her shoulders. 'He may be gone, but take comfort in the fact that his enemies failed to drag him down. He flies above our heads now.' Luisa's words were muffled, as though she were speaking through layers of wool.

❧

Margarita was close to the studio when her father, the King, passed, head bowed. He allowed her to follow him into the room. He told Luisa and Maribárbola to wait outside.

Velázquez's chamber smelled of incense and candles and something else Margarita didn't like and couldn't name. The windows were curtained, and candles glowed around the bed. The hooks for the chandeliers hung bare from the ceiling, casting shadows. She shivered and pulled her capelet tighter around her shoulders.

Margarita had never seen Velázquez lying down. His body was long, as he was a tall man. His face was riven with shadow, different. With his warm brown eyes closed he seemed distant, like a faraway land, but perhaps only sleeping. He had worked hard. He was tired. She placed a hand on his arm and pressed, watching his eyes for any movement. There was none. She walked the length of his body and stopped beside his feet. His brown leather boots were soft from much wear. One boot had a hole in the sole, and through it she could see a fingernail-sized piece of black stocking. She touched this spot with her finger and pressed. *Wake up.* Nothing.

The King came to her side and placed a hand on Velázquez's chest. 'My friend, you achieved nobility through your art.'

A red cross with an upside-down heart had been freshly stitched upon his black doublet. The symbol for the Order of Santiago, prized emblem of the nobility, an honour recently bestowed on the artist by the King.

To Margarita he said, 'We will not see his like again. He saw the truth. He saw us as we are.'

Velázquez seemed to have died reaching for something, for his elbow was bent and his hand slightly raised, fingers frozen in the suggestion of gripping. Margarita touched his hand lightly with her fingertips. The brown knuckles, round and lined. The lumpy veins that threaded the back of his hands. She stooped and kissed him. His skin was cold. Had he sought a paintbrush, or his mahlstick? Almost every time she saw him, or interrupted him, he was working – though he would always pause to answer at least some of her questions.

'He needs his mahlstick,' she said.

The King nodded. He gave an instruction to an attendant and within minutes the object was presented to the King, who gave it to Margarita.

Margarita balanced the stick between her hands. It was light and fine, beechwood. It gave him something called perspective, he'd told her. A special way of seeing. He did have a special vision. She moved around him and slid the mahlstick into place. It fitted easily and exactly between his fingers. Now he could rest. But how would they cope without him, the calm centre of the palace, their conductor?

An altar had been erected at the foot of Velázquez's bed with two huge candlesticks. Incense smoke curled upwards from a silver container. The King paused there, eyes closed, murmuring his prayers.

Margarita also said her prayers, to the Virgin Mary and to God, the Heavenly Father. God must guide her father, surely, now that Velázquez had gone. She remembered all the times the King had referred to Velázquez, had asked for his opinion, shared his own thoughts, though only ever in the studio, in private. There was no one else to whom the King spoke so freely. Theirs was a friendship. Silently, Margarita also prayed for protection from the curse. Then the King bade her leave. 'Lord, I am crushed,' she heard him say, as she left the chamber.

One afternoon that autumn, Margarita ventured with Luisa close to her mother's quarters. En route, they passed De Nieto bearing a collection of paper scrolls. Since Velázquez's death more of these were brought to her mother rather than the King. De Nieto smirked and gave the barest of acknowledgements. 'Not much longer, Luisa,' he said, and he laughed.

When he had gone, Luisa shook her head. 'All this sadness in the alcázar makes the devil smile.'

The King had retreated to his chambers and had not re-emerged since the death of his only friend. He took his meals in private in his chambers. Without Velázquez to marshal his movements about the palace, the King, it seemed, was lost. Margarita entreated the attendants to allow her to enter.

As the door to the privy chamber opened, she caught a glimpse of the King, standing half-dressed. His head and shoulders were slumped, long nose and chin pointing towards the floor . . . Without his usual garments, his capes and his padded doublet, he seemed thinner, as if stretched within his own outline. Margarita gasped and retreated. She did not recognise him. The door was slammed shut from within, and she was left staring at the solid oak panelling.

⌒

The next November, the curse took her brother, Felipe. He'd coughed and coughed and then it was over. She didn't believe it. Three-year-old Felipe did not fight. He was hot and limp at breakfast and gone by the bell for evening prayers.

'How goes the King?' a gentleman asked Agustina as Margarita passed.

'He takes the news hard, sir. Very hard.'

The cloying incense around Felipe's chambers caught in her throat.

Margarita had heard shouts and cries from the direction of both the King's and Queen's areas of the palace as she made her way with Luisa to vespers and to see the dead Felipe in his chamber for the last time. His body was illuminated by the candles surrounding his bed. The amulets the Queen had made for him still dangled from his cot. They had made a mistake, she was sure. The candles were flickering, and he was bathed in a golden glow. He was asleep. But as she touched him, his skin – though still moist – was cold. Beneath the surface he felt full, as if he might split apart; he was ripe, with that strange, sweet smell. Margarita wanted to shake the little boy awake. She said his name and touched his little round nose and his sweet pink mouth. His golden hair curled around his shell-like ear.

'Felipe,' she whispered. 'It's me.' Then, louder, 'Felipe! Fefe!'

Any minute now the little one would turn his head, grab her finger.

But he never stirred. Someone brought her a chair, and she sat with him, and patted his soft hand with its half-moon fingernails, and sang him a little song, the one Luisa had sung to her as a child. When she had finished, Luisa's hand on her shoulder told her it was time to go, and together they trudged, faces wet, the length of the several corridors to her own chambers.

The palace was in chaos for days. Margarita's rooms were a disordered mess. No one had tidied the bedclothes she'd discarded earlier, nor put away her things. The women wept. Luisa said tables had been overturned in the kitchens. There was no supper. No one had time for Margarita.

The girl sought refuge with her mother, who'd been in her rooms now for months, her belly swollen and ready to burst with another child. Her mother's red eyes and nose and choked voice frightened her. This was not her mother, but some kind of blubbery sea creature such as the courtiers spoke of with the fishmongers in the palace courtyard on Fridays. Luisa always said they were too far from the coast to eat fish. The Queen wailed over the death of Felipe and clutched at her enlarged shape; she said she wanted the child within to remain safe and then she complained about her huge girth, her enlarged ankles, the soreness of her back.

New strictures were imposed. Margarita watched with Maribárbola in the kitchens while their clothes were stirred in giant cauldrons, by women with wooden spoons taller than both of them. All her pretty clothes, now black, black, black; she remembered the play and the words about the maiden and killing. Had she hurt Felipe by loving him? Was it her fault he had died? The curse was blighting everything. Who would be next?

Alone in her bed at night, she dreamed of the Manzanares River, which was barely a trickle, rising and rising and washing away the walls of the palace, as if they were mere sand. And she saw Felipe's cot, tipped over and full of mud, and her own bed, empty, the covers ripped and trailing, perched on the edge of a cliff. She woke, sweating, with a thudding in her chest.

The Queen, in her advanced confinement, could not attend Felipe's funeral at El Escorial, and thus it was with the meninas and Luisa that Margarita rode in the carriage. For hours, the boys sang behind the priest, who intoned words she didn't understand. Everyone was solemn; even Pepito was distant, downcast. Her skirts were digging into her ribs, and she wriggled and tried not to yawn. The King, meanwhile, sat like a statue behind a screen, as if his blood had frozen in his veins and he had become stone.

Margarita held Luisa's hand and let slip some silent tears as the minister read the rites. Felipe would not like it in there, in that marble box, one of many among a carousel of infant graves. The box was pretty, capped with stone roses, but must be cold. Above them all, a marble angel whose gaze curved downwards; so many young charges for her to watch over – too many. Margarita tried to remind herself of what Luisa had said: that God took only the good ones and that Felipe was too good and therefore he died. But he was too little. And she was still alive; was she not good? Her father the King used to say she was the life of the palace, but life was leaking through the gaps in the walls of the alcázar. Like sunlight, it seemed it could not be contained for long. Shadows and sadness now festooned their walls.

After the ceremony, Margarita lingered with Luisa and Maribárbola and ran her hands over the smooth, white lids, imagining the little babes within.

Outside the church, Margarita stopped suddenly. Luisa tugged at her hand, but Margarita would not move. She was taller now, nearly as tall as Luisa.

'It's the curse, isn't it? That's why Felipe died, and Balthazar too.'

Luisa's eyes slid skywards towards the steeple as she crossed herself, before kneeling and squeezing Margarita's hand. 'Hush. No, no! Make the sign of the cross.'

Margarita obeyed.

'Do not speak of curses. Not on hallowed ground. Not ever. You might bring it upon our heads.'

At that moment, De Nieto, who had been walking a little ahead of them, turned. He cocked his head at Margarita and gave a twisted smile.

It is already upon us, she thought.

18

TUNNEL

1662

Winter. There was snow in the air; during the day the whiteness could be seen on the distant mountains. The corridors of the alcázar were cold. That night, a fire had been lit in her Majesty's room. De Nieto was attending to the Queen. Her ladies-in-waiting were out of hearing, no doubt murmuring about Prince Carlos, the feeble new babe. He sighed.

The Queen's lips were pale, and she wore a stricken expression. The twin spots of red flaring in the centre of each cheek were natural, not the result of make-up. He'd had never seen her like this.

'Can it be true?' She sank onto a chaise.

He wished to comfort her and imagined clasping her face within his hands. But he stood straight and pulled his shoulder blades together.

'He will drag our reputations in the mud,' said the Queen. 'The secret is gnawing at his soul. He thinks I do not know, but I have heard the rumours. Now he speaks of it in his sleep! Of her despair.

Her despicable . . . despoliation. Everything! He believes he has hexed himself.'

Her grasp of the nub of the events in question surprised him. She knew nearly as much as him. Villanueva had had the tunnel dug; even the abbess had given way.

He addressed the Queen. He wanted to serve her. 'Your Highness, anything you request.'

She rose and went to the window, clasping her hands behind her back like a man. He came closer; wanted to see what she could see. Her waist was small again. Snow was gathering on the windowsills and against the walls of the palace. A winter slurry, which would turn to ice overnight and be treacherous in the morn. The gates were shut, as they should be. Those with paper windows would be freezing in their beds. She was more intelligent than the King gave her credit for. She was too good for him. The Queen's breasts moved against the front of her bodice as she leaned forwards. He swallowed and squeezed the muscles of his inner thigh, enough to tease himself. This moment was exquisite. He exhaled slowly. Later he would imagine those breasts pressed against his chest, her yielding underneath him. He waited for her command. What would she ask him to do?

'You must find out. Go to the nunnery. You must suppress any record of it. The King has imposed perpetual silence in this matter. You must ensure it.'

❦

The following day, De Nieto halted his horse in a narrow lane next to a fine old two-storey brick building which abutted the Convent of San Plácido. He sat for a few minutes, checking that no courtiers or anyone of significance was in the vicinity. A boy with a grimy visage was holding a broom. The laneway was relatively clear of what remained of the snow. Perhaps it was the boy's work. As De Nieto dismounted, he threw the reins of his horse to the lad.

Surprising himself, he fished a maravedi from his breast pocket. The boy cradled the piece of silver, imprinted with the head of the King, in his palm. He smiled, revealing a few stubby teeth. 'Whenever you need me, sire.'

De Nieto knocked. A footman received him and ushered him in.

In the reception room sat a white-haired man in shirtsleeves and a waistcoat, with a mug before him.

'This was it, Villanueva's place? You're sure?'

De Nieto had only met Villanueva once or twice. He had fallen from grace, taking the blame for the schemes hatched during the King's wilder days, and had been banished.

The man nodded. 'Aye, he was the previous owner, sir.'

'You know what I want to see,' said De Nieto.

The man groaned as he rose from his seat. He led De Nieto along a corridor and down a few stairs. They came to an empty room with one internal window, shuttered. Perhaps it was a cupboard, for a set of wooden steps, like three boxes, had been positioned beneath. The steps creaked under the man's substantial weight. With difficulty he undid the shutter, ducking under it to let it swing over his head and preventing it from banging against the wall with the palm of his hand.

'Come on, come on, let me up,' said De Nieto, taking his turn at the watching place. Through the latticed screen he peered into the locutory of the neighbouring nunnery. The girls, young nuns in soft green gowns and wearing wimples over their heads, had languid expressions. Some of their heads were bowed over prayer beads, while others reclined in more relaxed positions. One's habit was only loosely tied and showed her ankles. They were unaware they were being watched. He was peeping into a secret female space, a sacred female space. It was as Duran had told him it would be, but still he was taken aback. De Nieto's breath caught in his throat – so many virgins for the King's pleasure. And with the Devil's help he had picked the choicest fruit – forbidden fruit – and thereby damned himself. He stepped backwards down the stairs. It was unbelievable, even to him.

As the shutter was closed, he said, 'The tunnel – show me the tunnel.'

If the story were true, there would be a tunnel somewhere within the house. The Queen would quail. Or would she? Was her mettle not toughening lately, as the King's fibre failed? Without Velázquez around to prop him up, the Regent was lost.

The man was leering at him. De Nieto pointed to the door.

The old man led him on down a flagstoned corridor into a room with a fine Moroccan rug on the floor. Kneeling, the fellow began to roll back the carpet. He was too slow. De Nieto kicked at the carpet. There was indeed a trapdoor in the floor beneath. The man grasped a rope handle that had been cleverly set into the wood and pulled. The trapdoor lifted to reveal a set of stone stairs leading down into the darkness. The man lit a copper lantern and swung it to illuminate the space.

De Nieto crouched down, feeling chilly air in the gap around his loins where his leggings tied to his codpiece. The tunnel was low-ceilinged and would require stooping. A tall, stiff man like the King would have struggled to pass through. Would have had to crawl. And yet pass through he had. De Nieto felt a grudging admiration for the intensity of the King's lust. He was as base as the rest of them. Diego's faith in him had been misplaced.

'It's five or six paces along, and up another stair, and hey ho, you came up practically under their skirts, which was how the gentleman liked it.' The man laughed, too loud.

At De Nieto's scowl, he said, 'They cannot hear us here, sir; the abbess had their end of the tunnel sealed some years ago – their virtue restored. It's a stone wall there for any member who tries his prick against it. And the new abbess herself on the other side. Now she really is impregnable. Ha-ha! But in the King's youth, well . . . like a rutting bull, he was. A bit of a Zeus, eh.' And he tapped his finger against the side of his nose.

A Zeus, he'd called the King. A Zeus! The man would have to go; he knew too much. Duran would take him. But for now De Nieto nodded and said nothing except, 'That's all.'

Retrieving his mount from the waiting boy, he cantered back to the alcázar. Perpetual silence had been the instruction. Perpetual silence it must be. He would see to it.

19

FILTHY WEATHER

Alex put her hand over the mouthpiece of the phone and turned towards Oscar, who was sitting with Flora at her pine kitchen table. Flora was preparing for her trip to Portugal; she would be leaving the following week. On the table were her storage bags, a dustpan and several water bottles.

'What is it? What's wrong?' said Oscar.

'Someone broke into the professor's place last night and went through all his papers; they were scattered everywhere.'

'Is he okay?' asked Flora. They had just finished telling her about their visit to Oxford.

'Yes, he's a bit shaken, but fine. His son is with him now. They want to fax me something, a poem Mum sent him.' The phone slipped from her hand. She caught it by the cord and held the receiver against her chest. To Oscar, she said: 'You know – he mentioned it as we were leaving. He's *found* it on the floor this morning in the chaos.'

'Give them my fax number,' said Flora.

A few minutes later, Alex watched as the machine in Flora's study dotted and hummed its way along each line on the shiny roll of paper. When it had finished, she tore the end. It felt like she was holding a modern scroll.

'Oh no,' she groaned.

The handwriting was in old Spanish, the individual letters tightly packed and spiky as barbed wire. Was that an R or a P? And that an L or a T? How would she make out the words? It might as well have been morse code.

Oscar came to look over her shoulder. 'Clear as mud,' he said. 'How does he know it's a poem?'

Alex frowned. It was a good question. The writing was not her mother's, yet Professor Leadbeater had been certain they came from Rosara. But who was the author?

'It could be any kind of verse,' said Flora, who had followed them up the stairs.

Alex sighed and rolled up the fax. Maybe she could find someone who would be able to translate it.

She rubbed a hand over her face and repressed a yawn. She'd found it hard to sleep the night before. First her backpack had been snatched at the market with her journal inside. Then there was the strange visitor at the professor's house – and now there was the break-in. The theft of her backpack had seemed random, but perhaps it was not. She'd sat up in bed and rewritten as many of her notes as she could, from memory, into an exercise book she'd bought at a corner shop for fifty pence. Had the professor's visitor been listening to them? How much had he heard? Why would he care? She swallowed. Had she put the professor in danger?

Was *she* in danger? She brushed the thought away; she didn't want to worry Flora.

'I've got to get going,' she said to Oscar.

'Going where?' asked Flora.

'To see the opposition,' said Alex.

'Me too,' said Oscar.

Alex had borrowed Flora's car, a Fiat. They made a few wrong turns and it was mid-afternoon when they arrived at the address. The driveway was flanked by two sweeping lines of oak trees clad in bright green leaves. The weather had deteriorated and low grey clouds now hovered overhead.

'Are you sure this is right?' said Oscar. 'It's not the university. Not even Cambridge exactly.'

'I think this is it.' She'd called Blunt that morning, before setting out; the great-nephew had said he could receive them that same day, and even suggested they consider staying the night. This was not Alex's intention, but she'd brought a small bag and Oscar had bought a toothbrush en route – 'just in case'. *What would Helen say?* Alex put that thought out of her mind.

She glanced in the rear-vision mirror as she pointed the car up the driveway, then checked the side mirrors.

'Will you stop looking? No one is following us,' Oscar said. 'It's fine. Relax. Bags get stolen at Camden all the time. Break-ins do happen. They're not related. They can't be.'

'But what about that man who visited while we were there?'

As Alex drove up the driveway she began wondering about the great-nephew of Blunt senior. If he had made the effort to contact Leadbeater, this man must have felt his great-uncle's work was important.

Alex slowed the car as they passed an unusual tree; seen out of the corner of her eye, its thick trunk appeared to have thin people leaning against it, reaching up towards the branches that flowed from its centre like arms.

Oscar had also noticed it. 'That must be really old. It's a yew, I think.'

'Aren't you the botanist!' said Alex.

'My dad,' said Oscar. 'He's a dendrologist; trees are his job. It's handy when it comes to identifying the different woods in the instruments.'

At that moment, Alex swung the car around a corner and a grand manor, surrounded by swathes of lawns, came into view.

'Wow,' said Oscar.

'I guess this is what they call "a bit of a pile",' said Alex.

They parked on the gravel in front of the house and crunched across it and up some stairs to an imposing front door. A family crest was carved above the doorway. Alex took a step back to see that the crest included an image of a tower and a closed book. Moving forwards again, she knocked.

As they waited, she wondered if the man they were about to meet might be able to help them translate the poem and what other material he might have. She knocked again; the sound sank into the dense wood. She wished she'd taken Spanish at university. She recalled phrases, but not enough – and the old writing she'd received was so hard to decipher.

Oscar tried the doorbell. They listened for its chime but could not hear anything.

'Flat battery?' said Alex. She cupped her hand to the glass of the small window beside the door. 'I can't see anyone,' she said.

'Maybe there's a back entrance?' Oscar suggested.

Just then, the door opened. A man in corduroy trousers, a crumpled linen shirt and with wiry brown hair stood on the doorstep. After the introductions – 'Call me Sebastian,' he said – he exhaled through his nose and pressed his lips together. 'I do wish the professor had got back to me sooner,' he muttered.

He ushered them into a large room with several sitting areas. Alex opted for a pink-and-blue-striped armchair. Oscar sat close to her, on a sofa. Their host stood in front of mahogany fireplace.

Tea was delivered by a housekeeper as rain began to beat against the windows.

Sebastian poured tea, handed them each a cup, took one himself and then joined Oscar on the couch, but addressed himself to Alex. 'Leadbeater called me yesterday – tells me you come in search of tales of the hapless Hapsburgs?'

'Well, sort of,' said Alex, mentally thanking the professor.

'Sort of?' Blunt raised a bushy eyebrow.

Alex cleared her throat. 'I'm actually interested in Velázquez and *Las Meninas*, and Picasso's suggestion that it was a picture painted with curses.'

Sebastian set down his cup. 'Curses? Interesting. Hmm. I don't know that I can help you there, but my great-uncle Algie could have.'

'Your great-uncle . . . Algie Blunt?'

'Yes. Well, Algernon Blunt. He's passed on, of course. Unfortunately for him, publishers had lost their appetite for the grand narrative style of history.' Blunt began talking at length about the academic achievements and then tribulations of his great-uncle, concluding with: 'He never published his masterwork, just a smaller volume, which is now out of print.'

'And his papers?'

'Well. That all depends. Anyway, it's filthy weather; you must stay the night. I'll get Wilson to whip up a meal. And she'll show you to your rooms. Separate or together?' The man was considering Oscar with evident interest.

'Separate, please,' said Alex, as Oscar telegraphed her a wide-eyed look of concern.

Blunt didn't notice. 'Oh good. It'll be nice to have some company. We'll eat early, I'm starving. It's nearly five; anyone for gin?' He rubbed his hands together and moved to the black-and-chrome drinks trolley.

⌒

Over a dubious dinner of boiled silverside, a clumpy white sauce and potatoes, and after several glasses of wine, their host became increasingly genial.

'Above the door outside – is that your family crest?' Alex asked. 'The tower and the closed book?'

'Hm, yes, closed book, that's a reference to the Cambridge crest,' Sebastian replied. 'Means wise counsel.'

Alex remembered the open book beside the professor's door. She'd checked. The open book *was* a symbol for Oxford. It meant manifestation. Passing on knowledge made things happen. Was Blunt going to help, or would he be too sozzled?

Their host opened a bottle of port and poured the amber liquid into three crystal glasses. 'I have good news and bad news,' he said. Then he laughed. 'Well, I have a confession.'

Alex didn't touch her glass. What was he about to tell them?

'I recently had a visitor, a man connected to a reputable Spanish archive. They've bought most of the papers and boxed them up to take away.'

Alex almost groaned out loud. She glanced at Oscar, who grimaced and shrugged in sympathy. They were too late. Why had Blunt suggested they come all this way, and even stay the night?

Their host chuckled. 'Oh, I *do* hate to disappoint. Don't despair. All is not lost. Come on, both of you, I'll give you a peek.' Sebastian led them up a grand staircase and down a long, carpeted corridor that absorbed the sound of their footsteps. Alex recognised some German lithographs, then they passed several oil paintings of horses and hounds.

'Not my thing,' Sebastian said casually, and waved them on. 'Do you ride?'

Alex shook her head.

'I can. I mean, I have . . .' said Oscar.

Their host had reached a pair of wood-panelled doors. He opened them with a flourish, and they entered a huge library crammed with books. Alex gasped. On two long tables, sealed boxes were stacked in piles. *There must be nearly fifty*, she calculated.

'I can't say there's an index,' Sebastian said. 'And I'm afraid we can't actually open them.'

'If those are full, it would take a lifetime to go through all of this,' said Alex.

'Quite. It *is* a lifetime's work. Or it was . . . Most of it is sealed now, but I'm intrigued that you're interested in this idea of curses. Did you know that the King, Philip IV, had himself exorcised?'

Alex nodded. 'Professor Leadbeater told us.'

'Did he know why?'

'He didn't say.'

'Well, I think my great-uncle knew.' Sebastian went to a shelf at the side of the room and extracted a clutch of manilla folders. 'I didn't believe in *all* of it going offshore, and something tells me Uncle Algie would appreciate your interest.'

Two hours later, Alex rubbed her eyes; she was sitting at a desk struggling to maintain her focus. Oscar was on the other side of the room, sitting on the floor with several stacks of papers in front of him. 'This lot's all about proceedings for the King's funeral – *exequies*, they called them,' he said.

Alex had been reading copies of letters from the King that had been translated from Spanish to English. They bemoaned the state of the kingdom and the nobles' never-ending requests for more money and titles.

'These letters show the kingdom was in a bad way.'

'Hey, wait a minute. What about this?' said Oscar, holding up a poem transcribed in both English and the original Spanish. 'It's about the King, by someone called Quevedo.' He read aloud:

'Hail, Philip, King whom all acclaim,
In fear the infidel to keep,
Awake! For in thy slumber deep
No one doth love or fear thy name.
Awake! Oh King, the worlds proclaim
Thy crown on lion's brow to sit,
Thy slumber's but for dormouse fit.
Listen! 'Tis flattery's artful wile
That sunk in sloth thy days beguile,
And calls thee, its base ends to foster,
"Pater Noster".'

'Bravo! Well read,' said Sebastian. Their host had left them for some time and now was back, standing in the doorway, watching and listening.

Quevedo was a writer during the era of Philip IV, Sebastian explained. 'Those Spanish royals must have hated him, he had what you might call a "rapier wit". You heard it – *Sunk in sloth thy days beguile . . . base ends,*' he added, repeating some of the lines Oscar had just read. 'Did you know that Philip was a naughty, naughty boy? He had more than thirty children, most of them illegitimate.'

'Thirty!' said Alex in disbelief. She wondered if Margarita had known. The poem said the King was slumbering like a dormouse, that no one loved or feared him. He was failing in his role, was 'sunk in sloth' – laziness; his citizens needed him to wake up.

Oscar was shaking his head. 'The King sounds like a bit of a loser . . .'

Alex scanned the papers. 'I can't see anything about Margarita, or a curse, or *Las Meninas*.' She was about to call it a night when she came to a plain sheet of paper with only two words written on it: *Toledo* and *Fuendacia* – the latter circled. This grabbed her attention. Her mother had been to Toledo. And Fuendacia? *He mustn't learn about Paz and F* . . . her mother had written in her notebook. Could Fuendacia be the mysterious F?

'Can you read old Spanish? I have this . . .' She extracted the faxed poem from her bag, which she'd brought with her from downstairs, and laid the rolled paper flat on the table.

Sebastian joined her at the table. 'Let me see. Is it signed?'

'No,' said Alex, then, 'Oh.'

'Yes,' Sebastian was nodding. Oscar came to stand behind Alex.

An inch or so from the bottom of the page was a funny mark. Alex pointed to it: 'A page number . . . a seven maybe?'

'Not a seven; that looks to me like an F, an old style, F – it's back-to-front,' said Sebastian. He set a book on each end of the roll then leaned over the words. Tracing the lines with his fingertip, he muttered, 'That's *the tunnel* . . . Something *the grille* . . . *His passion* . . . I think that's *love* . . . That's *faith* – perhaps a *betrayal*? Don't know what that is . . . *As the Planet* . . . Something, something . . . Could that be *An offering*? Something . . . *injustice*. Something else there I can't decipher . . . Ah, the last line is something about a curse. *An invisible curse . . .*' Alex stared at Oscar and held her breath as she waited for Sebastian to finish.

Their host was still studying the poem. '*An invisible curse we see, to damn his line for eternity,*' he said finally.

'That's it!' said Alex. 'It's about the curse!' This was evidence of something, but she still wasn't sure what. '*To damn his line for eternity,*' she repeated. 'But what does all the rest of it mean?'

'And why does it talk about a planet?' asked Oscar. 'Is that, like, to do with astronomy?'

'I suspect it might be referring to Philip, the Planet King,' said their host. 'Ruler of all.'

'Yes, that's right, Leadbeater called him that,' Oscar recalled.

'A tunnel, and an injustice? To damn his line?' said Alex, her excitement growing.

'With the Hapsburgs, my great-uncle said, you thought of the worst and then you multiplied it,' Sebastian told them. '*Decadence,* my uncle called it in his book. Well, *that* was a euphemism. You know what I think? I think this period in Spain, the seventeenth century, is where you will find the origins of the Illuminati.'

'The conspiracy theory?' said Alex. 'But that *is* just a theory, isn't it? Something titillating that isn't actually true.'

'With Hollywood actors . . . and pyramid symbols on dollar bills,' added Oscar.

'No,' said Sebastian, 'I mean, the *Illuminati* – the *real* Illuminati. The conspiracy theorists bark up the wrong trouser leg. They trace a trail that goes into Bavaria, or Germany, but it actually began in Spain. It had a different name. One no one has paid as much attention to . . .' He raised his eyebrows suggestively.

'What name?' said Alex.

'Wouldn't *you* like to know.'

Sebastian Blunt struck Alex as a bit of a nutter. He certainly seemed rather titillated himself. Why had they agreed to stay the night?

'*I* would like to know,' said Oscar, catching Alex's eye.

'They were called . . .' said Sebastian, coming closer, picking up the glass, which he'd put to the side, and swirling his drink before taking a sip.

'Yes?' said Alex.

'The *alumbrados*.' Sebastian hissed the *s*, as if to underline his point. 'That's Spanish for the "illumined ones".'

Alex wanted to bring the focus back to the poem. If this was about something that the King did, how was it linked to *Las Meninas*, to the painting? *A picture painted with curses . . .* A King whose line was damned? Why?

She imagined Velázquez at his easel. *He knew.*

But how would he convey such a secret?

20

PROVENANCE

Alex wished she'd brought an umbrella, as Flora had suggested when she dropped off the car. She should know London spring rain by now. Water dripped from her hair and raincoat onto the polished wooden floor of the corridor outside Greta's office in the Courtald.

She reached into her pocket for a tissue that wasn't there. Her fingers brushed her tube pass and the stiff invitation card. She pulled out the card and read it again: the invitation Helen had left for her at her flat. It was for the opening of a student photography show in the East End and Helen's was one of the names listed. Alex smiled and returned the invite to her pocket.

She rearranged her shirt collar before reaching up to knock on Greta's door.

'Just a minute!' called a voice from inside.

Her three weeks was almost up, but Flora had offered her a ride to France and Spain. It was an exciting prospect – she could meet the professor's contacts – Eva and Carla. Going to Picasso's old house would be incredible, and then Madrid – but what would Greta say? Would she allow it?

Greta opened the door. 'Alex. Come in.'

Alex explained that she'd just returned from meeting Sebastian Blunt in Cambridge and Professor Leadbeater in Oxford.

'Blunt? I've never heard of him,' said Greta. 'But I do know of Leadbeater.'

'The professor found a poem my mother had sent him. It's in old Spanish – we've only translated a few snatches – it mentions the curse. I think it's a lead,' said Alex.

'Who's it by?'

'I don't know. Well, there's an initial – F.'

'Just one initial?' Greta asked.

Alex nodded.

'When was it written?'

Alex shook her head. 'Don't know, but it's old.'

Greta sighed. 'We're going to need more than that. Is there anything specific linking the poem to *Las Meninas*?'

'Well . . . it talks about the Planet King, Philip IV.' Alex tried again: 'We found another poem too, in Blunt's great-uncle's papers; it's by a poet called Quevedo, who was writing at the time Velázquez was the royal artist. It says the King, Philip IV, was "sunk in sloth" – that he wasn't a very good king.' She hesitated and then took a deep breath and outlined her plan.

Greta looked impressed, then exasperated.

To Alex's surprise, Greta agreed that Alex could go. It was the mention of La Californie that did it. 'You can't pass up an opportunity like that,' she said. 'Hm. Anyway, before I change my mind . . .' Greta motioned for Alex to follow her to her workbench. 'There's something I want you to see.'

A framed work lay upside down on the table, with the details of its provenance noted on the back.

'That's not it,' said Greta. 'It's this – it was hidden inside the frame.' She reached over and lifted several layers of tissue to reveal a work on paper.

Alex came closer and stood before the drawing: the head and shoulders of a man. It was as if she were looking down into a pool, with a face from the past rising up to meet her. She smelled salty sea water and heard a rusty key turning in a lock.

Alex took a step back and looked towards the door. There was no key. No lock.

'What is it?' said Greta.

Alex swallowed. 'It makes me think of the sea, for some reason.' She felt herself swaying, as if she were on board a ship, and for a moment she had a vision of a distant coastline and the crenelations of a fort.

'Who was he?' Alex asked.

'I don't know,' said Greta. 'And I don't know the artist either – it's unsigned. It reminds me of Rubens, but it can't be.'

'Are there any marks on the paper?'

'Not that I've found,' said Greta.

'It's by Velázquez,' said Alex.

Greta sighed. 'Oh, Alex,' she said. 'Everything is about Velázquez to you, isn't it? We'll have to get you working on some other artists.'

'No, it is. See how the shading is the same as that on some of his drawings? I've seen this before. And look at the man's eyeballs – they're still shining after all this time.'

Greta put her hand to her chin, glanced at Alex and then back at the image. 'I do get a feeling from his expression. Do you?'

Alex nodded.

The man's eyes were alert, as if he were drawn in low light. 'Look at the size of his pupils,' said Alex.

'Like he's on drugs – well, that's not likely.'

'No, not drugs,' Alex said, wondering what Greta might get up to on weekends. She returned her attention to the drawing. 'I feel like it was night-time and . . .'

'What?'

'Something about his eyes. Look . . . Do you think maybe he was afraid?'

Alex waited at the intersection for the lights to change. Greta's message had requested that she dress smartly. She'd borrowed Helen's blue dress, the one with the bow at the neck, but she'd left it untied. 'Keep the dress for a while,' Helen had said as they said goodbye. 'I don't think I'll need it at art school.' Alex had grinned and given her the thumbs up as she waved her off. Black cabs streamed down the wet road and a Roadmaster bound for Islington splashed water onto Alex's stockings. A cycle courier rode past hands-free, shouting into a walkie-talkie, with only lycra and his balancing skills as protection against the traffic. She pressed the round silver button to cross and rubbed her wet leg. The nylon snagged on her fingernail, and a neat circle of flesh appeared through a hole in the stocking. Oh no – every time!

On the other side of the street, the doors of Christie's were open. Light spilled out onto the footpath, anointing the faces of patrons, turning grey coats and pale skins to gold.

The foyer was full of people and the air thick with perfume. Alex picked up a catalogue and flicked through the thick glossy pages, scanning the images of oil paintings, etchings, lithographs and even antique porcelain. Pencil and watercolour works were at the back and here, among others by Degas and Renoir, she found the sketch she'd seen in Greta's office of the unknown man. The picture was shown in a modest size, with no title and no certificate of authenticity. The artist was listed as 'Unknown', and after the word 'Original' was a question mark. No one had agreed with her suggestion that it was a Velázquez, but no one had discounted it either. Greta said the drawing was too much of a sketch for it to be identified with any certainty. Alex, glad for the question mark, wondered what Montano would say.

Wineglasses clinked, the hum of conversation and laughter becoming louder every minute. A waiter carrying a silver tray of champagne flutes moved past. A woman took two and handed one to her friend. This was fancier than the gallery openings Alex had attended with her dad, back when his students or colleagues had their exhibitions. She looked down: the toes of her shoes were soggy from the rain, inside and out. She tried to discreetly move the hole in her pantihose to a position on the back of her leg, but this created a tightness around her thigh. There was no time to find a bathroom to fix it. She gave up.

Greta was talking to two men in suits. Alex forced herself to move closer and waited for a break in the conversation.

'Ah yes, Alex. Good. I'm glad you're here. Nice dress – matches your eyes. Gosh, so it's raining out there,' said Greta, taking in Alex's damp hair. She placed her hand on the arm of the man to whom she'd been talking. 'Quite a big crowd.'

He nodded. 'Word has got around about your mysterious unsigned sketch.'

Alex looked at Greta, who met her eye briefly but maintained her focus on her companion.

'Excellent,' said Greta. 'Thank you. I did recommend to the vendor that it might be more prudent to wait, but she's a bit of a gambler, Miss Nettie.'

'Provenance would increase its value significantly. Exponentially. But, if there's even a possibility, people may still take a punt on it.'

Greta nodded.

'Can I ask – what did Montano say?' said the man.

'He was, ah, a bit distracted,' said Greta, with a slight frown.

'Shame. Security is edgy with all these people here tonight. The potential buyers have all registered.' He lowered his voice. 'You might be interested to know that a representative of the Spanish crown is in the house.'

Greta's eyes widened.

'You didn't hear it from me,' said the man, excusing himself.

Alex touched Greta's sleeve. 'They're not really selling it, are they?'

'Yes, I'm afraid so – but we've put a high reserve on it, so I'm expecting it to pass in. But . . .' Greta scanned the crowd.

'What is it?' asked Alex.

'It's interesting that the Spanish government has sent someone. There are only two people who saw the drawing in my office: you and . . .'

'Montano?'

Greta nodded.

'What did he think – by Velázquez, or not?' said Alex.

Greta put a hand over her face and shook her head.

'What is it? Greta?'

The buzzer rang and Greta drew Alex with her to join those hurrying up the stairs, across the landing, and into the large auction room.

The first part of the program was concluding. People held round wooden paddles with numbers on them, or fanned their programs.

On the display table near the front of the room was a collection of pewter tankards and jugs, which were now being moved by auction house staff.

'Georgian,' said Greta flicking them a quick glance as they passed.

Alex shook her head. Greta knew so much.

'It becomes familiar, eventually, if you stick with it,' said Greta.

If you keep your job, thought Alex.

Staff in black shirts and name tags were hurrying about with earpieces and microphones. Some patrons were leaving and others arriving. Alex caught a glimpse of a familiar-looking woman in a smart red suit. Her black hair was swept into an elaborate up-do. She had shared the stage here a few weeks ago with Montano,

Alex recalled. She turned towards Greta, but Greta had already seen her. 'Patrizia,' she whispered.

A few steps behind Patrizia was a man with dark hair and a clipped beard.

'And a bodyguard maybe?' said Greta.

Alex gasped.

Greta looked at her, concerned. 'Are you okay, Alex?'

Alex's mouth was dry. The man adjusting his black leather gloves looked very like the man she had seen outside Professor Leadbeater's house. Could it possibly be him? And if it was, would he recognise her? At least she looked different in her dress and stockings.

A voice over the intercom asked people to take their seats. Alex picked up a glass of water. It rattled against her teeth. She took a few sips and put it to the side. 'You're very pale,' said Greta.

'I'm fine,' said Alex.

The auctioneer appeared, unbuttoning his blue suit jacket. The lights in the room dimmed. He took his place at the lectern and they were soon underway. The preliminary items travelled briskly past the auctioneer's punctuating gavel. When he reached the final pieces, he paused. The image of the sketch appeared on the screen behind him. The man's forehead and eyes were round; he had a mole on the side of his nose. The auctioneer leaned on his lectern as if it were a bar.

'Well, ladies and gentlemen, this is interesting, isn't it? One for the curious collectors among us. It's an "is it or isn't it" question. Are you brave enough to trust your gut?'

The woman in front of Alex sat forwards on her seat, craning to get a better view.

'An unsigned sketch, undated but thought to be seventeenth century, on paper. The experts have reserved their judgement, they wanted more time – but our vendor, well, she's a law unto herself.'

There were murmurs and a few chuckles from the audience.

'It's notoriously difficult to attribute a work like this. This vendor is wonderful because she wants the market to decide. It was found hidden in the back of another work, bought in a second-hand sale. Yes, don't tell *Antiques Roadshow*. This could be the real thing. And I'm not talking Coca-Cola.'

Beside Alex, Greta fiddled with the timer on her watch.

Then the auctioneer was off, calling the numbers as if in a horse race: 'I have five hundred pounds, thank you. I have five-five, that's easy, how about a thousand?'

A man raised his paddle and the auctioneer nodded. 'I have one thousand – who'll give me one five?'

The auctioneer gestured. 'I have one thousand five hundred; anyone for two?'

Someone a few rows ahead of Alex and Greta was leading the bidding. The auctioneer seemed to know him well – he called him Steven. Another bidder, a handsome woman in a wraparound dress, was standing near the front of the room holding a phone to her ear, talking and watching. Her bids were casual, a slight raise of one finger. Her other hand toyed with the gold fob chain at her neck.

'Diane von Furstenberg,' said Greta.

'Do you know her?' asked Alex.

'Not her – the dress,' said Greta, smiling.

Someone new joined the bidding. 'Welcome, sir,' the auctioneer said.

Alex twisted to look across to the other side of the room. The new bidder was dressed in black. His sideburns pointed to an unsmiling mouth. He raised his paddle with a black-gloved hand. It was the man who had accompanied Patrizia, and now she was sure: he was the man who had visited – harassed – Professor Leadbeater.

The price slowed at twelve thousand pounds.

'How about twelve and a half?' asked the auctioneer. And away they went again.

Alex looked at Greta. Her head was tilted towards Alex. As the bids increased, she drew in a sharp breath and exhaled through her nose.

'This is getting too steep . . .' she said.

Too steep for a fake, thought Alex. *Could it be by Velázquez?*

They exchanged glances.

'Do you think . . .' said Alex.

'*Shh.*' Then, under her breath, Greta said, 'Oh, Nettie, why'd you have to put it up? But the reserve is twenty grand. It won't get there.'

Yet the bidding continued, in thousand-pound jumps. It was now between Steven, the woman with the gold chain and the man in black gloves.

With the bid close to reserve, Greta groaned and whispered, 'Someone knows something.'

Alex sensed people shifting in their seats around her.

Then the woman with the chain raised her paddle once more and bid twenty thousand pounds.

The auctioneer placed his hands on the lectern in front of him and looked out across the audience. There was a slight buzz from the crowd.

'We have reached reserve, ladies and gentlemen. Someone is taking this beautiful drawing home tonight.' A pause, then: 'I think the room wants you to bid again, Steven.' The auctioneer cradled the gavel in his hands and rocked back on his heels.

The crowd laughed.

Steven shook his head.

'That didn't look like a "no" to me,' said the auctioneer. 'That was a maybe.'

More laughter. Steven shook his head again.

'I have twenty. Who'll give me twenty and a half? You, madam? Thank you. I have twenty thousand five hundred pounds.'

There were no further bids.

'Damn,' said Greta quietly.

'Anyone? . . . Going once . . .'

The man in black held up his paddle.

'Is that twenty-one, sir?'

Alex craned her neck to see.

'On you, sir, at twenty-one thousand pounds.' The auctioneer turned to the woman with the fob chain. 'Madam?'

She shook her head.

'The bid is still yours, sir – going twice at twenty-one thousand pounds, I am selling . . . Going three times and *sold*.' The gavel came down.

'Damn it,' said Greta, as the crowd clapped. 'No one pays that much for an unsigned drawing. I think we might have our answer. But how do they *know*?'

Alex stood and edged to the end of her row, positioning herself behind a small group who were clearly gossiping about the auction.

She peered past them, trying to get a view of the man with black gloves as he moved through the crowd. His face and neck were mottled, almost streaky. Yes, he was the one who had visited Professor Leadbeater. Was he also the one who'd purchased records from Blunt in Cambridge?

One thing was certain: he had bought the drawing. He knew something about it.

'Come on, let's go,' said Greta, tucking her handbag under her arm.

As they reached the top of the stairs, Alex paused. The man with black gloves was a step behind the woman in the red suit, who was walking down the stairs. Her coat was draped over his arms as if he were holding her train.

～

In the car, Patrizia turned her chin to the window. José waited, but she did not speak. The outline of her legs through her trousers fascinated him. She wore these modern clothes so nonchalantly. He tried not to stare.

At her hotel, he followed her through a foyer studded with crystal lights. He raised a hand over his eyes. When she stopped in a carpeted hallway, he groped for the keys – the keys that once hung upon his belt. She gave him a withering look, slipped a rectangular card from her handbag and passed it in front of a plain panel above the doorhandle, and like magic – *click* – the door opened.

The room was dark, with long grey curtains. Candles were arranged around the bed.

José entered and kneeled beside the bed, head bowed. They had the drawing, or they would have it tomorrow – she had said so after he made the purchase. Maybe she would reward him.

Out of the corner of his eye, he watched as she lit the candles then took a black fabric strap from the doorhandle, folded it in half and threaded the ends through to make a loop. Her movements were slow and deliberate. As she placed the loop over his head, one of her hands brushed the lump which was his deformed ear.

'You are my dog,' she said.

'Madam,' he said, feeling a tingle up the back of his thighs.

'My hound.' She touched his hair. 'The drawing was of the messenger, Paredes.'

He ignored the fool's name and leaned into her, leaned into the familiar way she rolled her Spanish *r* a little too much. Oh, the elasticity of her tongue. His mouth filled with saliva. He swallowed.

She stood beside him, her fingers twisting his hair. His head was level with her belly as the cord tightened around his neck.

'What of the girl? We have the drawing, but is she still in pursuit of the secret? If she gets too close, you must stop her, José. Perpetual silence means perpetual silence. Should you fail, I will ask the master to condemn you . . . again.'

At the constriction of his throat, De Nieto thought of the luscious richness of air, real fresh air, and then, as the pressure in his head intensified, he also remembered what 'life' was like without it.

Sargatanas' waiting room was like the chimney of a furnace. At the memory of the heat, sweat sprang to his forehead and scalp. He wiped his upper lip and noticed a grey smear from his skin on the back of his hand. If he had to go back, he would lose this new skin, would never feel her next to him like this. He had been constrained on all sides, with heat rising from below. Little drips of him fell on the floor and sizzled. The stench of burnt leather, like smoked meat, travelled from the soles of his boots to his nose. He had been so parched he fantasised of water, cooling liquids, the ocean. He would have savoured the foulest puddle, lapped from it like a poodle. Dogs and water. He remembered the moment when his famous cousin first judged him. His little sister had found a soft golden puppy. The other children, including Diego, played with it as it gambolled about. They loved it as much as they ignored him. One day, when no one was looking, he lifted the soft furry creature to the side of the well. They sat together for a while, feeling the heat of the sun, he and the furry creature. The puppy licked his hand, he gave it a pat, then he held it in one hand over the water glinting at the bottom of the well. He let go, heard a splash, and heard the little yelps it made until it gave up.

His sister had searched for that puppy all day. The next morning, Diego had gone for water and pulled up the bucket.

Patrizia's voice brought him back to the hotel room. 'Well? Is she still on the trail?' she demanded.

'Yes,' he said. 'She's been to the professor, but . . .' He could not go back to the waiting room, to purgatory.

'Your time is running out,' she said. The strap tightened around his neck. At that moment he knew his mistress would do it without hesitation. Eternal purgatory would be his, unless he stopped the girl from sticking her nose into the King's business. Unless he ensured perpetual silence.

21

LA CALIFORNIE

Flora was driving and had been doing so since they crossed the Channel earlier that morning. From Calais, they had driven on towards the Champagne region. Flora had her tools in the back of the car. She would be visiting a site in Portugal and on her way would take Alex to Cannes and then as far as Madrid. Oscar was already in Spain, continuing his research work at the University of Barcelona.

That evening, they stayed in Troyes, sharing a twin room in a small hotel.

'So charming. It reminds me of Amsterdam,' said Flora. The old houses leaned against each other, all askew. After dinner – her first in France, which they celebrated with champagne – Alex collapsed into bed and re-read her mother's *Vogue* magazine. The article about Picasso was based on a 1956 interview with the artist at La Californie, his home in the south of France, towards which they were now heading. Peering at the article under the glow of the beside lamp, she noticed tiny pencil marks made by Rosara in the margin which she hadn't seen when she'd looked at it in Flora's attic. She pored over the piece and copied several of these excerpts – which were direct quotes from Picasso – into her new notebook:

> *I never do a painting as a work of art. All of them are researches. I search incessantly . . . A painting is a machine to print on the memory.*

And:

> *. . . often one does a painting really for a corner of the canvas that no one looks at.*

She underlined this and leaned against the headboard. She must remember to look in the corners. A machine to print on the memory. Searching and researching. The corners of *Las Meninas* were dark and shadowy, like the corners of this little room. The two pictures hanging on the wall had become dense dark squares; she couldn't make them out. 'Often one does a painting really for a corner of the canvas that no one looks at,' Picasso had said. Had Velázquez thought like that too? Picasso had learned from him. *Look in the corners*, she wrote.

⌒

They reached Cannes the following day. After topping up at a service station, they found a little pension and ate ratatouille at a local bistro.

Alex woke early the next morning, full of anticipation for her appointment at La Californie. Their hostess at the pension asked what they were planning, and when Alex told her, she put her hand on her hip and raised her eyebrows. The public couldn't visit La Californie, she reminded them; it was not a museum but a private house. Flora told her that they had been invited – Professor Leadbeater had seen to that – and the landlady nodded politely. '*Trés bien*,' she said. 'You are very lucky.' But her expression suggested she did not quite believe them.

In the hills above Cannes, the houses were grand, garlanded with ivy. Flora parked and they began walking up the narrow, winding street; the houses perched on the hills had stunning views to the bay below, where yachts and motor launches swung at their moorings, like white birds on a blue sea.

Alex pulled Professor Leadbeater's letter of introduction out of her bag and checked the address. 'This is it.'

The house had large metal gates with an intercom and an expanse of gravel leading to the front entrance. It didn't look like many people arrived on foot, let alone in frayed sneakers like Alex wore. This was a leather loafer kind of house.

A small brown sausage dog came trotting up the opposite footpath. Alex watched him sniffing at a few blades of grass that emerged from beneath the well-clipped hedge of the garden opposite. The dog raised his leg. When he'd finished, he looked at Alex and wagged his tail. She heard the noise of a motorbike coming fast up the hill. The dog was still focused on her, or on the house behind her. It began crossing the road just as the bike roared into view. 'No!' Alex leapt out, grabbed the dog and threw them both out of the path of the bike.

The motorcyclist careened to a halt.

Alex landed on her side on the kerb, with the dog clasped to her chest. He licked her neck.

The biker was still upright, helmeted. He gunned his bike and took off.

Flora rushed over.

'I'm fine,' Alex assured her, easing herself off the kerb.

The front gates of La Californie opened and a woman in a skirt, jersey and a silk scarf hurried towards them. 'Poochi!' she called. She released a stream of pointed French in the direction of the motorcyclist. 'Good riddance,' said the woman, then, 'He could have killed you both. They come here and they think they are in the Monte Carlo rally!'

The dog wriggled free of Alex's hold and ran towards the woman, who scooped him up.

'Ça va?' said the woman.

'I think so,' said Alex, rubbing her side.

'I was watching out of the window,' the woman said. 'Thank you for saving my dog; he's a little deaf these days. I didn't realise he'd escaped. He likes to explore, but he is, how do you say, a little naughty.'

The woman invited them in for a glass of water, and as they walked up the driveway, Alex explained that she'd been about to ring the doorbell. Handing her the letter of introduction from Professor Leadbeater, she said, 'I'm researching the Infanta Margarita and *Las Meninas*, including Picasso's versions.'

'Oh yes, of course, the professor's research assistant. I'm Eva Pierre – I've been expecting you.'

His research assistant! That was stretching it. Alex was taken aback but pleased. Flora winked at her.

'He's helped me with information about paintings, questions of provenance, a few times over the years,' Eva was saying. 'He's very knowledgeable, very helpful. You are welcome here at La Californie. I will show you the studio where the *Las Meninas* series was created.'

Eva ushered them inside. Picasso was a friend of her parents, she said, as she tucked her blonde hair behind her ears. The house was now a private home; she was helping the owner.

'Pablo's *Las Meninas* works are in Barcelona, at the Picasso Museum.' Eva explained that the works – all fifty-eight of them – were created in August 1957, around three hundred years after *Las Meninas* was painted by Velázquez.

'It was like a tribute, one great master communicating with another, but it was also personal . . .'

They entered a living room to the left of the foyer. The walls were hung with numerous Picassos, as well as prints by some other artists. Alex's eye was drawn to a painting she didn't recognise, which seemed almost childlike in execution. It was hung above the fireplace, along with several family photos. It was a colourful, realistic painting of a man, a woman and two children, all standing a little apart, as if waiting for someone to take their picture. The faces of the children were sweet; the woman had red hair and held a bucket. They were like a fairytale image of what a family might be.

Not mine, thought Alex.

Eva noticed Alex looking and came to stand beside her. 'That was painted in 1937,' she said. 'A family portrait by Pablo. It's a little different. Not many people recognise it as his work. He called it *La Familia*. And that name, *La Familia*, strangely enough, was also the early name of *Las Meninas*.'

Something registered in Alex's brain at those words, but she didn't allow herself to become distracted. She followed Eva up the stairs, keen to see the studio.

On the first floor, Eva opened another pair of ornately carved doors, then stood back and allowed them to enter.

Alex took a few steps into the white-walled room, saw the blue bay glistening through the two sets of narrow French doors and a mirrored wardrobe or armoire at the other end of the room. All other furniture, apart from a small table near the door, had been removed. An easel stood in the corner. Alex saw herself in the mirror, and between herself and her reflection she saw the parquet floor, a mosaic of wooden stars, each with eight points. Each within a little frame, a square of wood. The pattern repeated ad infinitum. Alex held her breath for a few moments. Margarita and her diamond and the frame. He'd painted her here, she knew. Casting back over three hundred years, from those August days in 1957, Picasso had found her, and he had found too the artist who had immortalised her, Velázquez. They had communed; jousted with mahlstick and paintbrush. They had sparred, painted and conjured the girl and her blue star dancing between them.

'There used to be many of Pablo's things in here, all his objects of inspiration, his relics, including photos of his own head. Gone now. He was a very superstitious man,' said Eva.

'But the stars,' said Alex, 'they are still here.'

Eva smiled. 'Yes, he loved the stars. He said they helped him dance, and paint. There are photos of him dancing in this room. Did you know that his first wife was a ballerina? He met her when they were performing a ballet of *Las Meninas* in 1916 and they fell in love. Her name was Olga.' She nodded gravely. '*Las Meninas* was very special for him. There's a lot of love in it, and grief, too. That's why he gifted the whole suite of paintings to the Picasso Museum. It was absolutely his intention that they remain together.'

Flora pointed to something in the bay through the French doors, and Eva went to join her on the balcony. The sound of their voices blurred to static white noise, as if someone was switching radio stations. A cloud passed over the sun and the room dimmed. Alex was alone inside the doorway, waiting. Grief, Eva had said. A lot of grief.

Something gathered in the darkest corner of the room. At first Alex thought it was a trick of the light, caused by a flutter of the gauze curtain. Then she saw them, at the vanishing point, shimmering like a mirage. Two figures: a stocky teenage boy, his head in profile, bent towards the palest outline, a mere wisp of a girl lying flat on a bed, her head on the pillow tilted towards his inclined ear. He was straining to catch her indecipherable words, grasping her hand, imploring her to stay.

Alex took a step towards them, hoping to see the girl's face, but the boy turned his head, his dark hair smooth. He held Alex in his challenging gaze, then his image quivered and was gone, and the girl, in her nightgown, trailed behind him like a silver cape and disappeared into the wall. The stars on the floor glimmered with a pale blue light. They led like a pathway towards where the vision had been.

She was tingling all over, and the hairs on the back of her neck were standing on end. She stepped onto one of the stars and felt a snap, like a small electric shock. The room began to move, a whoosh of heat ran up her body, she was hot and then cold, bile rose in her throat. She sank to her knees, and then was on all fours on the parquet floor.

A few moments later she felt her aunt's hand on her back, patting her gently.

'Sit down and put your head between your knees,' said Flora. 'That's it.'

Alex could see Eva's patent leather shoes in front of her. There was a wrinkle at the ankle of her nylon stocking.

'Has she fainted?' The voice came from a long way away.

'Yes, I think so – or almost,' said Flora. 'Alex, are you okay?' There was a frown of concern on her face.

Alex's stomach felt empty, as if all the air had been sucked out of her. She took several deep breaths. She was not sure what she had seen, but she didn't think she'd imagined it.

'I'm okay,' she said, kneeling.

'Let's get you downstairs for a glass of water,' said Eva. 'It's very hot today. Perhaps you are thirsty.'

'Dehydrated?' said Flora.

Alex took Flora's hand and allowed her aunt to help her up. But at the doorway she turned back towards where she had seen the pair. The stars were wooden again; their iridescent blue light had vanished. She left Eva and Flora and walked closer to where the apparition had been.

'Alex?' said Flora. 'What's going on?'

Alex crossed to the far corner. There was dust on the floor in the corner, undisturbed, and no sign of footprints. She touched the wall with her fingertips, and then her palm, both hands, then knocked. The plaster was flat and solid.

'What *are* you doing?' said Eva, her tone brisk.

Alex turned to them. 'I saw something,' she said. 'Here, in the corner.'

Eva said nothing, but led them downstairs, smoothing her hair as she went.

Flora raised an eyebrow at Alex.

In the salon downstairs Eva directed them to some small armchairs in the window alcove. She went off and returned a few minutes later bearing a tray with three glasses of iced water. Alex took a sip and regarded the two women over the top of her glass. She put it down on a little marble side table.

'Now,' said Eva, straightening her skirt over her knees. 'Please tell me what happened.'

Alex described what she'd seen. She did not leave anything out.

Eva listened intently, nodding. When Alex had finished speaking, Eva clasped her hands together. Flora's eyes were wide as she glanced between Alex and Eva.

Eva gazed out of the window, as if composing her thoughts. Finally, she spoke. 'Don't be afraid. I saw them once too, a long time ago, after he died. I've always wondered if I dreamed it.' She took out a handkerchief and dabbed her eyes.

Alex had not been expecting this. She thought of the ghostly girl in the bed.

'Conchita,' said Eva.

'Pardon?'

Eva raised her eyebrows. She took a cigarette from a blue-and-white Gauloise packet on the side table and lit it. She took a long drag then exhaled, directing the smoke away from them.

'Conchita was Picasso's younger sister,' Eva explained. 'Their father was an art teacher, and he moved the family from Málaga to La Coruña for a new job at the art school. They didn't have much money. Conchita caught diphtheria and died; she was only seven. Picasso was six years older than her, and he adored her.'

She explained that the young Pablo was at Conchita's bedside while she clung to life and was devastated by her death; he might have carried some guilt that she had died while he had lived, Eva suggested.

The vision of the boy and the dying girl had been so tender, Alex thought; Eva's words seemed to describe their poignant situation exactly.

After the births of his daughters, Eva went on, Picasso had become quite obsessive, highly concerned for their wellbeing. This, some of his family members thought, related to his unresolved agony over the loss of Conchita.

'I think the Infanta Margarita reminded him of Conchita,' said Eva. 'Maybe it was partly her light, her "life force", that he was responding to. He believed in a universal life force, you know.'

'So you think he saw Conchita in the Infanta Margarita as Velázquez painted her in *Las Meninas*?' asked Alex.

'Yes, indeed I do,' said Eva. 'A well Conchita, a happy Conchita. A living Conchita. As I said, I think those girls represented a life force.' She went to a wide set of plan drawers and extracted a small A4 sheet, and brought it back to where they were sitting. She held out a copy of a pencil sketch: the head of a young girl, in a lace-trimmed bonnet, with a sweet expression and hopeful eyes.

'Is that her?' asked Alex.

Eva nodded. 'Yes, this a copy of a drawing Pablo made of Conchita.'

'She does look like Margarita, doesn't she?' said Alex. A life force. Margarita had vibrated with it.

Eva sighed. 'There's more to this.'

Alex followed her gaze to the unusual unsigned painting above the fireplace.

'*La Familia*,' said Eva. 'Pablo was a great artist, but he did not leave a happy family.'

'*Salvare la familia . . .*' murmured Alex, as the words came back to her. 'Someone said that to me once, but I didn't understand what it meant.' She did not say that that someone had been Margarita.

'Well,' Eva said, 'it could mean "Save the family", or' – she gestured to the painting above the fireplace, the red-headed family with the bucket – 'it could mean "Save the painting *La Familia*".'

In other words, Alex thought to herself, *Save Las Meninas*.

'Did you know that Velázquez also had a daughter who died young?' said Eva.

Alex shook her head.

Eva continued: 'Her name was Ignatia. He sketched her too. Oddly enough, she also looked a bit like Margarita. She and Conchita and Margarita are all like reflections of each other.'

'The grief connects them through time,' said Alex, and as she said the words, the realisation hit her: it connected her, too.

Eva nodded and glanced at Flora. Alex did, too; her aunt was looking pale, she noticed.

'Grief, eh?' said Flora softly.

'Their life force connects them too,' said Eva.

'Doesn't the open door often represent the journey towards death, or the afterlife?' said Flora.

'Like the open door at the back of *Las Meninas*?' Alex thought of her mother, of how the loss had affected her. 'I had . . . an experience,' she said to Eva, 'at the Prado, when I was twelve, while looking at *Las Meninas*.'

Flora was nodding, encouraging her.

Eva put her hand on Alex's arm. 'Whatever happened, Pablo would probably have approved, or understood. He visited *Las Meninas* when he was young, too – fourteen, I think – with his father. Later he said it set the direction of his life. He was quite a mystical man. Art was alive for him. He – how do you say? – "communed" with Velázquez through the medium of their art. He became convinced that an artwork is a magical object, endowed with the properties of its subject. He respected the Indigenous peoples who held such beliefs. Perhaps through Margarita, Velázquez made his daughter Ignatia "live" again, and through Margarita, Picasso reconnected with Conchita.'

'Art helped him face death,' said Alex. It was meant as a question, but it didn't come out that way.

Eva nodded and leaned back in her chair. She explained that the young Picasso's talent was so prodigious that he eclipsed his father, and his father, recognising his son's brilliance, gave up painting and passed his brushes on to his son and thereafter concentrated on teaching.

Alex recalled how her own father had put away his brushes after her mother's death; he had taught art but he had never again drawn or painted for himself.

She felt a soft nudge against her ankle. It was Poochi, the dog.

'You've made a friend,' said Eva. 'He reminded me of Lump, Pablo's dog. You know, Lump is in Picasso's version of *Las Meninas*, too – his outline. Picasso loved a joke. If it's a painting about succession, then Picasso has put himself and Lump in there. He was a son of Spain, like Velázquez. An artist, like Velázquez.'

'Velázquez's successor?' asked Alex.

'Touché. Indeed. I believe he thought so,' said Eva.

When Alex and Flora said goodbye, they patted Poochi, and Eva kissed them both on each cheek.

In the car, Alex buckled her seatbelt.

'Art with impact, huh,' said Flora. 'Art with ghosts?'

Alex's mind was spinning with the new information. *Las Meninas* had been known as *La Familia*. '*Salvare La Familia*,' Margarita had said. Grief connected them. Grief.

She wanted to tell Helen, and Oscar.

'What is it?' said Flora.

'I'm wondering about *Las Meninas*, the one that was first called *La Familia*. She told me to save "*la familia*". Could she have meant the painting *La Familia*? Could it actually be in danger?'

Flora shook her head. 'I don't think that's what Eva meant.'

'No, not Eva . . .' Alex murmured.

'Anyway, it's safe in the Prado.'

Is it? Alex wondered.

❦

They had driven down to the edge of the sea and found a place to park. The Mediterranean was slumping onto the shore. Flora was sitting, hands on the steering wheel, gazing through the windscreen. She looked slightly dazed.

'Are you okay?' Alex asked.

Flora sighed. 'I'll be fine. I just need a moment. You know, I haven't told you, but I had a son. He died when he was three.'

Alex's mouth dropped open. She'd assumed her aunt had decided not to have children, or had never met the right person. She touched Flora's arm. 'I'm so sorry,' she said. 'I didn't know.'

'I never talk about him, do I? I should. I will.'

'What happened to him?'

'Leukaemia. He needed lots of blood transfusions.' Flora was a regular blood donor, Alex knew. Maybe this was why. Alex remembered the little silver cup she'd seen Flora polishing at her house in Clapham – a christening cup, she realised now.

'I've seen Louis in my dreams. I would give anything to see him again. But I've never seen him as a ghost. It wasn't even night-time today, yet you saw . . . Sometimes I look at young men in the street and imagine that they are him, at the age he would be now. I even followed one of them once . . .' She shook her head.

Again, Alex had a sudden memory of her mother sitting by her bedside, reading to her. She realised she could conjure that comfort whenever she needed it. Could the memory of loss become less anguished? Could she see it more clearly, slip inside it, remembering the good bits, like trying on a jacket in a market?

'Oh,' she said.

'What?' said Flora.

'Something about Mum. I remembered her reading a particular book to me at bedtime. It was clear. Good.'

'That's a nice memory,' said Flora, giving Alex's leg a pat, before starting the car.

'Yes,' said Alex, reaching for her sunglasses.

'We save the good memories. I read somewhere that it's up to the living to let the dead go . . . When we let them go, they can rest. And we learn how to live.' Flora put the car into gear. 'So, where to next? Madrid?'

Alex nodded. Back to *Las Meninas* and where it all began.

22

NOISES

1665

Margarita woke with a start. Something had disturbed her sleep; a kind of howl. Had she dreamed it? She didn't think so.

The sound came again. Could it be Terrón, the mastiff? Since the departure of her sister and the deaths of Velázquez and Felipe, she often felt on edge at night. She climbed out of bed and lit a candle, cupping its hot flame with her hand. Her reflection was ghostly in the glass windows. She picked up her dark blue shawl, wrapped it around herself and crept out of her room. Luisa was snoring lightly in the antechamber. Maribárbola was sleeping there too.

Outside in the corridor, she paused. She'd not slipped away like this since Velázquez died, and never at night. It was most definitely not allowed. It was dark in both directions. Her candle threw a pool of light into the licorice night. The flagstones were cold on her bare feet. Perhaps she should return to her warm bed.

She moved on until she came to the painting of Balthazar on his rounded pony with its gleaming flanks. Holding the candle aloft, she studied his face and took some encouragement from his familiar features and his eyes. Taking care to hold the candle in her other hand well away from the canvas, as Luisa had taught her, she touched his foot with her fingertips. She was only a year younger now than he had been when he had died. Velázquez's words came back to her. 'Don't let them suppress your inner light. It's yours alone.' She wished he were still alive.

Another howl came echoing down the corridor and she froze. It sounded like an animal in pain. She should go see. But what if Luisa woke, found her missing and raised the alarm? What would her mother say? The Queen had warned her that she must never be alone, lest her precious virginity be questioned. It was maddening.

'Margarita?'

She turned to see Maribárbola standing in the doorway behind her.

'Come back to your bed; it is late. You must not be here like this . . .' Maribárbola's voice was sleepy, her crumpled face even more scrunched than usual.

Margarita shook her head and continued along the corridor, realising she knew her way even in the darkness, though she was not exactly sure where she was going. To her relief, Maribárbola, ever obliging, sighed, yawned and followed.

Then the sound came again: a tortured, agonised squeal, like a fox caught in a trap.

'Stop – please.' Maribárbola reached for Margarita's arm. 'What is that?'

Margarita brushed her hand away and hurried on, the small woman muttering behind her as she struggled to keep up.

A glow up ahead. Huge shadows loomed on the stone walls. As she peered around a bend in the corridor, hiding her own candle behind her, she saw they were cast by hand lamps, and she saw several of the King's court attendants, poised like birds. They too were leaning towards the source of the sound. The sound was coming from the King's chamber. Guards stood on either side of the closed doors.

What is happening? Margarita wondered. The coldness of the floor was creeping up her legs towards her chest. She felt alone, small, her courage wavering. What if Luisa awoke and found them missing? Who would speak for her? Maribárbola? Velázquez was dead and no longer able to influence the King. When he was alive, they had lived in a golden bubble. The King was fading, unwell and increasingly invisible. And now? Was he worse? Had that noise come from him? She bit her lip. Imagined herself pounding on his door. The thought made beads of sweat form on her forehead. The Queen had become unrecognisable, so stern, so intent on the throne and pretending that poor feeble Carlos, her latest issue, was a perfect son and heir. Margarita's rooms were far away. De Nieto could be very close. He might find her and report her to the Queen. She would be angry to find Margarita here. As her father retreated inwardly, her mother seemed to become stronger; the balance between them had tipped. Margarita's only friends were Luisa and Maribárbola. And they were afraid. More afraid than she.

'Come.' Maribárbola tugged on her arm and Margarita returned to her room without protest. By the time she lay down in her bed and Maribárbola replaced her covers, the first cock was beginning to crow. Margarita closed her eyes and buried her face in her pillow. In the morning there was blood on her sheets and between her legs, and Luisa cried at the sight of it.

III
BASE GROUNDS

23

MALADIES AND REMEDIES

1665

De Nieto entered the King's bedroom, following the black-garbed Geronimo Duran, the acting Inquisitor General, his assistant, Alfonso, and Gomez, the King's confessor.

A bare-chested King Philip IV lay on a long board set upon trestles in the centre of the room. He raised his head and then dropped it back on his pillow. The sheet around his arse was spotted with blood.

Two physics were in attendance, in grey coats and gowns, and a marquis with a hundred maravedis' worth of silver thread in the sleeves of his doublet. Though his sleeves gleamed in glory, the marquis was not one to stand and fight for his lord. As they entered he took leave of His Majesty and scurried out, holding his nose. The room stank of piss and shit.

De Nieto suppressed a sneer. Weak stomach, weak will. He found a spot to stand near the unlit fireplace and avoided Duran's eye, lest the other man's lust give him away.

The physics presented their conserve of mallow leaves. 'A gloomy malady afflicts him with fever, pain and haemorrhage,' one declared. The other muttered about gallstones. A physical malady afflicted the royal body, but the remedy which would be applied by the agents of the Inquisition was of a different nature.

Duran directed a stern warning at all present: 'Satan is behind this.'

The physics glanced at each other. One coughed and the other buttoned his cloak. The pair retreated to the doors, promising to return in the morn, and hurried from the chamber.

Cowards, thought De Nieto.

Duran and his assistants remained. Duran, De Nieto knew, scorned the King for his actions with the nun and had demanded multiple confessions. He would hold strong and would give no quarter. They were a bonded triumvirate. Duran was to conduct the rites of the exorcism. De Nieto thought of the Queen, alone in her quarters, perhaps in her bed. She knew what was about to happen and had condoned it. He was her man. She had given him the authority. She had been fourteen when Philip had taken her for his own. Now she had the power. And through her, he, De Nieto, without his hated cousin, was at the right hand of the throne. De Nieto was almost the most powerful man in the kingdom. He hated that word 'almost'.

Our King is a dormouse, not a lion, thought De Nieto. No one loved him. They were reciting Quevedo's lampooning poem in the *mentideros*; everyone had heard it, except the King himself:

Hail, Philip, King whom all acclaim,
In fear the infidel to keep,
Awake! For in thy slumber deep
No one doth love or fear thy name.
Awake! Oh King, the worlds proclaim
Thy crown on lion's brow to sit,
Thy slumber's but for dormouse fit.
Listen! 'Tis flattery's artful wile
That sunk in sloth thy days beguile,
And calls thee, its base ends to foster,
'Pater Noster'.

Tales of the recent slaughter of their troops by the English and the Portuguese were sweeping the town. Eight thousand Spaniards had been killed within twelve hours. When Philip had received the news a few days ago, he'd cast himself on the ground, taking the news as another nail in his coffin, further proof of the hex in action. De Nieto and the Queen were present when this occurred. The King's heartbroken words then had chilled the chamberlain. 'Oh God, thy will be done.' Royal consent to the exorcism had followed not long after.

His countrymen were racked by despair and shame. De Nieto clenched his fist under his cape, watching as Duran prepared himself. Had an exorcism *ever* been conducted upon a King? It was unbelievable. This would not be happening if Diego Velázquez were still alive; he was too compassionate. What if Philip sat up and ordered them to the dungeons halfway through, what would they do? None of them would stop what was about to happen. None of them would help him. Besides the King, there were now only the four of them in the room, and they had sworn an oath earlier that day. De Nieto was still revelling in his new knowledge, trying to estimate how much the Queen, his mistress, knew . . .

They had met during the siesta, at De Nieto's tapestry workshop. In a private room, Duran had revealed more news about the situation at the nunnery of San Plácido; information he had gained from his predecessor, Sotomayer, who had 'retired' near Cordova. The King's 1638 soirée had not been the first incursion. Earlier that decade, an errant friar had declared no less than twenty-eight of thirty nuns at the same nunnery to be possessed by the Devil. On the pretext of exorcising the Evil One, the friar had been with them nearly day and night for three years. De Nieto had been drinking a draught of ale as Duran related this. Twenty-eight! He'd nearly choked. No one had invited him!

Duran was pacing up and down as he described how they forced the nuns to strip and had sexual relations with them, even the highest-ranking members of the nobility taking part. They were members of a secret society called 'the *alumbrados*' – 'the illumined ones' – and conducted, Duran said, 'fantastic irreligious rites'.

Three years, marvelled De Nieto.

Alfonso went off and returned with more ale. Duran took the drink and dismissed him.

Duran pulled his chair to face De Nieto and placed his hands on De Nieto's knees. His gaze was intent, his grip vicelike and his voice low.

It was just the two of them. Dangerous. Duran had a bead of sweat on the indentation above his upper lip.

'The highest-ranking nobility took part in this rampant sport,' he repeated. 'Their actions were . . . repellent.' The man's left hand slid up and under De Nieto's legging and neatly cupped his balls.

The highest-ranking? De Nieto was both thrilled and repulsed; repulsed by Duran's foul breath. Accepting his touch gave him powerful currency, but he could trust no one. Should he ask for names?

'The stories were so strange and caused such scandal that we, the Inquisitors, had to hold them to account. Evidence was gathered,' said Duran.

What happened to it? Brushing Durans' beringed digits aside, De Nieto grasped his own rod and gestured for the other man to do the same.

Duran's cheeks flushed and he licked his lip. 'The King himself had the evidence transported to the Holy See, in Rome, by a messenger.'

'And?' De Nieto had heard rumours of the messenger. But had the man succeeded? Had he survived the downfall of Olivares, the King's first chamberlain?

Duran's eyes were closed, his arm jerking up and down within his parted cassock, as if he was a bellows boy tending a blacksmith's forge.

De Nieto tugged out his own climax, then placed his sticky finger on the other man's upper lip.

Duran whimpered and his chin sunk to his chest as he finished with a grunt. He began straightening his garments. 'It remains under consideration. There are reviews. These things take time . . .'

But the King imposed perpetual silence, you fool, thought De Nieto, handing Duran a rag with which to wipe his prick. And, more importantly, so had the Queen.

⌒

Back in the alcázar, De Nieto's nerves had been on edge ever since the tryst. He paced the perimeter of the King's chamber, checking behind the curtains at the door and by the window. He crouched down and scanned under the King's bedstead. He felt Duran's eyes upon him. Noticed a white stain upon his black stocking. He gave it a rub. He checked that the doors were locked and closed the cover on the keyhole. Once satisfied the room was secure, he indicated as such.

Sweat trickled from Philip's brow. His head turned from side to side and a terrible grimace contorted his mouth. A paroxysm of fever gripped him. When it passed, he lay silent, exhausted.

Duran positioned himself at the King's feet. He held a short staff tipped with metal.

He formally introduced himself, his compatriot, Alfonso, who would assist, and their purpose, being the exorcism of the Demon from the King of Spain. De Nieto was there as a witness for his mistress.

At a nod from Duran, Alfonso removed the pillow from beneath Philip's head. Alfonso was a squat man, dressed this evening in a simple friar's robe. He then joined his master at Philip's feet.

Duran lifted his spike and pointed it towards the King's head and commenced incantations in Latin to defeat the Evil One.

The other churchmen's voices joined in: '*Vade retro Satana. Nunquam suade mihi vana. Sunt mala que libas. Ipse Venana bibas . . .*' Satan begone. Never tempt me with your vanities. What you offer me is evil. Drink the poison yourself . . .

Philip's breath rasped. His ribs showed, yet his belly was distended. He groaned and extruded a tarry stool, with some blood. A foul stench filled the room. Duran and Alfonso continued chanting.

De Nieto felt sweat trickle down his back; their Latin church words gave him an ache. He tried to open the neck of his doublet; he wished to leave the chamber but knew he could not. The incantations were not addressed to him, he reminded himself, but still something writhed inside him. He had to force himself to hold his ground.

Philip's mouth opened. 'The nun,' he gasped. 'Where is she? I sinned against her. I am cursed . . . release me . . .'

'*Vade retro Satana. Vade retro Satana. Vade retro Satana,*' the voices continued, louder now.

Philip's eyelids fluttered. He cried like a woman, clutching his side. None of those assembled mopped his brow.

The friars increased the urgency of their chanting.

After half an hour of this, the King lay silent, his eyes closed. De Nieto wondered if he had died or merely fainted.

Alfonso held his fingers to the King's neck. 'Alive.'

De Nieto breathed a sigh of relief. They must not kill him.

Duran placed a hand on the King's forehead. 'The demon burns inside him. We must beat it out.'

Duran took a birch twitch and held it into a candle flame where it flared, releasing a wildfire scent. He murmured prayers, then he beat the flames out against the stone wall above the fireplace with great vigour. De Nieto, startled, quickly checked for tapestries nearby, but there were none.

Taking the smoking birch to the King, Duran raised his arm and began to lash the pale body, leaving red marks on the royal hide. When the King made no protest, Duran hit him harder, till all could hear the minute flicks of his whipping. Duran's wrists were so supple, so adept at his task. Philip began to whimper. De Nieto felt a swell of admiration for Duran's focus and tenacity. He craned his neck, watching with interest the changing colours of Philip's flesh, as the incantations rose and fell around them.

The King had slipped into a trance. They desisted. Alfonso wiped his arse with the sheet, rolled it into a ball and threw it under the table. At a nod from Duran, De Nieto slipped his hands under the King's feeble arms and sat him up. Bracing himself, he pulled the King away from the bench, while Duran and Alfonso took a leg each. Thus they held the King of Spain between them, like a carcass, barely covered in a cloth, his chin sunk to his sallow chest. The remaining linen fouled with the King's blood and excrement fell to the floor. Duran's expression was strained, his eyes wide. A vein pulsed at his neck. Alfonso huffed and puffed. De Nieto had a strange sense of calm. The King was a tall man but weighed little now. His collar bones protruded and his long arms hung limp at his sides. This once proud pillar, dubbed the stone statue, was a rag doll in his arms.

As they hauled him onto the bed and rearranged him in a semblance of order, De Nieto's eyes went to the wall of the King's bedroom. The damned thing was there, still with its fudgy dark corners and brusque brushwork – here, in pride of place. Diego's frozen image observed him as if from the afterlife. His contemplative gaze gave De Nieto pause. And there was the Infanta, as she had been as a child, like a lamp in the darkness. Her purity and innocence made him squirm. *It is just a painting*, he told himself, and yet he knew it was more. He felt the venom rise in his throat. He hated how his own representation hovered, hesitating in the doorway. He recalled Diego and the King, who now lay sprawled upon the bed, how they had talked together for hours before this infuriating canvas, as if it contained secrets only they understood. The truth of it had eluded him. Diego was dead and the hidden meaning eluded him still! Or did it? The sight of the naked King draped in a sheet, on his back, reminded him. He was no 'Zeus' now but, as the old man who had shown him the tunnel had said, he'd been a Zeus in his youth.

And then he knew. *The Rape of Europa.* The secret! It was hidden, here, in the King's very chamber, under his nose. The painting must go. Soon he would replace it with tapestries at the Queen's behest. Soon the King too would be gone. In his mind's eye he saw *La Familia* burning, its edges curling like charred parchment, and a thrill swept through him and made his nostrils flare. All of those who so reviled him – Diego, the King, Maribárbola, the Infanta – one day all of them would be turned to dust. Only he and the Queen would remain. And the trace of the curse would be lost in the past, where it should be, and Mariana would be glad, and she would shine. His mistress would shine for him.

24

DEPARTURES

1665

'His Highness the King is indisposed; the physics have been with him day and night,' said the Queen.

Margarita had been summoned to her mother's quarters, with Luisa and Maribárbola in attendance. The Queen's face was shadowed. Her gown was black. She had not relinquished mourning garb since little Felipe's death and did not smile on seeing Margarita.

Margarita wondered if Maribárbola had told anyone about their midnight excursion. It seemed that she had not.

Margarita's newest brother, the infante Carlos, was four years old, but he could not speak, only drool. His enlarged lower jaw didn't seem to fit his face, and at times his neck struggled to support his head.

'Don't stare,' said the Queen.

Margarita could tell Luisa was also shocked at Carlos's state but trying not to show it. They hadn't seen him in person for months, as he seldom left his rooms. This boy would not make a king was the evident conclusion. Margarita sighed. It was true, he was an unhappy saliva-soaked puppet. The curse was all around them, afflicting them. What of her own children, if she had them? What would their fates be?

The women were attaching a steel frame to a belt around Carlos's middle to hold him upright. Queen Mariana winced and drew a sharp breath as they tightened the buckle, as if the belt were fastened around her own waist. Margarita drew in her own belly to try to release the pressure of her guardainfante. With her heavy brocade overskirt, the wooden frame dug into her skin. She hated it.

Her mother showed little sympathy for her complaints. 'Your papa is dying,' she said, her tone matter-of-fact. 'We pray, but I fear he may not have long. The three of us shall proceed now to see him.'

Margarita recalled the wailing of a few nights ago. It *was* her father she had heard. What had they done to him?

Agustina took the handles and began to wheel Carlos along on his trolley, like a limp doll. Margarita pitied him. He did not know her; scarcely acknowledged any of them. Queen Mariana gestured for Margarita to walk with her and for the others to follow with Carlos. The wheels of the trolley squeaked as they proceeded along the flagstoned floors towards the King's quarters at a sedate pace. No one spoke. Even Agustina was quiet.

Within his chamber, the King lay still on his bed, a sheet drawn up to his chin. His eyes were slits, the lids swollen and puffy. A basin beside the bed was covered with a linen cloth. A servant removed this as the Queen moved to her husband's bedside and drew Margarita and Carlos in beside her. Margarita shuffled. The size of her skirt, and that of the Queen, made it difficult to reach the bed. The King's nose was purply blue and so were his fingers. The tiny pores around his nose were enlarged, and the skin of his cheeks oozed a viscous yellow substance. He gasped, as if about to speak, but instead uttered incomprehensible sounds. His breathing was like a branch scratching on a window.

'The poison is coming out of him,' said the Queen, holding a handkerchief to her face. 'With God's grace he will be restored to us.' And she bowed her head. The counsellors and gentlemen of the chamber who lined the wall near the doorway nodded and murmured.

Margarita studied her mother's profile. Her tone and words contradicted what she'd said so boldly in private: that the King was dying. Her mother was speaking not for her now, she realised, but for the audience of attendants around them. The Queen wanted them to believe that *she* believed what she knew was untrue; this was the message that she wished to be relayed about the palace. This was play-acting. The double meaning of her mother's words and actions produced a hollow feeling within Margarita, as if her heart might fall from its perch.

The King lifted a hand a few inches from the bed. His lips moved, but no words came. Margarita's head was buzzing, her stomach ached. She remembered him in the studio, watching her and Velázquez. She reached out to the bed to steady herself. A hand on her shoulder made the tide of brown fuzziness recede.

Luisa suggested fresh air. Margarita followed her out of the room.

Three nights later the bells were rung, and Margarita knew he had died. The next day, they laid him in state in the studio, on a silver platform, in a silver coffin, dressed in a golden suit.

The conclusion of the English ambassador, who had come to pay his last respects – that the deceased King resembled a dish of mustard in a silver salver – flew around the palace. The servants drew straws for who would bear him to El Escorial, for they were reluctant to complete the task.

$$\sim$$

Soon after the King's death, her mother, now Regent – keeping the throne warm for infante Carlos – summoned Margarita. The Queen sat at a desk that had been installed in her chamber. Dry-eyed and poised, she had aged ten years in the last five. Her hair was covered with a wimple. Pretty curls and plaits were things of the past. Under her arched eyebrows, her round eyes were a stony grey.

'You must be brave,' she said. 'You are going into battle – a battle of love. It is better to make babies to sit on thrones than to have to fight for them.'

Her mother proceeded to outline Margarita's duties in Austria. The phrase 'you must endure his embrace' became etched in her mind. She detested the way the ladies of the court spoke of marriage and knowing a man. Agustina's more earthy descriptions of the couplings of horses in the royal stables had left her with rather more violent and unpleasant images, which she'd tried to banish from her thoughts.

On the day of departure, Margarita sat waiting, hollow as a drum, inside the carriage. She had refused to eat since her marriage by proxy three days earlier. The pamphlets publicising her marriage had littered the streets outside the alcázar; she'd seen them from the window of the golden tower, covering the ground like snow. Pepito had saved her a copy – and though she had been pleased with her printed likeness, she was not pleased with the prospect of her imminent departure. Maribárbola, who was with her in the carriage, was also downcast. Attendants who would become the members of her household in Austria were travelling in other coaches.

Margarita's eyes and nose were red. The night before she had cried until her pillow was wet. Luisa was on the steps, also weeping. Pepito leapt onto the carriage and blew kisses. Margarita thought they were for her, but then Maribárbola blew a kiss back and Pepito glowed.

Through the open carriage door, Margarita watched as the Queen raised a hand. This was it – she was about to tell them to cancel the journey, to nullify the marriage, for she could not bear to be apart from her daughter. But she issued no such order; instead, there was a sour irritation in her tone.

'Where is De Nieto?' asked the Queen. 'I haven't seen him all morning. Go and find him, Pepito. We have matters to discuss.'

Pepito made a sad face, raised a hand in farewell, and trudged off.

Her mother caught Margarita's eye, gave a single nod, then turned her head slowly and inclined her chin. They would write, she had reassured Margarita in private. They would write; that would be enough.

But it was not enough. It would never be enough.

The coachman rallied his team of horses. The carriage shifted slightly as the footmen climbed aboard at the rear. The side door was shut. The carriage was stuffy. Margarita threw her arm against the door and rattled the handle. This could not be. She would not go!

But it was too late. The entourage began to move. The wheels tipped backwards and forwards as the horses pranced and began to pull her over the cobblestones towards her future, towards the port of Denia and the waiting galleon that over the coming months would transport her via Italy to Vienna.

Margarita dug her fingernails into her palms and squeezed; she wanted to pierce her skin, to bleed, to shout and release the swelling roar within her head. But though she opened her mouth, no sound would come out until she had passed through the gate of the city.

25

ROSÉ

Alex double-checked the address on the envelope Professor Leadbeater had given her then pressed the buzzer for Carla Mertez's apartment building.

'Is that you, Alex? *Hola*, hello.' The door opened with a click.

While the main avenues of Madrid were grand, as befitted an imperial capital, Carla's neighbourhood was intimate and friendly. Locals carried their shopping in hessian bags and sipped coffee or wine at small cafes. People talked to each other from their balconies.

Alex ascended the wrought-iron spiral staircase to the third floor, where she found Carla, dressed in an elegant green silk shirt and black trousers, waiting in the doorway of her apartment.

'I'm glad to see you,' Carla said, greeting her with a kiss on both cheeks. 'Your mother was special. I was so sad when we lost her. I am sorry. But we have met before, I think. I saw you and your papa some years ago when I worked at the Prado, didn't I? And there was some trouble, they couldn't find you for a while – is that right?'

Alex nodded. 'Yes, that was me, when I was twelve.' So it was Carla her father had been talking to when they were reunited that day. She had a flash of him standing at the end of a corridor, gesticulating to two guards and a woman.

In the apartment, Carla moved about in the kitchenette, spooning some olives from a jar into a small bowl and cutting bread. Next came some soft cheese and a side dish with some olive oil.

They sat in two armchairs, with an antique chest between them. Carla had laid an embroidered linen cloth over the chest and placed two glasses of cold rosé and the food upon it. The blue-painted double doors leading to a small balcony were open. The terracotta roofs of the nearby houses and apartments stepped up a slope. Pigeons were cooing. Afternoon sunlight streamed in across the woven woollen rug. Carla's dark hair was loose. Her shirt was open at the neck.

As they sipped wine and ate, they talked about Alex's visit to La Californie.

'You are extremely lucky,' said Carla.

'Yes, very,' said Alex. 'But what about you, Carla, you knew Mum . . .'

'Yes, she would have loved to visit La Californie.'

'Mum was interested in what Picasso said about *Las Meninas*. That it was a picture painted with curses . . .'

Carla nodded. 'The curses, yes, she was fascinated by that.'

'My sense is that Picasso's version is like a lens to the original,' said Alex.

'You know, that is quite perceptive. Your mother would agree, I'm sure . . . You remind me of her. Your hair, your smile – even the way you tilt your head.'

Alex hadn't realised her head was tilted. She made a show of straightening it with a hand on either side of her head. They laughed.

'Rosara and I met at Oxford,' Carla recalled. 'Your mother was clever, intuitive. She was interested in what was going on behind the canvas, how pictures became the way they are. We worked as interns together at the Prado. It was an exciting time. They were doing a clean of *Las Meninas*, which as you know was her favourite work. It was a bit controversial because our supervisor was cleaning off layers of dust and varnish. I've never told anyone else of this, but Rosara told me that while she was close to the painting she heard Margarita *talking* to her – that she had spoken to her of the curse. We had been out the night before, drinking, and at first I thought she was fooling around, joking. But it wasn't a joke.' Carla shook her head. 'She was serious. The English and the Americans laughed at her, but in Spain, well, life imitates art. And vice versa. It's the way.'

So Alex hadn't imagined it; it had happened before. Some kind of transmission of soul occurred between people and art. Art was an expression of soul. Margarita had spoken of a curse – and Rosara had 'heard' her.

It wasn't hard to imagine her mother here with them, drinking rosé and reminiscing. Alex leaned back against her chair, suddenly aware of how relaxed she felt, how happy.

Carla gathered her hair into a knot and tied it up with a hair band. Her wrists were slim. When she smiled her almond eyes twinkled. Carla was so accepting and easy to talk to.

Alex sat up in her chair. 'I'm on this search to discover the hidden secrets of *Las Meninas,* to find out about the curses,' she said. 'And I feel like it's bringing me closer to Mum somehow.'

Carla reached over the makeshift table and gave her hand a squeeze. 'I'm glad for you,' she said. 'Rosara would be too.' She looked thoughtful. 'Your mother was particularly interested in the paintings in the background of *Las Meninas.* They were on the wall when the painting was made, we know this because they were identified in the early catalogues. I remember she was interested in the subject matter, which related to Greek mythology, but a leader on the team said that this was inconsequential, that the relevance was that it related to mortals challenging Gods, and *Las Meninas* was primarily a demonstration of painterly skill. Rosara didn't agree.'

'I went to a lecture in which Regi Montano suggested the same thing,' Alex said. 'But I don't believe it. Velázquez once said that he would rather be an ordinary artist than the world's greatest copyist. I don't think he was attempting to prove his superiority by copying Rubens and Titian. If it were, he would have done a better job of it. They are hardly clear; more like suggestions.'

'Rubens' *Pallas and Arachne* touches on the story of this myth and in the background is a copy of a Titian painting – *The Rape of Europa* – rendered as a tapestry.'

Alex frowned as she recalled Velázquez's *Las Meninas.* 'You see a rape?' she said, doubtful. She'd seen nothing that distinct.

'No, no – it's not done like that at all.'

Carla went to the bookshelf and pulled out several books. One was an art catalogue. She flicked through the pages.

'There,' she said, bringing it over to show Alex. 'You have to see the original – and even then it's not obvious. This is the Titian painting . . .'

A half-naked woman, draped in a white sheet, was being carried away on the back of a swimming bull.

'That's a rape?' said Alex.

'Well, that's what the title tells us. The bull represents Zeus, the king of the gods. This is the original, which is now in Boston, but copies of or allusions to that painting, a kind of homage, were included first in Rubens' work and then again in Velázquez's *Las Meninas*. It's very hard to make out in *Las Meninas*, but it was identified from catalogues of the royal collection detailing what would have been hanging in that room. If you look carefully, you can make out a suggestion of the shapes, though it's very obscure.'

'It's like Picasso said,' Alex mused. 'Sometimes you do a painting for a corner of the canvas that no one looks at.'

Carla's eyes widened. 'Picasso said that, did he? It's funny you should talk about that and the tapestry . . .'

Carla went to her shelf for another book and leafed through it. She found what she was looking for and placed the book open in front of Alex, pointing to a colour plate on a glossy white page.

'One of the works *I've* focused on in my research is also by Velázquez. It's called *Las Hilanderas – The Spinners*. It was painted around 1657: close to the time that *Las Meninas* was painted. In the background of *The Spinners* is a tapestry of Rubens' *Pallas and Arachne* – and again, you see, there's part of Titian's *The Rape of Europa*. There are some aristocratic or courtly women looking at it, as if they have come to the spinners' studio for a viewing. But that reference to Titian wasn't actually identified until the 1950s.'

'So long after he painted it?'

'Yes. Three centuries later. So you see, we are still learning new things about these works. They are rich in meaning.'

Alex looked at the reproduction. Beyond the foreground of women spinning and preparing yarn were several well-dressed courtly women viewing a tapestry hanging on the back wall. In it, a helmeted goddess stood over a woman. And in the background, beyond her, was a glimpse of a woman being carried off on the back of a bull.

'I see it! Isn't it a bit of a coincidence that this particular image occurs in two works painted within a year or two of each other? Why would Velázquez put the same tapestry in twice?' asked Alex.

Carla frowned. 'That's a very good question. Why haven't I thought of that?'

'Was he making a point?'

Carla fetched another book and opened it to a picture of Las Meninas. Alex studied the paintings included within the picture, on the back wall.

'If you hadn't told me, I wouldn't be able to recognise those paintings; they're so blurry. But they do seem to match. It's odd, isn't it? Was Velázquez simply including what was in the background of the room, or did he include them deliberately? Is this the corner of the canvas that no one looks at?'

She continued gazing at the background of Las Meninas: two rectangular paintings high on the wall at the back of the room, and below them the mirror with the reflection of the King and

Queen, the doorway with De Nieto and, behind Velázquez, another doorway, partially obscured; all of them were rectangles. Alex let her focus blur. Their outlined shapes together made five rectangles, just like in her mother's sketch! It was so obvious now. She reached into her bag, pulled out her mother's spiral-bound notebook and began flicking through the pages.

'Mum drew this . . .' Alex placed the open notebook on the chest between them. 'That's what this is, see? Two paintings, two doors and a mirror!'

Carla leaned forwards. 'Ah, yes – I can see it. It's cryptic, though, no?'

'She was trying to say something without saying it.' Alex said the words as the thought dawned on her. 'It was meant to be a secret. I think it relates to the curse.'

Alex flicked to the next page and began to laugh.

'What is it?' asked Carla.

'Cartoons!' said Alex. 'They're like thought bubbles – look.'

Carla studied the stick figure drawings with little clouds outlined above their heads.

'I don't see it,' she said, shaking her head.

'What if the paintings in the background express what is on the minds of the people in the picture?' said Alex. 'Literally, the matter hanging over their head.' As she said it, she remembered Bernarda's card reading. *Something is hidden which must be revealed. The crowning card, the situation hanging over your head.*

'We believe Velázquez was arguing for the nobility of painting as an art – that's the part about the mortals challenging the gods,' said Carla.

'Yes, but there's more than that,' said Alex. 'Why put *The Rape of Europa* in there? And why refer to it more than once? That's it, I think – it's the hidden secret!'

Carla nodded, but Alex felt like it was her mother nodding at her. 'Maybe,' she said, leaning forwards in her chair, eyes bright. 'You know, I've dreamed of your mother a couple of times, and in one of those dreams I saw her sitting at a spinning wheel.'

'We didn't have a spinning wheel at home,' said Alex. 'Maybe it's a clue. Maybe she wants us to look at that painting, at that tapestry inside those paintings.'

Carla cleared her throat. 'But she's not with us anymore . . . That's not possible, not logical,' she said.

'No,' said Alex.

Carla excused herself. She left the room and went into her bedroom. Alex heard drawers being opened and closed, and then Carla returned with a plastic duty-free bag and offered it to Alex. 'Rosara stayed with me when she was here in Madrid that last time,' she said quietly. 'She left these things behind. You should have them.'

Alex reached inside the white plastic bag and felt something soft – a silk scarf – and then her fingers closed around a glass bottle. Perfume.

She brought them out, opened the glass stopper and sniffed. Orange blossom and jasmine. Alex could not speak. She touched the patterned, pink-edged scarf. She smelled the scent of her mother as Rosara leaned against her, hair touching her cheek, and kissed her goodnight. Alex closed her eyes.

'She was very excited about her work, I remember.' Carla paused, her lips pursed. 'Since then, I've wondered if she was also a bit afraid. She was jittery. Several times she left Madrid and went to see Paz. I was busy and I didn't pay much attention to her comings and goings.' Carla gazed out the window and was silent for a few moments. 'Then I got the news from David.'

'Paz?' Alex said. *I give thanks for Paz*, her mother had written on her postcard. 'Who's Paz?'

'Paz Martínez – your mother's cousin. She was older; she became a nun.'

'I don't know Mum's family at all. I know they were Catholic.'

'Yes, and one branch of her family was from Spain. There was an aunt who adored Rosara and encouraged her to learn Spanish. She was a devout Catholic. She would have been your great-aunt – Rosara would've taken you to see her when you were little.'

Alex nodded. She remembered the goat and the figs.

Carla continued: 'Rosara's parents, who lived in England, were against her marriage to your father; they refused to attend the wedding. Your parents were upset, but they loved each other and went ahead anyway. They just went off to a registry office by themselves.'

Alex stared at her; she had never heard any of this before.

'Rosara's parents died before she did. One had a heart attack and, not long after, the other got pneumonia. I believe they would have come around eventually. They wanted grandchildren. They would have loved you.'

Alex's father had never said much about her grandparents; he had described them as very conservative, but that's all she'd ever known.

'Are you Catholic?' asked Carla.

'No, not really. Mum and Dad couldn't agree . . .'

'It makes these things complicated. Unnecessarily so. But yes, Paz was helpful to her, I believe. You didn't know about her cousin?'

Alex shifted to the edge of her seat. 'No, I didn't. She mentioned Paz in a postcard, but at first I thought it meant "paz", as in peace. "I give thanks for peace."'

Carla's eyebrows were raised. 'As I said, she was a nun – maybe she still is. She belonged to a reclusive order in Toledo, not far from Madrid.'

Alex recalled the note she had found among Algernon Blunt's papers, with just two words: *Toledo* and *Fuendacia*. And in her mother's notebook: *He mustn't learn about Paz, or F . . .*

'Do you know of a person or place called Fuendacia?' she asked.

'No, sorry.'

'What about these numbers? I'm guessing they are dates,' She checked the notebook. 'The first is 1638.'

Carla shook her head.

'What about 1734?'

Again Carla looked blank, then her face brightened. 'Oh – 1734 could be the great fire! That was the year the alcázar burned down.'

'It burned down?'

'Yes, it was Christmas Eve. They closed the doors to stop the looting and threw many of the paintings out of the windows to save them. *Las Meninas* was one of them; it would have been destroyed otherwise. We believe it's a little reduced on the right-hand side, as a result of being cut from its frame that night – there's possibly a strip missing. Hundreds of other paintings from the royal collection were lost. And many people died because they couldn't get out.'

The phone rang and Carla jumped up to answer it. She listened, frowning, and Alex had the impression that whoever was on the other end was asking numerous questions, as Carla kept repeating, '*Non*.' At one point she looked directly at Alex. '*Non*,' she said, 'I have never heard of that name.' Then: '*Sí*, let's talk again tomorrow.'

Carla returned to the living room and sat down. She reached for her glass and took a large sip of wine.

Alex helped herself to some cheese and took a sip of her rosé.

Some seconds later, Carla spoke. 'That was a colleague from the Museo Picasso, where I used to work. He received a visitor today asking about *Las Meninas*. He wanted to know what was in the archives. The thing is, that man asked about your mother and he asked about *you*, wanted to know about your interests. My colleague didn't know, and I didn't say.'

Alex felt her mouth fall open. She closed it and swallowed.

'Exactly. Do you realise that what you are doing – your search – could be . . . dangerous?' said Carla.

Alex gulped. 'I'm just here to visit the Prado – I want to see *Las Meninas* again.'

'But it's off display,' Carla said. 'Didn't you know?'

'Oh no! Why?'

'The official story is it's for restoration, but a colleague tells me there's something else. I'm not sure I should be telling you this, but it seems one of the figures in the painting has been fading – badly. Apparently, he's become almost transparent.'

'Fading? That's bizarre.'

Carla nodded. 'There is concern.'

'Who – I mean, which figure?'

'The man in the doorway,' said Carla. 'José De Nieto, the Queen's chamberlain.'

'The dark angel . . .' said Alex.

Carla tucked her hair behind her ears.

'I mean the one Picasso painted as the dark angel.'

'Ah.' Carla nodded. 'The very one.'

Realising she had been there some time, Alex stood to leave. 'Thank you so much for seeing me today,' she said. 'And for . . .' She held up the plastic bag containing her mother's scarf and perfume.

'It has been my pleasure,' Carla said. 'And please, now that we have found each other, let's keep in touch.'

Before Alex left, Carla insisted on helping her find out whether the convent where Rosara's cousin lived still existed.

'A lot of them have been closed down,' she explained. 'Young girls don't want to take that path anymore; they have other options.'

Alex tried to imagine being locked away with other women, spending hours every day in prayer. Like boarding school on steroids, but in a single room and a chapel. No travelling, no sitting next to boys like Oscar on the tube, no lying on your back in the park, no sangria in the sun. Not much fun.

Carla was speaking rapid-fire Spanish into the telephone: '*Sí, sí* . . . Paz Martínez. *Sí, gracias* . . . *Gracias*.' Then she dialled another number and another.

Finally, she scribbled on a piece of notepaper, hung up the phone and turned triumphantly to Alex.

'You're in luck!' she said.

26

TOLEDO

The Madrid Atocha station was bustling with early morning activity: people coming and going, whistles signalling departures, steel wheels squeaking to a stop. Oscar had arrived from Barcelona and was keen to join her on the excursion to Toledo; Alex found him waiting near the station entrance. They hugged awkwardly, and bought coffees at a little silver caravan.

'It's cool to hear you speaking Spanish,' he said, as she handed him his coffee.

She grinned. She'd been testing her rusty language skills.

The train to Toledo left at 9 am. They travelled in a carriage with a bunch of children on a school trip. In their uniforms, sharing bags of sweets, the kids were soon high on sugar and the liberation of noise.

Alex and Oscar were squeezed together on a bench seat. His thigh was warm against hers.

The train trundled past small, whitewashed train stations, with pot plants of red geraniums on the platforms. 'They've been tarting them up for the expo in Seville,' Alex heard the Englishman behind her say to his companion.

Alex shared with Oscar what she had learned from Carla about her mother's cousin Paz, the nun. She was still getting used to the idea that she was about to meet her. Carla had arranged the appointment. Today was Saturday – visiting day. Why hadn't her dad ever mentioned Paz? Maybe he'd never met her before either. He hadn't believed in going to church, Alex knew. Would Paz understand? What would she be like? Alex wiped her damp palms on her jeans and shifted restlessly on the seat.

'Do you want to get up?' Oscar asked.

'No, no,' she said. 'I'm thinking about . . .'

'Your mum?'

Alex nodded. 'She died near Toledo. It's weird to be going there, to be meeting a relative I never knew I had. A nun.'

'You're nervous?'

'I guess I am.'

'Was your mum Catholic too?'

'Yes.'

'And you?'

Alex shook her head. 'I think my parents argued about it. They couldn't agree. Dad was brought up C of E, but he wasn't religious.'

Alex looked out of the window. Saw a woman hanging washing on a line, and two men in singlets sitting in the shade under a tree, drinks before them on a small table. She leaned her head on Oscar's shoulder for a moment. He'd given her his number in Barcelona and she'd called him after seeing Carla, not really expecting him to answer – but he had *and* he'd suggested coming with her to Toledo. She'd needed someone to talk to, but he wasn't just someone, he was Oscar, come all the way from Barcelona to join her on this train. To sit beside her. Maybe Helen was right. Maybe . . .

He touched her forearm. 'She'll be pleased to see you, this cousin, she will. Anyone would be glad of a visitor, stuck in a convent all day.'

'But what if she doesn't want to be disturbed? Maybe I'll remind her of Mum and that will upset her.' Her voice wobbled, and she bit her lip.

'You're family. Don't worry. Were they close, she and your mum?'

Alex turned her palms upwards and shrugged. 'I'm not sure. I don't know my mother's side of the family at all. Dad never spoke about them. I'm cross with him about it actually. It's sort of hit me that I didn't just lose my mum – I lost all her relatives too. I'm going to talk to him about it. Thank goodness for Flora, though.'

'She's cool.'

'Yes, she's great. I love her. She's so positive and independent.'

'Like you.'

'Really? Thanks. I hope so. I don't always feel like that.' They were both quiet for a few moments.

'I've never been in a convent,' said Oscar.

'There's a reason for that,' said Alex.

'Oh, right.' Oscar adjusted his jeans. 'Such a man, I am,' he quipped, clearing his throat.

They both laughed.

'Please don't become a nun,' he said, adding, 'Just saying . . .'
Oscar's ears had gone pink.

Alex took a breath. She could feel herself blushing. He was so nice, but . . . distracting. She needed to focus on why she was here. She visualised her mother's notebook, the one she'd found in Flora's attic.

'My mum mentioned an "F" in her notebook, together with Toledo, but . . .'

'What is it?'

'In Cambridge we came across the name "Fuendacia".'

'And you think this Fuendacia could be the mysterious F?'

She nodded.

'And the other thing, there were these *numbers* in Mum's notebook: 16381734 . . . Carla told me about a fire in 1734 – the whole alcázar, the royal palace, burned down. They only just managed to save *Las Meninas*. They cut it out of its frame, along with a lot of other paintings, and threw them out the windows.'

'Who did that?'

'They don't know.'

'And 1638? Is that significant?'

'Carla didn't know – but I'd like to find out.'

❧

Toledo train station had a blue-and-white tiled floor and tall stained-glass windows, like a church. Tendrils of hair were beginning to stick to Alex's forehead in the heat. She pulled her hair back into a ponytail as they walked up the narrow laneways of the hillside town in the morning sun. Her gym shoes kicked up a fine brown dust.

Paz's convent was not hard to find. It wasn't far from the fort and cathedral, the steeple and turrets of which defined the skyline. Alex made her way there while Oscar went off to explore. They arranged to meet up later at the station, for the return to Madrid.

The convent was a collection of buildings centred around a tower and a chapel. The street-facing walls were forbidding, made of long, thin bricks, with sections of chunkier stone. The tower was square and squat, staunch enough to repel armies, and flanked by two cypress trees. Several windows had been filled in with brick and plaster, as had several old doorways, as if the walls had been reconfigured a number of times. After walking around two sides of the building, Alex found an entranceway on the side of the tower. The robust timber door with two ornate metal hinges seemed familiar. Alex stopped in the shade of the trees, drew her mum's notebook from her bag and found the drawing. Yes, it matched! Was this the last place her mum had visited . . . ?

She knocked on the door.

Nothing happened.

She knocked again, harder, and this time a querulous voice demanded to know who was there. Alex explained the reason for her visit and a bolt slid in a lock.

A diminutive woman in a jersey, knee-length skirt and white headdress opened the door.

'Paz?' said Alex.

The nun looked puzzled. 'You seek peace?' she said.

'No, sorry – Paz Martínez . . . She is a cousin – my mother's cousin.'

'Ah, yes, I see: Sister Paz. You have an appointment?'

Alex nodded.

The woman ushered her through a courtyard to a white-plastered room with wooden benches and a small opaque window. Terracotta tiles on the floor sloped and curved, as if softened by many feet. The room echoed. A simple wooden crucifix was the only decoration. *How should she greet Paz?* Alex wondered, jiggling her leg up and down. *Did nuns hug?*

A woman entered and Alex jumped up. 'Hi.'

'Alex? Oh! Look at you – I would know you anywhere,' the nun said in broken English, kissing Alex on both cheeks. Her skin was soft. 'My dear cousin – God took her too soon. You are her daughter; yes, you are.'

Paz was shorter than Rosara had been, and wider around the middle, but her steady brown eyes were familiar.

'Her death was very sad. I pray for her often. But now I see you – what a joy!'

'I would have come sooner if I'd known about you,' said Alex. 'I only recently found your name in her notebook. I'm interested in her research into the Velázquez painting, *Las Meninas*, and the Infanta Margarita and her family . . .'

Paz clasped her hands together and held them to her lips. 'How could you know?' she whispered.

'Know what?'

'*Do* you know?'

'I know my mother was excited about something she found when she saw you. And I know it had something to do with Toledo and F . . . Fuendacia, perhaps. Does that mean anything to you?'

259

Paz raised her eyes to the ceiling. Then she grasped the small cross around her neck and nodded.

'Maybe it's time,' she said. 'Fuendacia wants to be heard. Maybe the Infanta wants to be heard. Let's go out into the garden. I want to show you a little of my life here and I need to think.'

She knew about Fuendacia!

Alex followed Paz through several dark corridors to a back door, which opened with a creak. The light outside was dazzling. They were in a beautiful garden. Their shoes crunched on the fine white stones of the path. Paz wore sandals that closed with velcro, a strangely modern touch in this ancient place. Olive trees ringed the garden, which was terraced, and raised beds had orderly rows of herbs, lettuces and other vegetables. On a lower terrace was a grove of orange trees. In the far distance were bleached plains, speckled with dark green trees against a dry grey-gold landscape.

'We grow our own food here,' said Paz, running her hands over the lettuce leaves. 'The garden is one of my responsibilities. I love it. I'm very lucky.'

She perched on the edge of the herb garden. 'So you are also interested in *Las Meninas* – *La Familia* – and the Infanta.' She pointed across the plateau. 'Madrid is that way. That's where they lived, in the alcázar. It was a dark time for my sisters, for nuns, the seventeenth century.'

'Because of the Inquisition?' asked Alex.

'Yes, but also because of *him*!' Here Paz turned her head and spat onto the ground. 'Oh, the Hapsburgs . . .' Her tone was one of disgust.

'*Him?*' Alex was surprised by her vehemence. *Nuns don't spit*, she thought.

Paz's eyes were glinting in the sun. 'The King!' she said. 'Philip.' She placed her hands together in her lap and closed her eyes.

Alex wanted to touch Paz's arm but resisted the urge and waited.

'I don't like being the custodian of their secrets,' said Paz. 'Maybe it's time to . . . to pull the skeletons from the closet. You know, the number of nuns is declining. At fifty, I'm the youngest of us here. Most of the sisters are in their sixties and seventies; one is ninety-four. There aren't many young girls joining the order anymore. Faith is in decline.'

'Maybe it has found other avenues,' said Alex. She thought of how desperately the girls at her school had wanted to have sex, how the prospect of a nun's life of virginity and chastity would have made them shriek in horror.

Paz stood up and moved along one of the raised garden beds, full of basil, parsley and spinach. She pulled out several weeds.

'I enjoy the garden. I enjoy the camaraderie of my colleagues. It has been a good life for me here.'

Alex followed Paz down the path.

Alex stopped suddenly. 'Paz, where did it happen?'

Paz held her gaze, then sighed and gestured down the hill. 'That is the place. I say a prayer for her every day.'

Alex saw a steep slope, silvery green trees and a glint of water.

'Rosara came to see me several times. That last visit was just before . . . We sat together in the chapel. I wasn't allowed to bring her out here, like I can now with you. I gave her a rosehip from that rose over there to plant in her garden.' A large white rose climbed from the base of the tower to the second storey. 'I will give you one too, before you leave.'

'What was Mum doing here?'

'She came to study some of the materials in our archive. Our abbess, bless her, gave her permission. I helped her to translate. The Spanish was old, archaic. There were several poems, and some writing by a man known as Fuendacia.'

At the mention of the poems, Alex shifted forwards. 'Poems! I think maybe I have a copy of one of those: something about a tunnel and a grille . . .'

Paz nodded and stared into the distance. When she spoke, her voice was sombre. 'Rosara found some things that the church and the royal family wanted to keep hidden – things about the curse of the Hapsburgs.'

The curse of the Hapsburgs . . . Alex had never heard it called that. 'I found a note that Mum wrote – someone was following her when she came here.'

'*Dios mío*,' whispered Paz. 'I knew it. I didn't think it was an accident – the policeman who came here to tell me suspected that another vehicle had run her off the road. But they found no trace of that. And your Dad was . . . so distraught. He came to collect her body, but then returned to England. He needed to get back for you.'

Distraught. 'So you met him?'

Paz nodded. She took Alex's hands and held them.

Alex blinked back tears. Paz's hands were warm.

'Picasso said *Las Meninas* was a painting full of curses. My mum was fascinated by that. I am too.'

'Ah yes. She was always curious – since she was a child.' Paz shook her head and reached into her pocket. 'So many questions!' She smiled, touching a handkerchief to her nose. 'There seems to be a lot of her in you.'

'Do you know where those notes are? Can I please see them?' said Alex.

'Secrets, secrets – no good ever comes of them,' murmured Paz. 'Truth is golden. And elusive. And fragile, but also strong. Love and faith go hand-in-hand.' She rose. 'Come,' she said.

oc—

Alex followed Paz up a spiral stone staircase into a high-ceilinged archive with rows of shelves. Every shelf was crammed with books. Some were covered in leather, their spines imprinted with gold lettering; others were bound in cloth, row upon row of navy and grey volumes, their titles handwritten in a thick-tipped pen.

'Church records,' nodded Paz. 'I try to keep the dust off, but no one has referred to these for aeons, except . . .' Paz paused, her hand on the top of the books. 'We had a visitor yesterday. A man who wanted to talk to the abbess about our archive. She denied him access. He offered to buy *all* of our records. I'm worried she will change her mind and sell them. I caught a glimpse of him. I didn't trust him at all.'

'Was he tall, with dark hair and a beard?'

Paz nodded, surprised.

Alex recalled the man who'd stood so forcefully on Professor Leadbeater's doorstep, and his subsequent bidding for the drawing at the auction house. Had *he* been here, too? 'I think someone's been following me.'

Paz frowned. 'It's possible.'

If it was the same man, he might still be in Toledo. Alex wondered if he might return.

'Why would someone want your records?' She remembered Blunt; he'd sold those boxes to someone from Spain. But she didn't want to distract Paz by mentioning this now.

Paz pursed her lips. 'Fuendacia kept the secrets.'

In one corner was a wooden catalogue, with numerous small drawers. Alex expected Paz to consult this, but she did not. She went to the top of the stairs, listening as if to be sure no one was coming, then she disappeared behind a long row of files and books. A few seconds later, Alex heard a scraping sound.

'Can you help me?' called Paz.

When Alex rounded the end of the row, Paz was attempting to push a small bookshelf away from the stone wall. Alex took the other end and together they managed to shift it.

'Down there,' said Paz.

Alex kneeled. What was she meant to be looking at? Then she saw that one block of stone in the wall did not match the others; it was made of wood and had been stained and shaped to blend in with its neighbours. Clever.

'A little cupboard,' said Paz. 'Useful for special items not in the catalogue. You can open it if you press on the top left corner.'

Alex did so. The small door clicked open to reveal a fabric-wrapped bundle and some loose papers.

'Lift it out carefully,' said Paz, holding out her hands. 'This is Fuendacia's testimony, and those are Rosara's translations,' she said, clasping them to her chest.

Alex followed Paz to a small desk near the catalogue. Paz turned on a brass lamp and took a pair of reading glasses from a case. She lowered herself onto a wooden chair pulled up to the desk, and Alex carried over one of the high-backed chairs that stood against a wall to sit beside her.

'Looking after the archive has become my responsibility,' Paz said. 'I don't know who will succeed me . . . But I have faith someone will.'

Alex opened the bundle. Inside was a slim hand-sewn pamphlet titled: *Testimony of Fuendacia*. On the front page was a chiselled drawing of a tower. The paper was not like any Alex had seen before; it was thick and soft and the edges appeared to have been torn, rather than cut.

'A testimony?'

Paz nodded. 'A telling of the truth as he saw it . . . in poetry and prose. The hand is Fuendacia's. He was the keeper of the royal records, and he was Diego Velázquez's friend. Some people feared he knew too much about what happened in the 1630s.'

Alex tried to read the first page, which took the form of a poem, but the writing was spidery and the language very old Spanish. She pulled out the faxed pages from her backpack and held them alongside. They matched.

'My mum sent copies of these to her professor, and he sent them to me.'

'Your mother and I translated them together. I helped her, but I do not wish to read them again. You may read them here while I do some work on the catalogue.'

Paz placed several pages in her mother's handwriting in front of her, beside Fuendacia's testimony. Alex pulled her chair closer and began to read the first poem.

> *Through the tunnel,*
> *Beyond the grille,*
> *His passion draws him onwards still.*

It was the same as Sebastian Blunt had attempted to translate in Cambridge. She read on:

> *A love forbidden,*
> *A faith betrayed,*
> *A member not to be dis-swayed.*
> *The abbess looked the other way,*
> *As the Planet came to play.*
> *He found her there upon the bier*
> *Her hands clasped over her cordate habit.*
> *An offering to a higher power*
> *But what higher power could do such*
> *A blasphemous injustice.*
> *Alas, he cried,*
> *Alack, she wept,*
> *The cord is placed around his neck.*
> *And now an invisible curse we see to damn his line*
> *For eternity.*

Yes! '*An invisible curse we see to damn his line for eternity,*' she read aloud. 'This is it – the curse!' she said. 'It mentions a man and a nun . . . Who was the nun? What happened?'

Alex turned to see that Paz was murmuring a prayer.

'Amen.' Paz shook her head and sighed. 'Her name has been lost. I believe it would have been changed to hide her identity.'

'A cover-up?'

Paz nodded. 'The Planet is the King, the Planet King: Philip IV. His confessor lived not far from here for a time. The King did a lot of confessing, for he did a lot of sinning.'

'How did he sin?' asked Alex.

'He was unfaithful to his wife,' said Paz.

'Is that all?' asked Alex.

'No,' said Paz, sighing. 'It's not. Perhaps you should read the rest.'

Paz turned the pages. It was like a thicket of thorns – nearly indecipherable Spanish.

'I really can't read this,' said Alex.

'Yes, it took us a long time – and a magnifying glass,' said Paz. 'But don't be disheartened, my child.' She began riffling through the slim pile of papers in Rosara's handwriting, then offered some of the pages to Alex with a flourish. 'Here is your mama's translation . . .'

Alex placed the pages alongside Fuendacia's testimony and read.

Mi nombre es Fuendacia, y soy el guardián de los Royal Records. Dicen en la Corte que rigen el imperio el honor, el coraje, los principios biensonantes, pero en verdad lo rige el papel . . .

My name is Fuendacia, and I am the keeper of the Royal Records. They say in court the empire runs on honour, on courage, on

fine-sounding principles, but the truth is, it runs on paper . . .
We annotated our age, sought to preserve it on parchment, even
as we lived it, and I filed, bound and boxed with tremendous
dedication. But still now, I must admit, the picture, the puzzle,
is incomplete; it awaits a higher power to gather the files into the
correct order, to unite them, to discern the connecting strands.
Therefore, dear reader, do not take offence, I beg you, if my tale
does not entirely correspond to that which may have found its way
into the plays, recitations and history books. For from my humble
position, I do not seem to see events from the same perspec-
tive as our Regent – not that I could ever, of course, assume to
imagine how our Planet King might perceive. Already, in my task,
I risk once more attracting the attention of the Inquisidor. And
as you well know, his attention would be most unwelcome, an
eviscerating focus which can cause one's innards and even one's
toenails themselves to curl . . . Here my hand trembles on the
page; can you see the tremors which trouble the nib of my pen?
And yet, yet . . . still I am compelled. I write by candlelight, these
scribbles my only way forwards. Therefore, forewarned, and with
Our Lady's blessing, let us begin.

The hour is late, the door to my room is locked from the outside.
Like that of the unknown messenger who perished in Castle
Ovo. The light from my candle throws the chisel marks of the
masons who built this chamber into sharp relief. The bumps and
undulations of the dun-coloured stone put me in mind of the plains
I knew so well, and every trail upon those plains leads to Madrid.

'This part was transcribed in Mum's notebook,' said Alex. 'I've read
it before.'

'Go on,' said Paz, nodding.

My tale starts at the alcázar, the royal palace built upon Moorish roots, those they sought to obliterate, but which remain still in the mud bricks hewn from the hills. It centres upon our most sovereign Philip IV, and his little daughter, the Infanta Margarita. The King is the Planet King, the sun from whence the characters of our court are cast in light and shadow. I will not tell you of her birth, though it was joyous, and not of her infant years; suffice to say she filled the palace with her own light. The King, her father, called little Margarita the life of the palace, and at other times his little rascal, and in hindsight, after she was gone, how well we realised the truth of both of these descriptors. Why it is she, of all those people in the palace at that time – they were many and wondrous – who nudges at my elbow here in this tower, who wants to make herself heard, I do not know. But she bothers me, the little rascal, and she makes me brave, she makes me bold.

'The life of the palace,' breathed Alex, '. . . who wants to make herself heard.' Fuendacia had taken a great risk in recording these words.

There are two confounding events which I do not pretend to comprehend. The first was the creation of Velázquez's great work, La Familia de Felipe IV, with the Infanta at its fulcrum. This painting was created as a fabulous diversion for His Majesty, kept in his private chambers. It is an inversion of the traditional royal portrait. It was a sensation. Luisa was afraid of it; she believed it upset the order of things. And, in many ways, perhaps that was the point. It hid certain persons in plain view. At that time the King had demurred from further portraits of himself; a guilty secret was gnawing at his soul. Velázquez was inherently a conduit of the truth. Hence the King was present, but as a reflection in the mirror only.

Alex felt her throat go dry, but she pressed on.

The little Infanta, as she grew, became a close observer of events, as was my friend Velázquez, and we perhaps talked too freely in her presence. But she seemed engrossed in painting; she did not seem to attend to the gossip of adults. And there was a purity about her. When she said the rosary in the palace oratory, with her little bell, one of those with her wrote to her father: 'She will make saints of us all.'

How he wished that this be true. There was a rumour that circulated through the alcázar, and also the streets of Madrid, that our court was cursed, that the King and his line were cursed. Somehow the Infanta came to know this and, being of sweet nature, she desired more than anything else that the curse be lifted. Would that it were a simple task.

I believe she never learned the secrets that hounded the King unto his grave, which I will here reveal.

'He's telling the secrets!' said Alex.

Paz raised the cross that hung around her neck to her lips and kissed it.

While the King was a paragon of a man in public, in his private life he was exceeding promiscuous. His affairs were legion and resulted in as many as thirty illegitimate or bastard children, of whom eight were recognised.

Blunt had been right. *Thirty!*

So myriad were his indiscretions that the nuns of Agreda did penance for him, day and night, until their knees bled under their gowns. It was best the King did not know of this, for it may have aroused him to further sin.

The most scandalous secret of his reign is related to the cloister. In 1638 the King was told of a most beautiful nun who lived in the convent of San Plácido in Madrid. He became enamoured of her from afar and, with assistance of Villanueva, . . . he was smuggled in to see her via a secret tunnel dug betwixt the house of the King's accomplice and the nunnery, and she was made available to him: placed – by the abbess, no less – upon a bier. This perturbed the King and he retreated, but later returned to continue the amours . . .

Alex shook with rage. 'Amours? Sex with a nun?' she said, without looking up. This, and the line in the poem – *The abbess looked the other way.* 'Does it all mean . . . he . . .'

'*Sí*,' said Paz, barely audible. 'We believe it was rape. We pray for our sister who was so unjustly dishonoured. It devastated her.'

Alex read on.

One of those aforementioned illegitimate children is hidden in plain sight in La Familia. He was described in the inventories as a dwarf, one Nicolas P, but he was a normal child. Sweet and robust. He could have been, or perhaps was not, another son of La Calderana, the King's favourite. The King wanted the boy close but could not claim him for fear of upsetting his Queen

*and thereby risking the security of other as-yet-unborn heirs who
might emerge from her womb . . .*

*Monsignor Inquisidor learned of the rumours of the King's
enamours and, noting his morose state and blighted heirs,
concluded that someone had cursed the King. The King was so
burdened by guilt and misery that he concurred and had himself
exorcised. 'Twas not long after that he departed this life.*

*Here I hesitate. The flame of my candle is flickering and
long shadows slide from my hand and rise upon the walls of this
chamber. Night is upon us, the air is cooling and my throat is dry.
The Infanta found her spiritual ossuary within* La Familia. *She
abides there still. Dismiss my crazy wanderings. Disregard them.
I am naught but a loon. If you see the Monsignor Inquisidor, turn
on your heel and do not stop until you reach Italia.*

Alex gripped the sides of the desk and read the words a second
time. 'This is amazing,' she whispered.

A guilty secret was gnawing at his soul. That was what Fuendacia
had written. This was the basis of the curse that had frightened
both Margarita and her father, who felt he called it down on himself
by his actions. 'No wonder the King felt he was cursed. So there
was the curse of inbreeding, which was genetic, but the King was
also damned by his awful actions . . .'

Paz nodded.

Alex remembered Carla talking about *Las Meninas* in her
apartment. Did Zeus represent the King and Europa the nun in
Velázquez's painting? Was this proof? Velázquez the artist had
sent this message into the future at a time when others wanted it
suppressed. She was gripped by the meaning of this: Fuendacia had

called Velázquez 'a conduit of the truth'. Here he was, speaking up for all the world to see.

A bell began to chime somewhere, little peals of four bells in a row, then a break and the pattern repeated. Paz clasped her hands.

'I have to go, my dear. It's time for vespers. I want you to take your mama's translations of Fuendacia's writings. Perpetual silence was declared in the matter of the King and the nun, evidence was destroyed. But these belonged to her, and now they belong to you. They are not officially part of the archive.'

Paz gathered the translated papers into a pile, then paused. 'I must warn you, though – something about this work made Rosara very anxious. She was worried. There are still those who would not want these secrets to come out. I suspect the man who came yesterday has a connection to this.'

'But it all happened hundreds of years ago.'

'Yes, in 1638 to be exact.' Paz pointed to the date in the text.

Alex stared. That was the date in her mother's notes. This *was* what Rosara had uncovered just before her death.

'It may have occurred many years in the past, but it matters. The truth always matters. And, finally, it is coming to light.'

There was a creak of hinges as a door opened downstairs. A man's voice could be heard – a kind of interrogating tone. 'That voice – it is him!' said Paz, grabbing Alex's sleeve. 'You must leave . . .'

Paz pointed to a rectangular window above the highest book-shelf. 'There's a fire escape on the south wall. Be careful on the roof; the tiles are ancient.'

'What about you?' said Alex.

'I'll go to chapel with my sisters,' said Paz. 'He won't care about another old nun.' And she winked.

Paz thrust Rosara's translations at Alex, then bundled Fuendacia's chronicle back into the hidden cupboard. Alex helped slide the shelves back into position, stuffed the plastic folder with the translations inside her shirt and tucked the shirt into her jeans.

She started climbing, using the bookshelves as a ladder. The large tomes left her little room for her fingers and toes. Would the shelves bear her weight, or topple? As Alex climbed higher, Paz backed away. Soon Alex was at the top. 'Be careful!' Paz called after her, her face pale.

There wasn't much room. Alex swung a knee over and pulled herself up until she was lying on her belly along the empty top shelf. She reached up and grabbed the clasp for the window. It wouldn't budge. *Damn!* She glanced towards the stairs; the man might burst in at any moment.

Alex braced herself with a hand on the shelf below and, using her shoulder, she shoved at the window frame till it opened. Wriggling out headfirst, she placed the heels of her palms on the thin lips of the tiles on the roof. Gingerly, she inched her hands down, allowing the weight of her body to follow. A tile gave way beneath her hand and she lurched forwards, managing to stop herself from plummeting by hooking the toe of her right shoe on the windowsill. She was splayed starfish-like on the roof. She moved herself around until she could continue feet first. Roses waved at the edge of the guttering. Climbing over, she found the ladder and scratched her way past the rosebush, picking a rosehip on the descent.

At the bottom of the ladder she ran, leaping down the terraces. A high stone wall encircled the lower garden. She jumped and tried to catch the top but fell back. It was hard to escape from a convent. Stepping a toe into one of the crevices, she tried again, gripping the raw chunks of stone and launching herself over the top of the wall. The drop on the other side was further than she'd expected, and she fell to the ground, whacking her elbow on a rock. Her funny bone twanged. She lay for a few seconds, clutching her elbow, then scrambled to her feet and continued up the slope towards the road. She had to get to the station, where Oscar would be waiting. She had to get her mother's precious translations to safety.

27

FAWNS

1666

Margarita walked down the long corridor of the Imperial Palace in Vienna. She was dressed in a white nightgown with a frilled collar and lacy front. Over it she wore a cloak of dark blue wool, and over that an embroidered satin cape. Her hair fell loose about her shoulders. Freed from the constraints of a bodice, she could feel her breasts bouncing slightly within the thin folds of her nightgown as she walked, and the air against her skin, moving around her, carrying her towards her assignation with her new husband, Leopold, the Holy Roman Emperor. She wondered what would happen if she baulked, like an obstinate horse. Refused the summons. But she could not.

Staff lined the entrance to the chamber. The ministers wore serious faces; they were appraising her. The room was full of eyes.

The Emperor's bed was large, canopied in purple, but he was nowhere to be seen. The servants raised the white linen coverlet over her legs. She sat bolt upright and waited.

The celebrations following their wedding had continued for a week and were ongoing. He had composed an opera in her honour. Margarita had sat in the royal box at the opera house, in a red-and-silver gown, with feathers in her headdress. At the conclusion of the performance, the actors representing her and her husband had stood hand in hand as generation after generation of 'children' had emerged, to rapturous applause. She was sixteen, with a body that curved at breast and hip. Leopold's gaze rested frequently upon her figure. The expectation was no secret. He was eleven years her senior.

En route to Austria from Madrid, after she had recovered from her tears, she had asked for an image of him, a sketch, a portrait, but nothing had been forthcoming. After weeks at sea, and in horse-drawn carriages, his spoonbilled visage had come as a horrid shock. His eyes were bulbous. Tiny black dots pitted the side of his nose. He walked flat-footed despite years of dance lessons.

But in this room, in his bed, as she scanned the walls, the face she found herself staring at was her own. The portrait of her in her luscious blue dress hung opposite within a gilt frame. It brought a lump to her throat. Velázquez's tender representation of the pale pink flush of her cheeks. There she was, on the brink of womanhood, safe in Velázquez's studio, in the alcázar. The scene of her fondest memories; her home. Its haphazard structure was openly disdained by those in court here, as was her lack of German and refusal to learn. She remembered the golden lion and the story of Zeus as a bull, and the woman he carried off, Europa. Margarita stared at her beautiful younger self, remembering the confident twitch of her shoulders, her determination not to hold the fur muff.

How they had applauded her spirit. All for naught. The emperor's eye had been upon her even then. Her image had been captured, locked in this strange man's room. For years he had known her; he had coveted her even when she was but a child. She had had no such advantage.

There was a ripple at the doorway. He appeared, still wearing the long curly wig of the Viennese style. She could see wispy chest hairs through his open nightshirt. He climbed the steps onto the bed and gave her thigh a squeeze. He waved away the courtiers and the doors were closed.

Margarita lay still. She remembered the royal hunt one day in the park of Buen Retiro. The sun through the brilliant green leaves. The fresh smell of the cut grass. The servants had erected a large circular fence, made of heavy canvas and sticks, in a clearing, and the deer had been driven inside the enclosure. Many of the ladies of the court had ridden side-saddle to the event, and were watching from under the trees, with their gallants. Margarita and the Queen were in a carriage drawn up alongside the canvas fence.

The ties of the lace cap she was wearing loosened and some of her hair caught in her mouth. Margarita looked out of the corner of her eye at his jowls. Leopold's hand left her knee and began to slide up her thigh. He pulled the sheet down. He placed an arm on either side of her chest and attempted to straddle her, but the sheet tangled with his feet. She was still covered from head to toe with her nightgown. Was he actually going to try to climb on top of her? He was so awkward she let out a nervous giggle.

Margarita closed her eyes. He was tugging on her nightgown and had pulled it up around her hips. She could feel her cheeks burning. Then she felt his hands and his knee between her legs, shoving them apart. She turned her head away and screwed her eyes shut.

Margarita remembered that day in the forest clearly. The fawns had dappled brown coats, legs like spindly twigs. They paused, listened, and became the stillness.

The mother deer, close to the carriage, looked around. Her nose was up, sniffing the wind. A fawn nuzzled her, reaching for her teats.

He was on top of her now, his breath hot in her ear, his wig scratchy and pungent against her cheek.

She remembered the thudding flurry of hooves, how four riders had entered the clearing, wheeling their horses and blocking the path of the deer and her fawn. It had been her father, the King. The mother deer looked at Margarita and at the fence. As Margarita wondered if she might jump to freedom, the King's hand loosed his arrow. The deer fell to the ground. The fawn ran away and then back to its mother, collapsing to its knees and touching its nose to hers. One of the riders dismounted and grabbed it, and, taking a knife from his belt, lifted it for all to see. Margarita thought, *They are to save her, she will be a pet for me.* But he was quick with his knife; he laid it against the fawn's neck, the small creature's legs kicking in the air, and sliced. The man's boots were splashed red.

Something sharp pricked her between her legs, and then he was inside her, jerking. He was panting; his neck was sticky. It didn't last long.

The emperor rose and gathered his robes. After he had gone, one of the servants indicated she must climb out of the bed. Her maid accompanied her as she limped back to her room, the woman carrying the stained sheet bundled in her arms like a swaddled babe.

28

TOLEDO II

Alex paused at the road. She should go through the town to get to the station, but the road invited her in the opposite direction. It curved down the hill. This road. This road to Toledo. Her feet seemed to know where they were going. She began walking.

On her right, the hill rose up, and on her left the edge dropped away steeply. A small stone wall bordered the lip of the road, but lower down this stopped, and there was nothing to prevent a car leaving the narrow ribbon of tarmac.

The cicadas rasped louder and louder. She checked behind her. She could see the garden of the convent, where she'd sat with Paz. There was no sign of anyone following her. Her shirt was sticking to her back. The plastic folder was like a slippery corset on her front, but she didn't care. She could be close to where her mother had died.

When she reached the point where the wall ended, she paused. Below her was a steep bank, speckled with a few olive trees and low grey shrubs. She glanced back up the hill at the clock tower. She still had time before she was due to meet Oscar.

Alex stepped over the edge and lurched as her shoes slid on the dry dirt. This place could almost be a desert. She picked her way down the ochre bank towards the river. There was no sign of a car, or a car crash; no tyre tracks, no twisted metal. She walked across and down the slope, setting off little gravel landslides with each step. Something caught her eye, glinting further ahead, to her right. She ran a few steps and skidded on the gravel. A car's rear-view mirror lay in the dirt, under a thyme bush. She dropped to her hands and knees, leaning over it. Reflected in the cracked mirror, the sun dazzled her. There was a metallic taste in her mouth, like blood. Momentarily blinded, she touched the glass.

Had this mirror reflected her mother's face?

'Mum. *Mama*.'

She would finish Rosara's work. She had to speak up.

Blinking, she took the rosehip from her pocket and placed it beside the mirror. Then she scrabbled in the dirt until she'd dug a small hole, the depth of a hand. She touched the rosehip to her cheeks, now wet with tears and sweat, then placed it in the hole along with the mirror and covered them over. She sat there for some time, noticing the dryness of the air, the scent of warm thyme and the dome of blue above her.

She patted the earth gently, then trudged back up the hill.

⌒

José was met at the door of the nunnery by the abbess, who wore a wooden crucifix around her neck.

'Is there a girl here, an Alex Johns?' he asked.

The abbess shook her head.

'Your archives, can I come in and discuss them?' he said placing a foot upon the step.

Again the abbess demurred. 'There will be no purchase; no male visitors.'

José tried another tack: 'I see your roof has a few patches; my client can offer a handsome sum.'

'Thank you, but the archives will remain here.'

'The girl?'

'I told you, she's not here,' said the abbess, thrusting her crucifix into his face.

⌒

José paced through the narrow lanes of the old town, then pushed his way through the crowds outside the cathedral – he scanned for blonde heads, saw two, but they were not her. Skirting around the holy ground he continued until he reached his bike. The doors of the train were closing just as he ran onto the platform of the station; he caught a glimpse as her profile rolled past, behind glass. Gunning his accelerator, he pointed the bike north, to Madrid.

29

CONFLAGRATION

The walls of the tapas bar were covered with photographs of bulls and matadors. There were also Picasso's drawings of bulls, toreadors, and a photo of Picasso at the bullfight. The man at the counter was slicing *jamón*. The white paper frill on the pig's tiny hoof, was like a little girl's sock.

It was evening and the bar was lively and welcoming. Thanks to Flora, Alex had a flight booked for the next day – this would be her last night in Madrid. Oscar had just arranged to stay at the same hostel, where he was offered one of the dormitory rooms. She had shared something of her experience of finding her mother's crash site while they were on the train.

She leaned across the table now and, lowering her voice, told Oscar about Fuendacia's revelations.

When she'd finished he placed his hands behind his head and leaned back in his chair. 'Jeepers!' he said.

Alex thought of Margarita: how she had wanted to lift the curse, but she had never known about the nun – that had happened before she was born.

'I wonder if the King became depressed,' she said. 'I've read that he wasn't painted by Velázquez after 1656 – he didn't want any more portraits. That's the last image of him, and it's not a portrait but a reflection in a mirror.'

'Maybe he didn't want to see what he'd become?'

'Exactly. And there's more. The scandal was covered up – kept secret. Which makes me think – Carla told me about the paintings in the background of *Las Meninas*.'

'Yes, you said. What about them?'

'There's a reference to a copy of another work, Titian's *The Rape of Europa*, in *two* of Velázquez's paintings: *Las Meninas* and *Las Hilanderas*. Maybe the King knew, and including that reference, that allusion, was a way for the King to "admit" his guilty secret, to get it off his chest, without actually revealing it. Or perhaps the King didn't know, and Velázquez left a clue in his canvas in the hope that future generations would understand.'

After several more glasses of red wine, they asked the barman for directions to the Convent of San Plácido.

'It's a monastery now, and it will be closed,' he advised, shaking his head.

'*Gracias*,' she said to the man, and to Oscar, 'I just want to see it.'

After Alex and Oscar had departed, a man approached the barman, asking where the young couple had gone. The barman shook his head, polished a glass with a tea towel.

José slid some pesetas over the bar.

The barman did not pick them up.

José frowned. These Castilians, they were proud and stubborn. He felt a grudging sense of admiration for his countryman. Where were men like this, men who kept secrets, when his Queen had needed them?

He pulled out his knife and traced its tip along the wooden bar, leaving a long scratch, then started cleaning his fingernails with it. The barman was weakening, he could tell, but the girl would have a head start.

The barman began wiping the countertop. José didn't have time for this. He slammed the tip of his blade into the man's hand, feeling it strike tendon and bone.

'*Aieee!* The Convent of San Plácido,' spluttered the barman.

José wiped his knife on the man's cloth and flicked the coins onto the floor. He picked up a random hat from a hook, then headed for the exit.

⌒

After consulting a map, Alex and Oscar wandered through the cobbled streets to San Plácido, their path lit by a full moon. To her surprise, Alex recognised the place from her mum's drawing. A stone wall abutted the edge of the lane. There was a bell tower. The door to the chapel was locked and the windows barred.

'This is it! Mum must have stood right here,' said Alex, as she located the perspective point from where the drawing had been done.

'Somewhere under there is a tunnel,' she said to Oscar. 'It's probably been filled in.'

'*The* tunnel! Well, it's all locked up now,' he said, 'but we can come back in the morning.' He nudged Alex. 'Let's go this way. There are some dodgy-looking types around here.'

Two men were lurking nearby; the face of one was hidden under the brim of a black felt hat.

They moved on, conscious of being watched, heading in the direction of Alex's hostel. They came across a building with clusters of people gathered outside, waiting to get in. With its neon sign, it seemed out of place in this old part of the city. Oscar moved to avoid them, but Alex grabbed his elbow. 'Look!'

The neon sign read: THE ALCÁZAR.

An unusually short man stood beside a bouncer at the entrance. He seemed out of place, as if dressed in costume. His wide lace collar was a greyish white, and he had a cheeky grin. He seemed familiar.

'Come one, come one,' he said to Alex.

'Doesn't he mean, *Come one, come all?*,' said Oscar. 'Or, *Come on, come on?*'

But Alex was already moving towards the dwarf and the open doorway.

Inside, a man was playing flamenco guitar and two couples were dancing. *Helen would love this*, thought Alex.

'I'll get us some drinks,' said Oscar, moving towards the bar.

The dwarf approached and gestured for Alex to follow him.

'But what about Oscar?'

'It will only take a moment,' said the dwarf.

'Who *are* you? Haven't I seen you before?'

'Pepito is my name. Come this way. She needs you.' He slipped through a curtain at the side of the stage. *She needs you.* Like the sign outside the National Gallery in London; that was where she'd seen the dwarf – Pepito – before. *No,* she thought. *It couldn't be him.*

She hesitated, willing Oscar to turn his head, but he was chatting to the barman.

She slipped through the curtain after Pepito.

He led her out through a side exit, across a lane, and into an old workshop.

'Have a seat.' Pepito gestured to two armchairs with a crate between them for a table. He picked up a slim silver case, engraved with unusual patterns, and tapped it. The case unfolded to provide a silver tray with two teacups. Pepito poured something from a flask into each cup.

'Drink,' he said.

Alex shook her head. 'No, thanks.'

'The alcázar is going to burn. She needs you.'

She! He meant Margarita; Alex was suddenly sure of it.

She picked up the teacup, sniffed, then sipped the liquid; it was hot, sweet and slightly grainy.

'Beware De Nieto. You have seen him in the present.' It was not a question.

'I have?' Her tongue felt numb.

Pepito nodded. 'José De Nieto takes many forms. The dark angel has been released from the past once more to keep their secrets.'

His words were strange but also compelling.

De Nieto; the man in the doorway in *Las Meninas*. What had Carla said about a figure in the painting fading?

Pepito nodded and tapped the side of his nose.

Alex leaned back in the chair. The muscles in her face were so relaxed. Pepito was standing before her, passing her something. She gripped the silver and ebony handle of a large knife as the dwarf began to count in Spanish: '*Uno, dos, tres, cuatro . . .*' And she began to lose herself and fall and fall.

❧

When Alex came to, Pepito had disappeared and she was in another place, with two chandeliers hanging from the ceiling above her. The candles must have been recently extinguished because she could smell smoke. Wispy trails of it wandered across the cracked and plastered ceiling. She was lying on the floor, still gripping the knife. Sitting up, she passed the knife from one hand to the other. The blade reflected her face, like a mirror. Through two paned windows she saw the night sky, stippled with patches of grey and amber. She clambered to her feet and turned. They were waiting for her. For *her*! The painting hung nearly floor to ceiling. The inhabitants were as they had been when she first saw them at the Prado: the Infanta Margarita, Velázquez the artist, the meninas, the attendants, Maribárbola, the dog and the boy. Like a scene on pause, they were frozen, fixed, holding their breaths – but she was not. Each of the group was touched with silver, but none more so than the Infanta Margarita, who was approaching incandescence. Alex's eyes were drawn to their hands, like Oscar's flight of musical notes, holding with the lightest of touches the invisible cord, or chord, which ran between them. But someone was missing – the man in black at the back of the room. The doorway was empty. De Nieto had gone.

Pepito had warned her. De Nieto, the dark angel, had left the painting. Where was he now?

The doors of the salon were open; a hot breeze was coming from somewhere inside the building. In the distance, bells were ringing. Alex sensed she was in the palace – Margarita's alcázar – but it was creaking and groaning like an ancient ship; its bones, laid down century after century, were quailing.

Alex moved forward and touched the canvas; it was hard, waxy. Though it moved under her fingertips, there was no viscosity to the surface, no way in. She didn't know whether she was relieved or disappointed. Why was she here, like this, now? What was she supposed to do? Banging, crashing and tinkling reached her ears. Again she smelled smoke, and now she heard raised voices. Crossing to the window, Alex opened the latch.

Below her, all was pandemonium. Courtiers in frockcoats and servants in long skirts were scattering about the courtyard, their faces stricken. Voices were shrill, and tones urgent. More people were emerging from a church nearby. A crowd had gathered at the entrance to the palace. Some kind of argument was going on. Soldiers in old-fashioned garb stood barring the doors.

Men were filling wooden buckets from a fountain and sloshing water towards the floors below. She calculated she was on perhaps the second or third level. Other people were standing, watching, hands shielding their eyes as if they were peering at the sun. And then the realisation hit her; they were protecting themselves from a wave of heat and smoke. The original alcázar, the royal palace, was on fire! And she was inside it! Alex couldn't see flames, but billows of smoke were drifting across nearby fields.

Alex heard pounding footsteps. A man in breeches, vest and flowing shirtsleeves burst into the room, gasping for breath. He had several large rolls of canvas under each arm and, with only a slight hesitation, he crossed to the window and hurled them out. Alex took a step towards him. He stopped and stared, but when he saw in the knife in her hand, he nodded.

'*Bueno.* Yes! We must save as many as we can. You do this one, *La Familia* . . . Use it!' He indicated the knife. 'Stupid fools locked the entrances to stop the looters; out the windows they must go! I've done the *salas reservados.*'

La Familia – the family. *We must save as many as we can.*

'*Salvare La Familia?*' she heard herself say aloud.

'*Sí, sí!*' It was a command.

'Where is the Infanta Margarita?'

He stared at her. 'She's long dead. Save the painting!'

While he was speaking, three wild-eyed women dashed past the doorway, skirts held high around their knees. One of them tripped on some boards in the hallway and went sprawling, then picked herself up and ran on.

'Not that way!' shouted the man.

Alex poked her head out into the corridor. The women were gone. Both ends of the corridor were dark and smoky. The air was close, warm and acrid. She could see no flames. Alex coughed. She backed into the room. The man slammed the doors then rushed to the window and climbed onto the sill.

'Wait,' she called. 'Stop. What year is it?'

He stared at her over his shoulder as if she were mad.

'Use the knife; save the painting!' he yelled. And then he jumped.

Alex ran to the window. The man lay in a crumpled heap, his leg jutting out at an odd angle. The people crisscrossing the court-yard ignored him as they dashed to and fro, many carrying pieces of furniture and pots and plates, tapestries. Alex shouted to one of those running by, but no one paid any attention to her.

The rolled paintings had unfurled as they fell and now lay spilling the fleshy female forms of Rubens' fantasies across the cobblestones. A man in a green coat rushed over, rolled up the reclining naked women and hurried off with them. As he passed, he stooped over the fallen man, then waved to two soldiers, who came and lifted him between them.

Away to the right, the people were standing much further back now, their faces lit by a golden glow. A small crowd was still arguing with the soldiers who were guarding what might have been the main doors.

The room began to hiss, as if a record was still going around and around after the song had finished. Alex's eyes were stinging. Fingers of smoke crept through the cracks around the doors, spilling across the ceiling and filling the upper reaches of the room.

What would happen if she died in a fire hundreds of years before she was meant to be born? No one knew where she was; it was up to her. The key to it all was here, in this room. She backed away from the window, turning the knife over in her hand, touching her fingers to the sharp shiny blade.

Within the smoke, by the fireplace, a form began to appear. A wheel spun, a foot worked a pedal up and down, and a spectral form spun itself forth from the grey smoke – a woman, her hair tied at the nape of her neck, the thread silken smoke in her hands. Her hands were Alex's mother's hands, and her face one the daughter recognised. 'Mum,' whispered Alex. 'Mum, it's me.' Warmth flooded her chest and throat.

The ghostly figure, who was even now beginning to fade, pointed at the masterpiece on the wall. Alex knew what to do.

The top of the painting was high above her head. She needed something tall to climb on. There was a heavy sideboard against the opposite wall, with a golden bowl on top of it. She ran to it and, putting the knife beside the bowl, pushed against the wood, but her gym shoes slipped on the smooth floor and the sideboard would not budge. An armchair with a high back stood in one corner of the room. That might suffice. She snatched up the knife once more and, after placing it on the seat, grabbed the rolled velvet top of the chair, which was the height of her shoulders, and pushed, but again her feet slipped on the wooden floor. Bracing her back against the wall, she gave it a hard shove. It slid about a metre. She shoved again, this time using all her weight. Another metre. Grunting, she kept shoving determinedly. She glanced up at the painting. She would not let it burn!

Finally she was close enough. Taking the knife in her left hand she stepped onto the seat, then put one foot on an arm of the chair and the other onto the chair's wide back. As she launched herself up, she balanced with a hand against the canvas, accidentally touching the area by Velázquez's shoulder. All the red in the painting seemed even redder than she'd remembered it: the red of the artist's lips, the red on his palette, on the cross on his chest, on the blood-red flower bursting from the chest of the Infanta, on the beribboned cuff of one of the waiting ladies. The Infanta Margarita was like a silver angel, hovering beside her. Golden light was flooding in from the window, making the surface gleam. Margarita nodded. *Her ossuary.* Alex remembered Fuendacia's words. Yes. She understood. The Infanta's spiritual ossuary: resting place of her soul.

What Alex had to do next didn't bear thinking about. She raised her right arm, glancing down at the image of the master artist frozen within his own canvas, and at the girl, the Infanta.

'I can't,' she said.

Margarita's voice called to her: 'Do it. Do it, or we will burn. *Salvare La Familia!*'

Alex stuck the knife into the top corner of the painting with some difficulty and sliced through the canvas down the side of the frame. She cut carefully, holding the outside of the frame with her left hand, but not leaning on it. She had to saw a little with the knife, although it was very sharp. Little strands of resistance, threads within the canvas, gave way one by one, pinging beneath the blade. With whispered apologies, she skimmed the knife past the painted back of Velázquez's easel on one side.

When she could reach no further, she stepped back and off the chair, and finished the rest while standing on the floor.

She wrenched the chair across to the other side of the frame and climbed up once more, balancing again on the top while cutting a straight line down the right-hand edge of the frame, behind the backs of Maribárbola, the courtly dwarf who was dressed like the Infanta, and behind the heel of the boy. The mastiff was alert. Watching. Was Margarita smiling, nodding? Sweat stung Alex's eyes. The right-hand side of the painting seemed different from her memory of it at the Prado. When she was halfway down she realised there was another girl, with loose blonde hair and a dark blue skirt, standing within the painted canvas at the window's edge, behind the young boy with his foot on the dog. She was awkward yet familiar. If her lungs had not been filling with smoke she would have laughed with delight as she recognised a painted version of her younger self. But there was no time to pause. A twinge shot down her arm as she sliced herself out of the picture.

Now both sides of the canvas were hanging free. She glanced up at the top of the painting and repositioned the chair in the centre, about six inches away from the front of the canvas, then stepped up onto the seat. When she cut, at some point, the weight of the canvas was going to fall towards the ground; the danger was that it would rip. What could she use to support it? She glanced towards the fireplace, but there was no sign of the ghostly spinner. She needed the man who had jumped, or arms like Oscar's or Helen's – it would be much easier with someone else there.

Then she saw it in the corner: a long stick, made of metal, with some kind of taper; it must have been used for lighting the chandeliers. Alex leapt off the chair, still holding the knife aloft, and landed on her feet. Smoke was now entering the room from the cracks around the doors and through the empty fireplace. The painted back of the double doors was blistering. The doors might explode at any moment.

She grabbed the pole. The top was pointed – too sharp; she picked up the golden bowl and placed it on top, then, carrying these above her head, hurried across the room, crashing into a chandelier. Shards of crystal rained down over her. She closed her eyes, shook glass from her hair, and kept going. Tearing off her jacket, she draped it over the top of the pole, tying the arms around it to cushion the end.

She placed the handle of the knife between her teeth and climbed, using one hand to balance and the other to hold the pole. When she was standing on the back of the chair once more, she moved the knife to her right hand and, holding the pole up towards the top left corner of the picture to support the canvas, she began cutting along the edge from the top right corner. She stretched as far as she could, feeling her ribs lift and extend and her straining arms scream. The top right corner of the painting dropped now, curling like an old map towards her shoulder. She had to work fast. Switching the pole into her right hand, and the knife into her left, she stretched to support the canvas where it was beginning to bend and continued slicing across the top in the opposite direction as close to the frame as she could.

As the last strands gave way, she dropped the pole and allowed the painting to curl over her like a heavy wave. She caught it and backed off the chair, supporting the canvas above her, and then she laid the painting, right side up, on the floor. It was not damaged, as far as she could see, apart from the slightly crooked cut made down the right-hand side, but there was no time to examine her handiwork. She glanced up at the bereft frame. A thin strip of canvas dangled from the right-hand side; she stepped around the painting on the floor and grasped the thin strip between her fingers. Holding it taut, she flicked the knife through to cut as close to the frame as she could and stuffed the sliver of canvas into her back pocket. Her eyes were stinging and she began to cough; smoke descended like a thick cloud. She returned to the painting on the floor and began to roll it in on itself, keeping it loose, praying that the old paint would not flake and fall off.

The painting was now a long fat tube of rolled canvas. She kneeled, slid her hands and forearms beneath it, and lifted. It was heavy; it felt as if she were holding a body in her arms. She crossed to the window, still coughing, and turned side-on to ease it through. Tears streamed from her eyes. This was the moment.

Her mother. The weight of missing her. The scent at the nape of her neck. Alex didn't want to let go.

But then she did. She watched as her burden flew heavily but safely to the ground.

At that moment, the doors behind her splintered and burst open. A shadowy figure entered, his face streaked with soot and his cloak in tatters. His movements were effortful and jerky. Smoke furled around his charred and semi-skeletal form. The corridor behind him was ablaze and collapsing. He stared at the empty frame where the painting had hung then swung his attention to Alex. It was the man who had tried to force his way into the professor's house; the man from the auction, the man from the doorway of the painting. They were the same. José De Nieto: the dark angel.

She sank to her knees and scrabbled around on the floor in the smoke, eyes stinging. Her fingers found something solid, something metal – the handle of the knife.

He came closer, his hand flexing and grasping at the air above her. She felt a tugging deep inside, as if her heart was a fish caught on a hook. Gripping the handle of the knife, she swung it between them, above her head. It snagged on something as light as silk, then gave way; De Nieto staggered backwards.

She crawled to the windowsill and hauled herself onto it. With a flick of his arm a whirl of smoke and cinders shot towards her like a fiery tendril. Embers flew past her. Fireflies in the night.

Alex stood. Below, a handcart was being pulled across the court-yard, overflowing with bedding and linens. It was a narrow target. She held the knife aloft, trying to find her reflection in its silvery blade, took a deep breath and jumped.

⌒

As the girl leapt out of the window, José fell to his knees. She had freed her mother, the last spinner. He no longer cared for spinners; their ravelling was a thankless task, as was his. He tried to spit, but all that emerged from his parched mouth was a gnarled tooth. He surveyed the husk of himself, from his bony knuckles to his hollow rib cage, from which dangled gobbets of flesh. His skin was as ragged as his cloak. This transition had not been a kind one. Every failure took a toll. He pictured Patrizia – or Mariana as she once was – the perfection of her pale skin. Inviolable. Forever unattainable.

If he returned himself to the flames streaking towards him now, there would be nothing left of him for them to send back. She would not have to live with the sight of this . . . revenant. And he would be . . . did he dare hope?

He staggered to his feet. And took his last steps.

30

RETURN

'Alex!'

Alex opened her eyes to see Oscar running across the lane. He kneeled beside her.

'What are you doing out here?' Oscar's voice sounded urgent. 'I couldn't find you.' He touched her cheek.

Alex raised herself up on her elbows. She was in her T-shirt and jeans, lying on an old mattress in a cobblestoned lane. Above her, silver stars filled a black velvet sky. She felt her forehead, then her neck and moved her legs.

'Alex, are you okay?'

She prodded the mattress beneath her. It squelched. Both she and the mattress were wet.

'Yuck.'

Oscar exhaled.

Two firemen stood conferring about twenty metres away. Their hoses lay slack on the ground. Another man began dragging the hoses into long straight lines. Behind them, the back entrance of a building was blackened and charred. A few cabbage leaves had washed into the middle of the lane and lay marooned, like boats on the hard. A kitchen hand sat in the alleyway, smoking a cigarette, his knees up in front of him.

'What's that?'

Alex sat up and followed the direction of Oscar's gaze to see Pepito's knife, which lay nearby on the cobblestones, its blade broken in two. She remembered Pepito passing her the handle. And the charred incarnation of De Nieto staggering towards her through the flames. She shivered and sat up. What had happened to him? There was no sign of him. Had the dark angel returned to the painting?

'What is it?' Oscar asked. 'What are you looking for?'

She coughed, trying to get rid of the taste of smoke.

'It's okay, it's okay.' Oscar took hold of her shoulders. His hands were warm; they anchored her in the present. She was not going back.

'What's with the knife? Was there a fight? Did someone hurt you? Is it from the kitchen?'

She shook her head. 'Pepito brought me out here and . . . I had to jump . . .' She craned her head and peered up. The alcázar, the old palace, and the window she had jumped from, had gone. The remains of the club that they had been in earlier were smouldering. A group of people had gathered at the end of the lane.

'Who?'

'The dwarf, Pepito.'

'Dwarf?'

'You saw him, didn't you? In the club?'

Oscar nodded. 'Yes, but he's not here now.'

'There was a fire,' said Alex.

'Yes, there was a fire in the club,' said Oscar. 'Someone said it started in the kitchen.'

'In the alcázar,' said Alex.

'Yes. I thought you'd gone to the loo. I couldn't find you anywhere when the alarm went off . . . Are you okay?'

'Yes,' said Alex. She inhaled deeply. 'Everything's good now, I hope. Is the painting all right?'

'You mean *Las Meninas*? That's in the Prado. It's fine, I'm sure. Hey, do you think you might have banged your head?'

❧

She woke in her hostel room. She was in the bed and Oscar was sleeping in an armchair, his legs slung over the side. When she got back from the bathroom, he was awake, rubbing his face.

'The ambulance officer who checked you last night said to keep an eye on you, in case you had concussion,' he said.

'I'm okay. I think you might look worse than me.' His hair was tousled and there was soot on his cheek.

He went to the mirror. 'You're right,' he said.

Alex pulled open the curtains. The sun was high in the sky.

'Oh no!' She grabbed her head with her hands.

'What's wrong?' Oscar asked.

'What's the time? Is it Monday?'

'Yes, Monday – why?'

'My flight! It leaves at lunchtime.' Flora had shouted her a ticket back to London, she couldn't miss it.

While Alex waited for the bus to the airport, Oscar stood beside her on the footpath, cradling a takeaway coffee. That afternoon he would be taking the train back to Barcelona where he would stay for a few more weeks before returning to England.

'We'll see each other again soon, won't we?' he said, as the bus pulled up to the kerb. 'Alex, I . . .' He swallowed; his Adam's apple moved in his throat.

She stepped directly in front of him so that the toes of her shoes were touching the toes of his boots. She studied his face, his gold-brown eyes, the curve of his eyelashes. The bus door slapped open. She ignored it.

She leaned into him a little and he drew in a breath. She reached up and cupped her hand around the back of his neck and gently pulled his head closer until their lips met. She'd never wanted to kiss someone like this before. As much as this.

'Watch the coffee, Romeo,' shouted someone from the bus, in English.

They pulled apart, grinning. There was a puddle of latte at her feet.

'*Vamos!*' said the driver.

'I wanted to do that last night,' she said. 'Thank you. Thank you for everything.'

She picked up her suitcase. 'London,' she said, touching Oscar's hand, then stepping aboard the bus.

At Madrid airport, she checked in for her flight and passed through customs. She was on her way to the gate lounge when a thought struck her. She found a public phone and called Carla. 'Could you please ask one of your old colleagues at the Prado to check *Las Meninas*? Ask them to look at De Nieto, the man in the doorway – the one you said had faded. Make sure he's still there, and all the rest of them, too. Please. And the Infanta – I need to know she's okay.' She gave Carla the number of the phone booth. 'I'll wait for you to ring me back . . .'

Carla sounded bemused by the request, but she agreed to do as Alex asked.

For the next hour Alex paced back and forth beside the phone booth, anxiously guarding the receiver. Her flight was called but she stayed by the phone. It was only as the final boarding call was made over the loudspeakers that the phone rang.

'*Todas presentes*,' said Carla, 'All present and correct. Isn't that what the English say? All is as it was. They have put De Nieto's fading down to a "temporary aberration", an instability. I'm not sure why you were so worried, but be reassured. The painting is as it should be, safe in the museum.'

'Thank you,' said Alex, feeling almost weak with relief. 'I'm glad to hear it.'

31

WISHBONE

1673

The strangest part about being dead was not being able to move her limbs. Margarita's soft, white fingertips, which had so recently felt the perspiration of her own clammy forehead and the dampness of her bed linen, now lost the sensation of touch. And yet her seashell ears found sound, for she could still hear the murmured prayers of the nuns and servants in the antechamber. As she'd travelled in and out of her fever, once or twice she had shouted for them to stop, to stop, for the noises and the people in her room, all of her antecedents, had seemed to advance and retreat, growing grotesquely large and loud and then receding – and, like the tide, they were gathering to carry her somewhere she was not ready to go. All her life she had had no power to resist. She had been bred and traded to wed and bed. She wished for her native tongue, for her home. Would that she could have stayed there. And had her babies there, around her; alive, not trapped in marble tombs.

She was no longer inside her body. A cruel separation, but also a blessing. She could see herself far below, lying in the bed, tiny. The colours had drained away; everything was in grey and white. One of the servant women moved to her bed and removed the darkly stained bedding. A cry came from the room next door. There was a pause, then it came again, a mewling sound, like a cat hungry for milk. Margarita felt the sound through every part of herself, although she was no longer herself, but she was in the air and the sound vibrated with her and through where her breasts had been and left her with longing.

She had had a baby, and another and another and another, and all but one had died. She was dust inside before this latest death. She tried to make a noise: to cry; to curl up; to clench her fists; to shout. But there was nothing.

A woman in the room said quietly, 'Hear the wind keening for Her Highness and her little babe.' And the attendants paused, listening.

And then the men were there, in robes, in another place, with a marble table and stone walls, and the men had knives and silver in their hands, and there was her body, washed and still damp and shining, and smoke from candles curling upwards, and there the priest, saying Latin prayers, and she was naked, and they were drawing a line down her chest, and she could see but not feel it; but the line was not a line, the line was blood, and while everything else was black and white this line alone was red, and they were cutting and cutting through her belly and pulling her open, levering themselves with a foot on the hard marble as her body yielded and yielded and yielded and they cut, cut, cut. Her ribs clasped her heart until they cracked like a wishbone, and she made her last wish.

She spun, she tumbled in the air, she writhed, and she took herself to another time, to a room, in a golden light, with a halo of hair, with clear, fresh-tasting breath brimming from her chest and mouth, and laughter, and the smell of oil paint and red wine, and of candle wax and warm dog. And in that moment, she returned there and settled herself, poised perfectly between the mirror and the canvas, into the pigments of the very painting that had held and embraced her, had been waiting for her, for all those years.

32

ROUNDTABLE

'I would rather be an ordinary painter working from life than be the greatest copyist on earth.'

DIEGO VELÁZQUEZ

The Royal Academy of Fine Arts was a venerable institution, known for its conservatism. The meeting was held next door, in one of London's oldest clubs.

'You have to show your findings, I absolutely insist,' Greta had said.

Now they were here, and Alex was among an august group, which included senior staff from the National Gallery and the Tate, as well as the Prado. Regi Montano was present, and Greta too, representing the Courtauld. They were gathered around a large mahogany table.

These were the people in front of whom she'd embarrassed herself so acutely only a month ago. She had had something to prove. It wasn't just her own small reputation on the line, but her mother's too – and, more than that, it was the security and respect of the painting, of *Las Meninas*, and the voice of the artist who created it.

Could she speak here of Pepito, the dwarf, or dancing in Margarita's shoes, or of the fire in the alcázar?

Alex had a small box with her – a shoebox, to be exact. Others had Filofaxes and manilla folders. Montano had a small leather moleskin notebook, and he cupped his hand over it, as if to protect the contents. Alex slipped her shoebox under her chair.

Greta was wrapping up her remarks. 'So I ask you to please hear what she has to say . . .' She gestured to Alex.

Alex stood up. 'My mother was Rosara Johns. She was an academic researcher who was doing some work related to *Las Meninas* – or *La Familia*, as it was first known – when she died unexpectedly.

'She wrote to me and my father about how Picasso had said *Las Meninas* was, and I quote, "a picture painted with curses". Some of you will remember me saying that at Christie's, and stating my belief that the painting contained hidden meanings. But I lacked the evidence to back up my assertion . . .'

The gazes of those present interlocked around the table, like a game of cat's cradle. Alex began to unpick each strand, until all eyes were on her.

'I've taken up the trail where my mother left off. And I've discovered, among other things, that her death in a car accident near Toledo in 1977 might not have been an accident. I believe someone wanted to prevent her discoveries from being brought out into the open.'

The woman from the National Gallery pressed her fingertips together. The man from the Prado placed his forearm on the table, one shoulder slightly slumped. Montano shifted in his seat and touched his hair.

'Since I've begun this research, I have also encountered . . . obstacles,' Alex continued.

The director of the National Gallery glanced at the senior curator from the Prado, who raised his eyebrows.

The man from the Prado said stiffly, 'These are serious suggestions, or is this more than that? You British are not usually so dramatic.'

There was laughter, then silence.

Greta pushed back her seat and went to stand by the slide projector. She nodded to Alex.

'Let's take another look,' said Alex, pressing the button on the remote to turn the carousel.

The image of *Las Meninas* appeared on the screen above the fireplace. Margarita sparkled like a Christmas angel on a tree. Those assembled swivelled and adjusted their positions.

'You all know this painting very well . . .' She took a breath. 'I have discovered that there was a scandal that was covered up in Velázquez's time. It was a scandal that haunted the King. He decreed that all evidence relating to it should be destroyed and that there should be "perpetual silence" relating to this matter.'

Greta was nodding.

'I believe Velázquez has included a reference to this scandal in his canvas. This is the allusion in the Rubens' painting to a tapestry version of Titian's *The Rape of Europa*, depicting the rape of a mortal woman by Zeus, the king of the gods. Ovid had written about this story, and it seems that just as Ovid used allegory to comment on events of his day, so too did Velázquez.

'I have discovered historical evidence which suggests that, in 1638, King Philip IV . . . well, it was with a nun. They think he had sex with a nun.' She hesitated, then said, 'It seems we could be talking about rape here. He gained access to the Convent of San Plácido in Madrid via a tunnel built between the convent and the house next door specifically for this purpose of clandestinely admitting the King. The adjoining house was owned by the King's co-conspirator and confidant, a man called Villanueva. This sounds extraordinary, I know, but it was not the first time that high-ranking nobles were involved in a sexual scandal at this particular convent.'

The delegation from Madrid began talking among themselves. She heard someone repeat the name San Plácido.

Montano was frowning.

Alex paused and looked down at her notes, then at Greta. She was grateful for her supervisor's encouraging smile.

Alex hesitated. 'The thing is . . .' she said. She had the attention of everyone in the room.

Alex took a deep breath. 'What I suggest is this: Velázquez has literally painted the King's guilty conscience into the canvas, into "the corner of the canvas that no one looks at", to misquote Picasso. Those shadowy rectangles on the back wall of *Las Meninas* are like cards in a tarot reading – cartomancy was popular in the court at that time – or like thought bubbles in a cartoon. Velázquez is indicating the matter hanging over their heads. The menacing hooks in the ceiling emphasise it further. And yes, the Inquisition had been very interested in this and other affairs with nuns. The torture alluded to by the hooks is perhaps the King's psychological torture. The secret was a burden – one that I think Velázquez also found intolerable.

'While the King was, ah, rutting around and bewailing the lack of a successor, his heir apparent, the silvery Infanta, was in fact standing right in front of him. Velázquez was presenting her to him. But in a sense, the King could barely see her, would not accept her as a successor, was obsessed with siring a son.'

'San Plácido,' said the man from the Prado, rubbing his chin. 'That's the convent for which the King commissioned Velázquez to paint his Christ.'

Alex nodded. 'This one?'

She flicked through several slides until an image of Velázquez's crucified Christ appeared on the screen. The room fell silent at the sight of the slender naked man with the crown of thorns.

'The date of this has always been a little uncertain, but we think it was commissioned for the convent by the King,' said the man from the Prado.

'Could it have been something like a penance? An apology from the King?' asked Alex.

'That is an unusual suggestion, but . . .' He shrugged. 'There is a new theory,' the man continued, 'that Velázquez could have been Jewish, and had hidden his heritage in order to climb at court.'

'Wouldn't that have been in order to save his life?' said Greta. 'Remember, Jews were still being exiled, along with Moriscos.'

'To gain the Order of Santiago . . . to attain nobility . . .' This was Montano.

'The cross on his chest . . . ?'

'And safety for him and his family?'

'*Jesus of Nazareth, King of the Jews* – it's inscribed on the sign at the top of the painting in Hebrew, Latin and Greek,' said Montano.

'Remember the doctrine of *limpieza de sangre* – purity of blood,' said the man from the Prado.

'Ovid tell us Pallas was angry with Arachne, not just because of her skill, but because she was revealing the "lewdness of the Gods"' – this from Greta.

Discussion exploded around the table, as the experts digested Alex's presentation and shared their own thoughts, like musketeers before a seventeenth-century stage play.

⌒

Alex peered at the faces around the table. She liked how it felt to see them all attentive, leaning in to hear more. 'The other thing,' she started, sensing how her own curiosity had given her the power to speak in a way she never had before, 'is that this was not the first time Velázquez had referred to *The Rape of Europa*. As others have pointed out, this image is also depicted in the tapestry at the back of *Las Hilanderas – The Spinners*. So we have that same reference used in two paintings, within a couple years of each other. It's symbolic. And in *Las Hilanderas*, one of the women who is in the background is turning towards us, the viewer, as if to say, *Have a look at this . . .'*

She let that sink in before continuing. 'Perhaps Velázquez was surprised people didn't latch on to his reference the first time he used it, and so he dropped it in again. But aside from that, what happens is that the King becomes increasingly miserable and convinced that he is possessed. He can't shake his guilt. It consumes him. He believes he is hexed. This climaxes in an exorcism of the King in 1665, and he dies shortly after.'

Alex saw raised eyebrows and nods. 'There's a quote of Velázquez's that really made me think. He is supposed to have said, *I would rather be an ordinary painter working from life than be the greatest copyist on earth* . . . He wasn't interested in outshining Rubens and Titian – rather, they were speaking the same symbolic language.'

The man from the Prado shook his head. 'Sometimes I think every generation comes up with its own interpretation of the great iconographic works. They defy classification and invite debate.'

'But there's more, isn't there?' said Greta. 'You question the identity of the dwarf, front right, with his foot on the dog?' She picked up a ruler and pointed.

'Yes, that's pretty simple,' said Alex. 'I don't think he was a dwarf, but rather an illegitimate son of the King, whose identity was being kept secret.'

'We need to see your evidence,' said the man from the Tate.

Alex nodded and looked around the table. 'I will offer my sources. But first, something has . . . come to me, during my research, which I would like to return to the Prado Museum.' She picked up the shoebox, put it on to the table and opened the lid.

'Been shopping, have we?' murmured Montano to the woman beside him as he tipped his chair back.

Alex looked to Greta, who produced a pair of gloves and put them on. She reached into the box and gently unwrapped the tissue.

A thin strip of painted canvas was unrolled. The frayed edges were darkened with age. As its colours, cream to brown, and contents – the pictured edge of a pointed elbow, a lick of the back of a red doublet, and a glimpse of a heel – came into view, there were gasps around the table. Montano and the Prado curators leapt to their feet to gain a better view. It was, unmistakably, the missing strip from *Las Meninas*. Like Cinderella's shoe, the strip was a perfect match to the painting.

EPILOGUE

1656

Diego Velázquez stood alone in the studio. He glanced up at the copy of Rubens' *Pallas and Arachne* above the mirror. The king of the gods in the background. The resisting maiden. The sallow face of his own king swam before him. The evidence of Philip's crime was long gone, the papers entrusted to the messenger burned to cinders in the King's bedroom. He remembered the poor young man who'd sat nervously in his living room late one night. And what of the woman, the unnamed nun? He'd never met her, but he prayed for her. He shook his head and rubbed his chin and cheek with the knuckles of a fist. The King had decreed perpetual silence in the matter.

Velázquez contemplated the unfinished canvas before him. He imagined Ovid's metaphorical rapist hanging from the hook. Pictures were silent, but through them he could speak.

He took up his brush.

AUTHOR'S NOTE

This is a work of fiction.

The sections of the novel set in seventeenth-century Spain are based on historical research. Most of these characters – Diego Velázquez, the Infanta Margarita, King Philip IV, Maribárbola and so on – were real people, and I have tried to be true to the facts of their lives. Velázquez's full name was Diego Rodriguez de Silva Velázquez, but I have followed the style of *The Prado Guide*, which refers to him as Diego Velázquez, except in the first instance.

Margarita's maid, Luisa, and Pepito are fictitious, based on similar characters of their era. Luisa's role is something of an amalgamation, for novelistic purposes. Duran, too, is an imagined character, as is Fuendacia, the keeper of the royal records. His journal and poem were penned by the author as works of fiction, in part based on sources noted below. Fuendacia was inspired by the real keeper of the royal records, Gaspar de Fuensalida, who was a friend of Velázquez. While 'Nicolas' is generally described as a dwarf or midget (Nicolasito Pertusato), I see him as a boy, plain and simple – based purely on Velázquez's depiction of him – and have written his character accordingly.

José Nieto, or, as I have styled him, José De Nieto, the Queen's chamberlain, was a real person. He appears in *Las Meninas* as the figure in the doorway. I owe him an apology, as I have given him a fictional afterlife. My elucidation of the tension between he and Diego Velázquez is based on my reading of historical sources, analysis of the hierarchy of the palace and of the hierarchy between the two art forms of tapestry and painting. His fictional character was also shaped for me by Picasso's treatment of his form.

The Infanta Margarita was born in 1651 and died in 1673, aged twenty-one. Her father, King Philip IV, *was* exorcised not long before his death in 1665. The first two sentences of Margarita's letter, in Chapter 5, are an extract from a real letter written by the Infanta in 1659, located by the author on a historical document auction website. (The source is not included in the bibliography, as it is unfortunately no longer available online.)

The story of the King and the nun comes primarily from M. Hume, *The Court of Philip IV*, published in 1907. Hume was originally known by the surname Sharp, and under that name published as a renowned Cambridge scholar, who also edited the Spanish State Papers. He was fluent in Spanish, lived in England and Spain, and spent years trawling through Spanish archives. He became a little jaded, it seems, by the 'decadence' of Philip IV's reign, which he alludes to in his notes to his text.

In *The Court of Philip IV*, Hume relates the scandals at the Convent of San Plácido. Hume implicates the King as well as Villanueva in the second 'scandal', for which he cites contemporary manuscript sources but footnotes only one, which is appended within *El Antiguo Madrid*, by Ramón de Mesonero Romanos. According to Hume, Archbishop Sotomayer, Philip's confessor, 'took the King to task severely and repeatedly for his crime'. But subsequent trials by the Inquisition, discussed in other sources and beyond the scope of this novel, focused only on Villanueva. Sotomayer was 'encouraged' to retire.

Hume cites Quevedo, a poet, on the subject of Philip IV and his kingly attributes, or lack thereof. Quevedo's poem in Chapter 19 comes from Hume.

H.C. Lea's *A History of the Inquisition of Spain* (1906–07) does not mention the King as party to any of the events at San Plácido. There is no trace of the conversations between Sotomayer and the King (as referred to by Hume) to be found in Lea's trawl through the records of the Inquisition. Is this because such records never existed, or because they were destroyed? Lea does confirm the existence of the tunnel into the convent. He notes that efforts were made to 'erase from human memory all that had occurred', and edicts were published requiring the surrendering of any documents, 'many of which were fabulous', about what went on at San Plácido. Lea also states: 'Philip went on to say that the affair of San Plácido had never ceased to give him concern.' But this does not mean he was implicating himself.

It should be noted that Hume's scholarship was questioned by his successor as editor of the Spanish State Papers, however this related not to his book about Philip IV but to his final volume of the state papers, which was incomplete when he died.

Hume's sources on the 'convent scandal' are not listed in full –
an omission on his part. However, I find it difficult to believe
that a scholar of his standing would have gone out on a limb on a
matter like this, especially concerning the King, without substan-
tive evidence. In a footnote, he does allow for ambiguity over the
continuance of the 'intrigue'.

J.H. Elliot, the pre-eminent English historian on Olivares and
the Hapsburgs, does not link Philip IV to the events at San Plácido.
Elliot refers obliquely to the 'events' as 'one of the darkest diabolical
mysteries of the Olivares regime'. However, his view differs from
Hume; for example, he writes: Olivares' penchant for consulting
the prioress [of San Plácido] and asking for prayers 'gave rise to all
manner of scabrous stories about immorality in high places'; he
cites Olivares as claiming he was 'overawed by [the nuns] sanctity'.
Elliot cites Hume's book and describes it as 'excessively melodram-
atic', but he does not say that Hume was wrong. Elliot touches only
lightly on Philip's affairs, but does describe him as 'notoriously
unfaithful'. Elliot's biography of Olivares concludes with Olivares'
death in 1645.

Lea details the several trials (over many years) of Villanueva in
relation to the events at San Plácido. These proceedings continued
into the 1650s. Lea corroborates the existence of the tunnel. He
writes of protagonists 'playing for time' in lengthy correspondence
between Rome and Madrid about the affair – and in this official
correspondence, only Villanueva's name is mentioned. Finally, in
1652, the Pope states in a letter to the King that 'owing to the
importance and prolixity of the case, he has not been able to reach
a conclusion'. Was Villanueva the only guilty party, as some sources

would have it, or was he a scapegoat? Or was he both a guilty party and a scapegoat – or neither? What *really* happened?

Spanish historian Carlos Puyol Buil writes of a confused historiographical trail, in which different accounts were given at different times, for different purposes, and which has left a knotty situation for historians, filled with 'insurmountable underlying anachronisms'. Puyol Buil nevertheless describes Hume's work on Philip IV as a classic of its time, though he puts the story of the King and the nun in the realm of fantasy and legend, and is critical of Mesonero.

Regarding the paintings *Las Hilanderas* and *Las Meninas* and Velázquez's inclusion of a reference to *The Rape of Europa* in both, the supposition here, and any errors therein, are my own, but the simple fact of the repetition of the image within two significant Velázquez paintings – in themselves, raising the theme of rape – completed within a few years of each other (closely following the conclusion of the Villanueva trials) and the King's commission of a work (Velázquez's *Christ Crucified*) for the Convent of San Plácido in the 1630s, combined with Hume's research and associated sources, appear to me to be linked to the scandal that was covered up. My 'thesis' is that Velázquez was troubled by this, and included an allusion in his most famous artwork(s). The close relationship between Velázquez and the King, the integrity of Velázquez's artistic vision, and Philip IV's struggles with his own conscience as seen in his correspondence, seem to me to strengthen this possibility.

The story of the messenger and his capture and imprisonment in Italy, plus the suggestion that his portrait was sketched by Velázquez, is alluded to by Hume and others.

I have read and owe a debt to many scholars who have written about the works of Velázquez in general and about *Las Meninas* in particular, including Kenneth Clarke, Michel Foucault and Jonathan Brown, as well as others. Ironically, it wasn't until I began studying *Las Meninas* that I also learned the term 'ekphrasis' – a work of art based on another work of art. Picasso's versions of *Las Meninas* fall into this category, as does my humble offering, and many others. I'm not the first to be inspired by this painting and I won't be the last. Debates about its meaning and content will continue. This is a testament to the power of the work.

A key text about the paintings of Velázquez was *The Prado Guide*, published by the Museo Nacional del Prado (third edition, revised, 2011), plus seventeenth century writing of the artist's contemporaries, Francisco Pacheco and Antonio Palomino. I noted Michael Jacobs's comment, in his introduction to a Getty Publications reprint of Pacheco and Palomino's texts: 'Present day art historians, anxious to establish their own intellectual credentials, find it hard to accept the old-fashioned idea of Velázquez as an innocent eye, responsive solely to his pictorial instincts. Yet the early written sources alone strongly suggest that this was the case . . .'

This chimed with a comment by Arnold Schoenberg, who wrote in *Theory of Harmony* (1911): 'It is indeed our duty to reflect over and over again upon the mysterious origin of the powers of art.' He argues that 'art propagates itself through works of art and not through aesthetic laws'. This sense of propagation between artists interests me, as does the creation of art as a means of expression. Artists are subjective beings, just like the rest of us, regardless of our various attempts to achieve objectivity.

For descriptions of life in seventeenth-century Madrid and about court life and the picaresque, I referred to Marcelin Defourneaux, *Daily Life in Spain in the Golden Age* (1970; 1979).

In the modern sections of the novel I have included various direct quotations by Pablo Picasso. The first, which refers to 'a picture painted with curses', comes from P. Daix, *Picasso* (1965). There is some ambiguity in the text as to which painting this refers to, but I believe it was *Las Meninas*. Unfortunately, the quote is not footnoted. Daix also writes about Picasso's artistic dialogue with Velázquez. I spent a lot of time comparing and contrasting Velázquez's *Las Meninas* and that of Picasso.

Other quotes attributed to Picasso – in Chapter 21 and elsewhere – come from a profile of the artist published in a 1956 edition of *Vogue*. I am also indebted to Timothy A. Burgard's 1991 article 'Picasso and Appropriation', published in *The Art Bulletin*.

Regarding theories that Velázquez had Jewish heritage, I referred to K. Ingram's *Converso Non-Conformism in Early Modern Spain* (2018).

For a superb analysis of the interplay between art and life and art and theatre in Spain, I acknowledge L.R. Bass, *The Drama of the Portrait: Theatre and Visual Culture in Early Modern Spain* (2008). The direct quotations from a seventeenth-century play, as watched by the royal family, in Chapter 12, were cited by Bass as part of her discussion on the historical/referential dimensions of portraiture. I also drew on Bass's work for Chapter 14, in which Professor Leadbeater quotes Alberti, who is cited in *The Drama of the Portrait*.

C. McCormack's book *Women in the Picture* (2021) is a breath of fresh air in the field. I felt a tingle of recognition as I read her introduction, having by then finished my manuscript, and would direct readers to her chapter on 'Maidens and Dead Damsels', which discusses Titian's *The Rape of Europa*. McCormack writes that it was dawning on her, in the closing phases of the Harvey Weinstein trial, that 'such gilded images . . . seemed able to say so much more about sexual politics than we [art historians] were giving them credit for as purely aesthetic masterpieces' and that 'the usual art historical reverence for brushwork, beauty and composition no longer felt right'.

Las Meninas did nearly burn and was rescued from the flames of the alcázar when the palace burned to the ground in 1734.

Although I have taken the liberty of using the names of the Prado Museum, Christie's, the Courtauld Institute of Art, and Oxford and Cambridge universities, all of the characters in the novel and activities within those institutions are entirely fictional.

Select bibliography

Bass, L.R., *The Drama of the Portrait: Theatre and Visual Culture in Early Modern Spain*, Pennsylvania State University Press, 2008.

Berger, J., *Ways of Seeing*, Penguin Books, London, 2008.

Brown, J., *In the Shadow of Velázquez: A Life in Art History*, Yale University Press, New Haven and London, 2014.

Burgard, T.A., 'Picasso and Appropriation,' *The Art Bulletin*, vol. 73, no. 3, 1991.

Clark, K., *Looking at Pictures*, Holt, Rinehart, Winston, USA, 1960.

Daix, P., *Picasso*, Thames and Hudson, London, 1965.

Defourneaux, M., *Daily Life in Spain in the Golden Age*, English translation by George Allen & Unwin Ltd, Sydney, 1970; reissued by Stanford University Press, 1979.

Elliot, J.H., *The Count-Duke of Olivares: The Statesman in an Age of Decline*, Yale University, 1986.

Foucault, M., *The Order of Things: Archeology of the Human Sciences*, Routledge Classics, UK, 2001.

Gilot, F. and Lake, C., *Life with Picasso*, Virago, London, 1990.

Hume, M., *The Court of Philip IV*, (1907) Outlook, Germany (reproduction), 2020.

Ingram, K., *Converso Non-Conformism in Early Modern Spain: Bad Blood and Faith from Alonso de Cartagena to Diego Velázquez*, Springer Nature, Switzerland, 2018.

Lea, H.C., *A History of the Inquisition of Spain*, vols 1–2, New York, 1906–07.

McCormack, C., *Women in the Picture: Women, Art and the Power of Looking*, Icon Books, 2021.

Pacheco, F. and Palomino, A., *Lives of Velázquez*, Getty Publications, Los Angeles, 2018, (reprint of two historic texts, one from 1649 the other from 1724), includes an introduction by Michael Jacobs. Also, Pallas Athene, United Kingdom, 2006, 2008.

Puyol Buil, C., 'Inquisición y política en el reinado de Felipe IV: Los procesos de Jerónimo de Villanueva y las monjas de San Plácido 1628–1660', Biblioteca de historia, 1993.

Romanos, R. de M., *El Antiguo Madrid*, (1881) reprint by Forgotten Books, London, 2018.

ACKNOWLEDGEMENTS

I would like to acknowledge and thank my inspiring parents, Cilla McQueen and Ralph Hotere, for taking me to art galleries as a child and for exposing me to a wonderful world of words, images and aroha. Through them I connect to Te Aupōuri, Te Rarawa and England and Scotland. I'd also like to acknowledge the genius of Diego Velázquez; *Las Meninas* is a great taonga – a treasure. Thanks to the Creative Hub, to my classmates and John Cranna, to my mentor for the first draft, Dame Fiona Kidman; to Gotham Writers, New York, and writer Thaïs Miller, for constructive and thoughtful assistance; also to Benjamin Buchholz, for critique. My gratitude to writers Alexander Chee and Marilynne Robinson for their separate and inspiring workshop sessions at the Auckland Writers Festival. My appreciation to the Prado Museum, including its online offerings; the Museo Picasso; the Kunsthistoriches Museum, Vienna; Rijksmuseum, Amsterdam; and Auckland City Libraries, especially the Grey Lynn branch. Special thanks go to Jane Reeves, Angela Norman, Delia Woodham, Lana Oranje and

Susan Gower for moral support and cups of tea. Thanks, also, to Marilyn Aitcheson, Helen McNeil, Bronwyn Calder, Emma Neale, Ali Knight, Anna Rogers and Tina Shaw. My gratitude to Michelle Elvy, for valuable help with editing. A thousand-and-one thanks to my agent, Catherine Wallace, and Vicki Marsden and Nadine Rubin of High Spot Literary. To my wonderfully perceptive publisher, Alex Craig, editor, Alisa Ahmed, and the Ultimo Press team, including the meticulous editor, Ali Lavau, proofreader, Rebecca Hamilton, and fabulous cover designer, Sandy Cull. I can't thank you all enough. My love and gratitude to my husband, Richard, for his encouragement and support, as well as to our children, and the Naish and Hotere whānau and friends who have provided fellowship and aroha during my writerly peregrinations.

Andrea Hotere grew up in Ōtepoti, Dunedin, and lives in Tāmaki Makaurau, Auckland, with her family. She studied history at the University of Otago, journalism at the University of Canterbury and has worked as a historical researcher, journalist, TV producer and author.